CHINESE CLASSICS

ROMANCE OF THE THREE KINGDOMS

Luo Guanzhong

Retold by Wang Guozhen

CHINA INTERCONTINENTAL PRESS

图书在版编目（CIP）数据

三国演义故事：英文 / 王国振编著. － 北京：五洲传播出版社，2012.1
（2021.5重印）
ISBN 978-7-5085-2233-3

Ⅰ．①三… Ⅱ．①王… Ⅲ．①章回小说－中国－明代－英文 Ⅳ．①I242.4

中国版本图书馆CIP数据核字(2011)第279760号

英文改编：王国振
策划编辑：荆孝敏
责任编辑：郑　磊
设计总监：闫志杰
封面设计：叶﹑影
设计制作：蔡育朋

出版发行：五洲传播出版社
地　　址：北京市海淀区北三环中路31号生产力大楼B座7层
邮　　编：100088
网　　址：www.cicc.org.cn
电　　话：010－82005927，010－82007837
印　　刷：中煤（北京）印务有限公司
开　　本：889×1194mm　1/32
印　　张：10
版　　次：2012年2月第1版　2021年5月第4次印刷
定　　价：88.00元

CONTENTS

In the late years of the Eastern Han Dynasty (AD 25—220), because of the corruption of the state administration exacerbated by years of famine, the ordinary people lived a very hard life. In Julu county, local man Zhang Jue, together with his brothers Zhang Liang, and Zhang Bao, managed to enlist some 500,000 people from today's Hebei, Henan, Shandong, Hubei and Jiangsu provinces, into a rebel force and they launched a joint attack upon government troops. Several days later, from every side people joined the army of the rebel Zhang Jue. The rebel army began to wrap yellow scarves around their heads and this quickly became their signature. As the strength of the rebel army increased, the imperial troops became less and less able to control them.

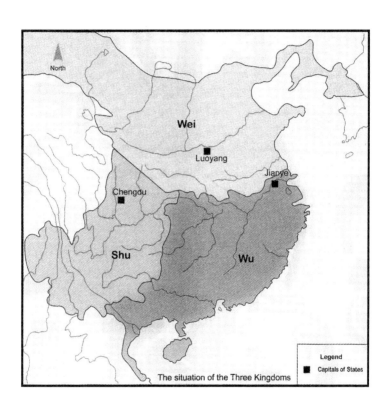

North

Wei

Luoyang

Jianye

Chengdu

Shu

Wu

Legend
■ Capitals of States

The situation of the Three Kingdoms

CHAPTER 1

Dong Zhuo Monopolizes Power

In those days, the Emperor had ten eunuchs as trusted advisers. Emperor Ling placed far too much trust in them, with the result that the rule of the Eastern Han Dynasty was in serious danger.

High Counselor Liu Tao passionately advised Emperor Ling to dispense with the ten eunuchs, but the Emperor instead imprisoned Liu Tao and threatened to have him executed. The Minister of the Interior Chen Dan beat his forehead against the steps of the throne in protest. The Emperor grew angry and ordered his imprisonment with Liu Tao. That night Liu Tao and Chen Dan were executed. From then on, no officials dared to raise their voices in protest again.

In the summer of AD 189, Emperor Ling became seriously ill and summoned He Jin into the palace to arrange for the succession. The Empress Dong had long tried to persuade her son to name Xian as the Heir Apparent, and the Emperor did indeed

have great affection for the baby and was disposed to do as his mother desired. When he fell ill, one of the eunuchs, Jian Shuo, said, "If Liu Xie succeeds to the throne, He Jin must be killed to prevent countermoves." The Emperor saw this too and summoned the Imperial Guardian He Jin.

He Jin came from a humble family of butchers, but his sister had become a concubine of great rank and had borne a son to the Emperor, named Liu Bian. After this she became Empress He, and He Jin was appointed to the powerful position of Imperial Guardian and Regent Marshal. On his way to his audience with the emperor, at the gates of the palace, He Jin was warned of the danger he was in. He rushed back to his quarters and called on the ministers who supported him. They met to consider what to do and how to kill all of the eunuchs. Emperor Ling soon died of his illness. He Jin mustered five thousand royal guards, commanded by the Imperial Commander Yuan Shao, and they entered the palace. In the hall where lay the coffin of the late Emperor they placed LiuBian on the throne.

Liu Bian succeeded to the throne, but Empress Dong, the mother of Emperor Xian, was not happy. The eunuch Zhang Rang gave her some counsel. She was very happy with this advice. Next day she held court and issued an edict to make Liu Xian Prince of Chenliu and Dong Chong General of the Flying Cavalry. She also allowed the eunuchs to once again participate in state affairs.

When Empress He saw this, she prepared a banquet to which she invited her rival Empress Dong. In the middle of the feast, when all were merry with wine, Empress He rose and offered a cup to her guest advising her not to meddle in state affairs. Empress Dowager Dong lost her temper and began to shout at her young rival.

Empress He too became enraged. That night Empress He summoned her brother to the palace and told him what had occurred. He went out and met with the principal officers of state to discuss how to remove the Empress Dowager Dong and Dong Chong. Next morning a court session was held and a memorial was presented, ordering that the Empress Dowager Dong be removed into her original fiefdom of Hejian. The secret emissaries of He Jin poisoned Empress Dong in her residence in the country. Many guards were placed around the Imperial Uncle Dong Chong's dwelling. They took away his seal of office and he, knowing this was the end, killed himself in his private apartments.

Commander Yuan Shao went one day soon after to see He Jin and advised him to destroy the ten eunuchs as early as possible. Soon after He Jin told Empress Dowager He of his plan to put the eunuchs to death. Empress Dowager He had a lot of time for Zhang Rang and some of the others, so she did not approve. Yuan Shao presented his scheme to He Jin, asking him to summon his forces to the capital and kill the eunuchs. But Counselor Chen Lin thought that nothing good could come of it, nothing but chaos and disorder and he objected. Then Cao Cao, one of the court secretaries, clapped his hands, and laughed.

He Jin asked Cao Cao why he laughed. Cao Cao said, "A gaoler would be ample force to employ against this kind of evil. Getting rid of the main culprits is quite sufficient. Why increase the confusion by summoning troops from the regions?" Hearing this, He Jin was very angry and said in a sneering voice that perhaps Cao Cao had some scheme of his own that he sought to advance. Cao Cao left the meeting, proclaiming, "the one throwing the world into chaos is He Jin!"

Dong Zhuo, a warload, leading a force of 200,000 troops, was sent to Xiliang in northwest China. He was a man of great ambition. One day, he received a summons from He Jin and was very happy. He ordered his son-in-law Li Ru to draft a memorial stating plainly their aims and intentions so that ministers would be clear about where they stood. Then they proceeded to the capital Luo Yang.

Zhang Rang and the other eunuchs knew this move was directed against them and they recognized that their only chance of survival was to strike the first blow. So they hid away a band of fifty armed bandits at the Gate of Grand Virtue in the Palace of Happiness, then they went in to see Empress He, and asked her to summon the General. Not knowing that it was a trap, she summoned He Jin to the palace. He Jin felt that the Ten Regular Attendants would not try anything against the man who had the fate of the empire in the palm of his hand. Many advised him against this foolhardy course of action, but he was deaf to their counsel. At the Gate of Grand Virtue, he was met by Zhang Rang and Duan Gui, and then the assassins appeared and cut He Jin to pieces.

Yuan Shao and Cao Cao waited for a long time. By and by, impatient at the delay, they called out, "The carriage awaits, General!" In reply the head of He Jin was flung over the wall. Yuan Shao and Cao Cao were very angry. Brandishing their swords, Yuan Shao and Cao Cao broke into the palace and slayed the eunuchs with no regard for age or rank. Fires raged, destroying the buildings.

Meanwhile, Zhang Rang and Duan Gui had spirited away the Emperor and the Prince and had escaped. They burst through the smoke and fire and traveled without stopping till they reached the Beimang Hills. It was then the third watch. They heard a great shouting behind them and saw soldiers in pursuit. Zhang Rang, seeing that all was lost, jumped into the river, where he drowned.

The Emperor and the Prince of Chenliu were found amidst the heap of straw and the guards turned to escort them home. The cavalcade had not proceeded far when they saw coming towards them a large body of soldiers with fluttering banners hiding the sun and raising a huge cloud of dust. The General leading this great force was Dong Zhuo. Dong Zhuo escorted the Emperor and the Prince of Chenliu to the palace and made camp outside the walls. Every day he was to be seen in the streets with an escort

of armored soldiers so that the common people were in a state of constant fear.

He also went in and out of the Palace armed with his sword. The next day Dong Zhuo threw a feast and invited many guests. He suddenly proposed the overthrow of the Emperor and the installing of the Prince Liu Xie in his place. The assembly listened in perfect silence, none daring at first to utter a word of dissent. Ding Yuan, Imperial Protector of Jingzhou stood up in his place, smote the table and vehemently opposed the proposal. Dong Zhuo drew his sword and made straight for the objector. But he had noticed standing behind Ding Yuan a particularly dangerous looking bodyguard, who was now handling his halberd threateningly, and whose eyes were blazing with anger, so he suddenly halted his murderous charge.

But the next day he learned that Ding Yuan had left the city with a small army and was challenging him to a battle. Dong Zhuo, with his army, went forth to accept the challenge. The two armies were drawn up in proper array. The battle went in Ding Yuan's favor thanks to the reckless bravery of Lu Bu and Dong Zhuo fled for his life.

Afterwards Dong Zhuo called his officers to a council. Li Su mentioned that he was a fellow villager of Lu Bu and knew him well. As long as Dong Zhuo was willing to give his fine horse, Red Hare, and gold and pearls to Lu Bu, he could persuade him to come over to his side. Dong Zhuo agreed.

Lu Bu bade the guards lead out the horse. It had a coat like the glowing red sun; not one hair of another color. Lu Bu was delighted with the horse. Next day, with the head of the murdered man as his gift, Lu Bu betook himself to Li Su, who led him to Dong Zhuo. Lu Bu bowed to him as his adopted father.

Thence Dong Zhuo's power and influence increased rapidly. He overthrew the previous Emperor giving him instead the title of Prince of Hongnong, and placed on the throne the Prince of Chenliu.

The new Emperor was nine years old and had no capacity to rule the country. Dong Zhuo became Prime Minister, and grew even more powerful and arrogant. When he bowed before the Throne, he would not take off his sword. Ministers were ordered to just do his bidding.

One who had opposed the plot to depose the Emperor and place the Prince on the throne in his place was Yuan Shao. He went to Jizhou Region in a state of great anger. Dong Zhuo thought it politic to pardon Yuan Shao and offer him the governorship of Bohai.

After this the deposed Emperor, his mother, and the Imperial Consort, Lady Tang, were removed to the Palace of Eternal Calm. The entrance gates were locked against all comers. The deposed Emperor showed his resentment through the poems he wrote. Dong Zhuo was told of this and so he had the emperor poisoned. The Empress He was thrown out of her window.

After this Dong Zhuo's behavior became more atrocious

than before. He spent his nights in the Palace, defiled the imperial concubines there, and even slept on the Dragon Couch. Once he led his soldiers out of the city to Yangcheng on a hunt when the villagers were all assembled for the annual spring festival. His troops surrounded the place and plundered it. They took away booty by the cart load, and women prisoners and more than one thousand severed heads.

CHAPTER 2

Cao Cao Plots to Assassinate Dong Zhuo

Dong Zhuo was so atrocious that the other resentful ministers plotted to remove him from office. At Bohai, Yuan Shao heard of Dong Zhuo's misuse of power and sent a secret letter to the Minister of the Interior Wang Yun, asking him to seek an opportunity to undermine the prime minister's position. One day Wang Yun invited several ministers to his home. When he could see there was no chance of gaining agreement to move against Dong Zhuo, the host suddenly covered his face and began to weep. Then they all wept with him.

Seated among the guests, however, was Cao Cao, who did not join in the weeping but clapped his hands and laughed aloud. Wang Yun turned on him angrily and asked him how he could laugh. Cao Cao said that he would borrow Wang Yun's sword with seven precious jewels, go into Dong Zhuo's palace and kill him. Wang Yun was very happy and gave the treasured sword to Cao Cao.

The next day Cao Cao, wearing this short sword, came to  the palace of the Prime Minister. Cao Cao went in and found his host seated on a couch. Dong Zhuo asked Cao Cao why he was calling on him at such a late hour. He replied that his horse was so old and slow. Dong Zhuo told Lu Bu to go and pick out a good horse as a present for him. Now there was only Dong Zhuo left in the house, and Cao Cao was about to draw his sword and strike, but he knew Dong Zhuo was very powerful, and so he hesitated.

Now Dong Zhuo's corpulence was such that he could not stay sitting for a long time, so he rolled over on the couch and lay face down. As Cao Cao drew his sword and prepared to strike, Dong Zhuo happened to look up and in a mirror he saw the reflection of Cao Cao behind him with a sword in his hand. Dong Zhuo turned around suddenly and asked him what he was doing. Cao Cao dropped to his knees and said that he had a precious sword which he wished to present as a gift to the distinguished Prime Minister.

And at that moment Lu Bu returned leading a horse. Cao Cao rode in haste out of the eastern gate. He traveled toward Qiao, his home county. Dong Zhuo was told of this and quickly realised that Cao Cao had planned to kill him. Pictures of the fugitive Cao Cao were sent everywhere with orders to arrest him. On the road at Zhongmou, he was recognized by the guards at the gate and was taken prisoner. They took him to the Magistrate. The Magistrate was deeply affected by Cao Cao's loyalty and uprightness, and he abandoned his office and joined him.

The two sought shelter in the house of Lu Boshe, a sworn-brother of Cao Cap's father for the night. Cao Cao suspected that Lu Boshe might report him to the officials. He and Chen Gong killed the whole household, male and female, in all eight people. Soon they met their host Lu Boshe coming home. Cheng Gong said that to kill deliberately was very wrong, Cao Cao said, "I would rather betray the world than let the world betray me!" Hearing this, Chen Gong was frightened and left in silence.

After returning to his hometown, he enlisted soldiers while issuing a decree to all lords, asking them to dispatch troops to attack Dong Zhuo. Heeding the call, the Governor of Beiping, Gongsun Zan, led three generals, Liu Bei, Guan Yu, and Zhang Fei to join Cao Cao's forces.

In AD 190, when all had arrived, Cao Cao, as the leader, prepared some sacrificial bullocks and horses and called all the lords to a great assembly to decide upon their plan of attack. At the assmebly, Yuan Shao was elected as the chief lord. He ordered the Governor of Changsha, Sun Jian, to go to the River Si Pass and provoke a battle. Yuan Shu was appointed Chief of the Commissariat, responsible for supplies.

When news of these actions reached Dong Zhuo's adviser Li Ru, he at once went to his master, who was much alarmed and called a great council. Lu Bu wanted to fight with various confederate lords. Hua Xiong volunteered to be a vanguard general. Dong Zhuo looked up and his eyes rested on a stalwart man of fierce mien, lithe and supple as a beast. Dong Zhuo rejoiced at Hua Xiong's bold words and at once appointed him Commander of Royal Cavaliers and gave him fifty thousand horses and soldiers. Hua Xiong hastily marched towards the River Si Pass.

Sun Jian's general Cheng Pu killed Hu Zhen on the spot with a thrust through the throat. Then Sun Jian gave the signal for the main army to advance. Yuan Shu feared that should Sun Jian take the capital and kill Dong Zhuo it would increase his power, and this would be disadvantageous to him. He refused to send him grain. Soon Sun Jian's hungry soldiers showed their disaffection through their indiscipline, and spies bore the news to the defenders of the Pass. Hua Xiong's troops arrived about midnight and the drums signalled an immediate attack. Sun Jian's army were thrown into confusion and fled in disorder.

Hua Xiong was soon hurling insults at those within the stockade and challenging them to fight. But soon came the direful tidings that General Pan Feng too had fallen. The faces of the gathering lords paled at this. Guan Yu proposed going and cutting off Hua Xiong's head, and laying it before them. Yuan Shu looked down upon Guan Yu and ordered that Guan Yu be driven out of the tent.

Cao Cao thought this man was no common person. He asked Guan Yu to heat some wine and offered him a cup as he went out. Guan Yu took the cup and put it on the table, saying, "Pour it out. I shall return in a little while. Guan Yu went with his weapon in his hand and vaulted into his saddle. Guan Yu returned, throwing at their feet the head of the slain leader, their enemy Hua Xiong. The wine was still warm

After Dong Zhuo was told the story of Hua Xiong's death, the other one hundred fifty thousand of his troops under Dong Zhuo himself went to Tiger Trap Pass. Lu Bu was a conspicuous figure leading the troops.

Then all eight of the lords led forth their armies to his rescue, and Lu Bu retired to his line.

While the council was in progress again Lu Bu came to challenge them, and again the commanders moved against him. This time Gongsun Zan, flourishing his spear, went to meet the enemy. After some skirmishes Gongsun Zan turned and fled. Zhang Fei was elated, and he rode forth with all his energy. They two were well matched, and they fought for a long time with no advantage to either side. Guan Yu attacked Lu Bu on the other flank. The three steeds formed a triangle and their riders battered away at each other for thirty bouts, yet still Lu Bu stood firm. Then Liu Bei rode out to his brothers' aid, his double swords raised ready to strike. Finally, they defeated Lu Bu.

Lu Bu's defeat dulled the edge of his army's desire for battle. Dong Zhuo's final orders as he left his capital Luoyang were to burn the whole city; houses, palaces, temples, and everything was devoured by the flames. Bringing the Emperor and his household, Dong Zhuo moved off to the new capital.

All the confederate lords entered Luoyang. Cao Cao went to see Yuan Shao and advised Yuan Shao to follow and attack the rear without delay. But all the confederate lords seemed of one mind, and that mind was to postpone any further action. Cao Cao was disgusted and with his generals and sixty thousand troops started in pursuit.

Dong's son-in-law Li Ru ordered the Governor of Yingyang City to set an ambush outside the city, to trap Cao's army. Cao Cao almost lost his life. They gathered together the few hundreds of soldiers who survived the ambush and returned to Luoyang.

As they extinguished the fires and made camp for the confederate lords, Sun Jian's soldiers found the Imperial Hereditary Seal of the Emperor in a well. Yuan Shao was informed of this and asked Sun Jian to return it to the government. Sun Jian pointing toward the heavens and swore said that he had never seen it. Sun Jian left camp and marched to his own home place.

Yuan Shao was not satisfied. He wrote to Jingzhou and a message to tell the Imperial Protector Liu Biao to stop Sun Jian and take away the seal. With the confederacy breaking up, the lords broke camp and left. The troops going on a punitive expedition against Dong Zhuo departed. Liu Bei, Guan Yu and Zhang Fei returned to Pingyuan county.

CHAPTER 3

Li Jue Attacks the Capital on Jia Xu's Advice

Those generals Li Jue, Guo Si, Fan Chou, and Zhang Ji whom Dong Zhuo had left to guard Meiwo fled when their master, Dong Zhuo, was slain and went to Liangzhou Region. Thence they sent a petition pleading for amnesty. But Wang Yun would not hear of it. The messenger returned and told the four there was no hope of pardon, so they conscripted the people into a force of some 100,000, and they set out to raid the capital Chang'an (today's Xi'an City of Shaanxi Province). Lu Bu was not able to withstand these enemies, so he urged Wang Yun to flee with him, but Wang Yun would not leave. Lu Bu himself fled to seek refuge with Yuan Shu.

Li Jue and Guo Si's troops reached Chang'an, surrounding the inner palace. The alarmed courtiers begged the Emperor to proceed to the Gate of Pervading Peace to try to quell the rioting. Li Jue and others requested the Emperor to let them have Wang Yun, and they would withdraw their troops. The Emperor was conflicted and he hesitated. But his faithful minister leaped from the wall, crying. And Wang Yun was slain at the foot of the tower. From this point the power of the court fell into the hands of Li Jue and Guo Si.

Now that they exercised real power, they were very hard upon the people. One day a report came that the Governor of Xiliang in northwest China, Ma Teng, and the Imperial Protector of Bingzhou, Han Sui were rapidly approaching the capital with one hundred thousand troops with the intention of attacking the rebels in the name of the Emperor. Ma Chao, Ma Teng's son, was only seventeen years of age, but he was a very brave fighter. Both boastful generals fell under the hand of this young man. Sure enough after a couple of months the supplies of the Xiliang force were all exhausted and the leaders began to think about retreating.

Then Cao Cao was made a general in charge of the eastern expedition, because of his service in quelling the remnants of the

Yellow Scarves. Cao Cao encouraged all able people to assist him, and he had advisers such as Xun Huang, Xun You, Cheng Yu, Guo Jia and Liu Ye on the civilian side and valiant generals such as Yu Jin and Dian Wei in the army.

As a dutiful son, Cao Cao sent people to Langye to escort his father to Yanzhou. Hearing that the family of the great man was passing through his region, Tao Qian went to welcome them, treated them with great cordiality, feasting and entertaining them for two days; and when they left, he escorted them to the border. Furthermore he sent with them one General Zhang Kai with a special escort of five hundred soldiers. Zhang Kai however was treachorous and he murdered the whole family of Cao Cao, stole all their treasure and fled. When he heard it, the enraged Cao Cao led his main army to Xuzhou to avenge this terrible deed.

At this time Chen Gong was also on friendly terms with Tao Qian. Hearing of Cao Cao's plan to massacre the whole population, Chen Gong who had once saved Cao Cao in the past came in haste to see his former companion, advising him not to attack Xuzhou. Cao Cao would not listen. Chen Gong felt that he could not face Tao Qian as he had failed to persuade Cao Cao. So he rode off to the county of Chenliu and offered his service to the Governor Zhang Miao.

Tao Qian wanted to give himself up as a prisoner and allowed Cao Cao to wreak his vengeance on him. His adviser Mi Zhu proposed that they go to Beihai and beg Governor Kong Rong to help them. Tao Qian agreed and wrote two letters. He asked Chen Deng to go to Qingzhou and, after he had left, Mi Zhu was formally entrusted with the mission to the north.

Just at this moment another uprising of the Yellow Scarves broke out, as 10,000 bandits carried out robbery and murder at Beihai. Thus Kong Rong sent in haste to Liu Bei.

Liu Bei was known as a humane, righteous, and compassionate

leader. Together with Guan Yu and Zhang Fei, he held off three thousand troops and set out to help raise the siege.

When Liu Bei's troops reached Beihai, Guan Yu's martial ability proved the difference as his dragon saber rose and fell, and killed the rebel leader Guan Hai, and raised the siege. Kong Rong invited Liu Bei to rescue the victims in Xuzhou.

Liu Bei went away to his friend Gongsun Zan and lent him two thousand horses and soldiers. He also wished to have the services of Zhao Yun. Gongsun Zan agreed to this. They marched away. Liu Bei and Zhang Fei leading one thousand troops dashed through Cao Cao's army. Liu Bei was asked to write to Cao Cao to entreat him to raise the siege.

While this was going on, a horseman came with news of great misfortune: Lu Bu has invaded Yanzhou, and now held Puyang. Cao Cao was greatly disturbed by this. His advisor Guo Jia advised him that the best thing would be to become friends with Liu Bei at any cost and return to Yanzhou. Accepting Gua Jia's plan, Cao Cao broke camp and returned to Yanzhou to deal with Lu Bu.

News that the enemy had left was very gratifying to Tao Qian, who then invited his various defenders including Kong Rong, Tien Kai, Guan Yu and Zhao Yun into Xuzhou City and held banquets and feasts in their honour to show his gratitude. Tao Qian renewed his offer to cede the region of Xuzhou to Liu Bei, but Liu Bei kept refusing. Tao had to invite Liu

Bei to camp at Xiaopei so that he could keep guard over Xuzhou. They all with one voice begged Liu Bei to consent, and finally he gave in.

Cao Cao had marched toward his own region. Now as he neared Puyang, he made camp. Lu Bu led an army of fifty thousand and they lined up in a circular formation. Seeing him approach, his generals, Xiahou Dun and Yue Jin both fled, but Lu Bu pressed on after them. Cao Cao's army lost the day. Retreating some ten miles, they made a new camp.

At dusk he and twenty thousand horses and soldiers left that night by a secret road for a camp of Lu Bu to the west of Puyang .So arrangements were made for defense. The fight became desperate. Cao Cao dashed at the enemy lines. The din was terrible. Arrows fell like pelting rain upon them, and they could make no headway. Cao Cao was desperate and cried out in terror for someone to save him. Cao Cao was in great danger. However, help came. Xiahou Dun with a troop of soldiers located his chief, stopped the pursuit, and battled Lu Bu till dusk. Rain fell in torrents swamping everything; and as the daylight waned, they drew off and Cao Cao reached camp.

When Lu Bu reached his camp, he called in his adviser Chen Gong. Chen Gong proposed a new stratagem. In Puyang there is a rich, noble family called Tian, whose clan numbered thousands of people. Chen suggested making one of these people go to Cao Cao's camp with a forged secret letter about Lu Bu's ferocity, and the hatred of the people for him, and their desire to be rid of him. Chen proposed ending the letter by saying that only Gao Shun was guarding the city, and they would help any one who would come to save them from Lu Bu.

And so fooled by this stratagem during the first watch Cao Cao led the way into the city. But when he reached the main residence, he noticed the streets were quite deserted, and then he knew he had been tricked. Wheeling round his horse, he shouted to his followers to retreat. Cao Cao attempted to reach the north gate, but sharply outlined against the brightening sun, he saw the figure of Lu Bu coming toward him with his trident halberd ready for the kill. Cao Cao covered his face with his hand, whipped up his steed and galloped past. But Lu Bu came galloping up behind him and tapped him on the helmet with his halberd merely asking where Cao Cao was? Cao Cao turned and pointed to a dun horse well ahead. Thus reprieved Cao Cao set off for the east gate.

Cao Cao returned to his camp and gave orders to spread a false report that he had been burned in the fire, and was dead, and that the soldiers were all in mourning. He himself laid an ambush for Lu Bu in the Maling Hills. Soon Lu Bu heard the false news and he assembled his army at once to make a surprise attack. As they were passing the hills, they were attacked by the ambushing soldiers. At that time a plague of locusts suddenly descended, and they consumed every green blade on view. Troops of both sides suffered and therefore the fighting ceased.

In Xuzhou, Imperial Protector Tao Qian, who was over sixty years of age, suddenly fell seriously ill. He requested Liu Bei again to take over the leadership of this region, but Liu Bei again declined firmly. Before long, Tao Qian passed away. When the ceremonial mourning of the officials was over, the insignias of office were brought to Liu Bei. The following days the inhabitants of the town and country around crowded into the state residence, bowing and crying, calling upon Liu Bei to take over. Finally he consented to assume the administrative duties.

The news of the events in Xuzhou duly reached the ears of Cao Cao, who was very angry. Orders were issued for the army to prepare for a new campaign against Xuzhou. But Adviser Xun Yu remonstrated with Cao Cao, and advised that it would be more advantageous to attack the remnants of the Yellow Scarves in Yingchuan and requisition their grain. Cao Cao captured Runan and Yingchuan as per this plan. Xu Chu submitted to Cao Cao and recieved the rank of general.

Thus Yanzhou and Puyang fell under the power of Cao Cao. Lu Bu who had no way out went over to Liu Bei, who had assumed power in Xuzhou. Liu Bei's heart was kind and he allowed Lu Bu to lead his troops there and take up residence in Xiaopei.

CHAPTER 4

Li Jue and Guo Si Duel in Chang'an

Cao Cao had subdued the region east of the Huashang Mountains. He informed the emperor and was rewarded with the title of General Who Exhibits Firm Virtue and was made Lord of Feiting.

At this time the rebellious Li Jue was the real power in the court. His and his followers conduct was abominable but no one dared to criticize them. Emperor Xian ordered Imperial Guardian Yang Biao to try to remove the two. Yang Biao said, "Guo Si's wife, Lady Qiong, is very jealous, and we can take advantage of her weakness to bring about a quarrel."

Yang Biao asked his wife to tell Guo Si's wife that there was talk of a secret liaison between the General, her husband, and the wife of Minister Li Jue. Late in the afternoon some presents arrived from Li Jue's palace, and Lady Qiong secretly put poison into the delicacies before she set them before her lord. Guo Si was going to taste some food but she said that it was unwise to consume things that come from outside. Let us try it on the dog first she advised. They did and the dog died. This incident made Guo Si doubt the kindly intentions of his colleague. One day, at the close of business at court, Li Jue invited Guo Si to his palace. After Guo Si arrived home in the evening, rather the worse for wear after too much wine, he was seized with colic. His wife said she suspected poison.

Thinking that Li Jue really wanted to injure him, Guo Si felt angry, so he began to ready his guards for a sudden attack. This was told to Li Jue, and he in turn grew angry. He too mustered his guards and came to attack Guo Si. Both houses had ten thousand men under arms, and they fought a pitched battle under the city walls. Li Jue abducted the Emperor and Empress while Guo Si imprisoned sixty other officials.

Thereafter the two adversaries fought every day for nearly 50 days with both sides suffering heavy casualties. Li Jue's commander, Yang Feng, was angry with Li and planned to kill him. Unexpectedly Li Jue was told about this by someone who had overheard the commander. Li Jue himself led his troops in search of the traitor Yang Feng. A melee broke out, which lasted till the fourth watch. But Yang Feng got away and fled into the hills.

But from this time Li Jue's army began to fall away. One day came news that Zhang Ji, leading a large army, was coming down from Shanxi to make peace between the two factions. Zhang Ji vowed he would attack whoever refused to parley. Li Jue tried to gain favor by hastening to inform Zhang Ji he was ready to make peace. So did Guo Si. Li Jue set free Emperor Xian while Guo Si set free all his captive officers, Zhang Ji petitioned the Emperor to go to Hongnong near Luoyang.

Just as they were about to approach the county of Huaying, the trampling of a large force was heard. Guo Si hoped to outwit Zhang Ji, seize the Emperor, and hold him in Meiwo. When the alarm was raised, Yang Feng led Xu Huang to attack them. When they had time to see their helper, they found he was none other than Dong Cheng, the uncle of the Emperor. Troops led by Yang Feng and Dong Cheng escorted the Emperor and Empress across the Yellow River. Yang Feng found a bullock cart and transported the Emperor and Empress to Dayang. On the way, they suffered much hardship. In the seventh month, they arrived at Luoyang.

Within the walls all was destroyed. The palaces and halls had been burned and the streets were overgrown with grass and brambles and filled with debris. The palaces and courts were all broken roofs and toppling walls. That year was a year of grievous famine. The Luoyang people, even though there were only a few hundred of them left, did not have enough to eat and they prowled about stripping the bark off trees and digging up the roots of plants to try to avoid starvation. Officers of the government went out into the country to try to gather fuel. Many people were crushed by the falling walls or burned houses. Fearing that Guo Si and Li Jue would come again, Emperor Xian issued a decree that Cao Cao be invited to defend the ruling house. Cao Cao immediately hurried to Luoyang and defeated Guo Si and Li Jue.

Next day at court Cao Cao said that Xuchang was a noble city, with a plentiful supply of food and resources lying close to Luoyang.

He requested that the court move the capital to Xuchang. The Emperor dared not disagree and the officials were too overawed to have any independent opinion, so they chose a day and set out for their new capital.

Cao Cao was then the main man at court. He wanted to attack Liu Bei and Lu Bu, to consolidate his administration of Xuzhou. His advisor, Xun Huang, proposes a ruse known as the 'Rival Tigers and One Preyplan'. He told Cao Cao to get a decree authorizing Liu Bei to govern the region, and when to enclose with it a private note telling him to get rid of Lu Bu. If he did that, then he would lose a vigorous warrior from the other side, and he could be dealt with as necessary. Should he fail, then Lu Bu would slay him. Cao Cao agreed to the plan.

Liu Bei called in his councilors to consider the letter. Zhang Fei imprudently disclosed the letter to Lu Bu. Then Liu Bei had to tell Lu Bu the whole story and showed him the secret letter. Lu Bu wept as he finished reading and again and again expressed his gratitude.

Liu Bei did not kill Lu Bu, so Cao Cao had to try another scheme. He told Yuan Shu to say that Liu Bei has sent a secret memorial to the Emperor to the effect that he wished to subdue the southern regions around the Huai River. Then he formally ordered Liu Bei to dispose of Yuan Shu and so set them to destroy each other. Lu Bu would certainly see that here was his chance and he would turn traitor. This was the 'Tiger against Wolf' trick.

Liu Bei realised that this was another of Cao Cap's tricks, but the royal command could not be disobeyed. So the army was prepared and the day fixed. Zhang Fei was left to guard the city. Zhang Fei in a drunken fit lost control of his temper and beat Cao Bao. Cao Bao went away burning with resentment, and sent a letter to Xiaopei relating the insults he had received from Zhang Fei. The letter told Lu Bu of Liu Bei's absence and proposed that a surprise raid should be made that very night.

As soon as the news of Lu Bu's successful seizure of his protector's region reached Yuan Shu, Yuan Shu sent promises of valuable presents to Lu Bu to induce him to join in a further attack on Liu Bei. But Liu Bei heard of the threatened attack, so he used inclement weather as an excuse to move his few soldiers out of Xuyi to Guangling, before the attacking force arrived. Lu Bu sent letters to Liu Bei asking him to return and take up his quarters at Xiaopei.

If Liu Bei was not removed from the equation, Yuan Shu could never rest easy. One day, Sun Ce sent letters to Yuan Shu, demanding the return of the Imperial Hereditary Seal. But Yuan Shu, who was secretly very ambitious made excuses and would not return it. Yuan Shu hastily summoned about thirty of his officers to a meeting.

An adviser of Yuan Shu's said to him that because Lu Bu was now Liu Bei's patron, first of all he should send Lu Bu a present in order to buy his acquiescence while he dealt with Liu Bei. He could see to Lu Bu after this was done, when Xuzhou was his.

Then Yuan Shu attacked Liu Bei, and Lu Bu sent invitations to both Liu Bei and Ji Ling to come to a banquet. He tried to force the two sides to make peace.

Yuan Shu offered his daughter to Lu Bu in marriage so as to arrange a marriage alliance with Lu Bu. Thereupon in spite of his many infirmities Chen Gui, father of Chen Deng, went to see Lu Bu. Lu Bu was much disturbed to hear this. So he hurriedly sent Zhang Liao to escort the wedding party, which had been ten miles away, back to the city.

Zhang Fei and his soldiers stole half of three hundred horses brought from Shandong by Lu Bu. Lu Bu was very angry at this and began to prepare an expedition against Xiaopei. Liu Bei abandoned the city and took refuge with Cao Cao,

Cao Cao's adviser Xun Huang advised his master to destroy Liu Bei. Cao Cao thought that if he put him to death he would alienate all good people and put fear into the hearts of all his able advisers. Thus on the contrary he sent him 3,000 soldiers and petitioned the Emperor to give Liu Bei the imperial protectorship of Yuzhou, thus facilitating a joint attack upon Lu Bu.

CHAPTER 5

White Gate Tower

In 197 AD, when Cao Cao was about to make an assault upon Lu Bu, Zhang Xiu, a nephew of Zhang Ji, sent troops to attack Xu Du. Cao Cao had to send 150,000 soldiers to Yushui to attack Zhang Xiu. Following the plan of his adviser Jia Xu, Zhang Xiu pretended to surrender to Cao Cao.

After Cao Cao entered Wancheng, he indulged in gluttony and pleasure-seeking with the wife of Zhang Ji. Extreme resentful at this, Zhang Xiu launched a late night attack on Cao Cao's battalions. Cao Cao escaped, but Dian Wei, one of Cao's major commanders who helped Cao Cao to escape, Cao Ang, the son of Cao Cao, and Cao Anmin, the nephew of Cao Cao, were all killed.

Cao Cao held a memorial ceremony for Dian Wei and he wept bitter tears. He said to his officers, "I have lost my first born son and nephew, but I grieve not so heavily for them as I do for Dian Wei."

Yuan Shu got the Imperial Jade Seal and declared himself emperor. He led an army of seven divisions under seven commanders to attack Lu Bu. However, with the help of Guan Yu, Lu Bu defeated Yuan Shu.

Cao Cao decided to gamble and attack Yuan Shu. Firstly he

sent people to contact Sun Ce, Lu Bu and Liu Bei in the South Land. Secondly, he sent 170,000 infantry troops southward. Yuan Shu just held his ground and didn't dispatch troops. He intended to wait until Cao Cao would be forced to retreat due to shortage of provisions.

Since the army of Cao Cao was huge, the provisions soon ran low. Voices of discontent were heard among his soldiers. Cao Cao decided to retreat. But to assuage the resentment among his men, he killed the officer in charge of provisions who was surnamed Wang. Thus, the morale of troops did not get too out of control.

When Cao Cao was preparing to attack Huaibei and give chase to Yuan Shu. Zhang Xiu also attacked Cao Cao. On their route march, Cao Cao gave an order that anyone who trampled on wheat would be beheaded. Unexpectedly, his own horse was frightened and trampled a large stretch of wheat. Cao Cao cut a lock of his hair off in lieu of his entire head.

Cao Cao's army laid siege to Nanyang. Jia Xu saw Cao Cao scout the city wall for three days running. Knowing Cao Cao would look one way and attack another, he laid an ambush of handpicked troops at the southeastern corner of the town. Cao Cao played into his hands, and suffered casualties of 50,000 soldiers. Suffering a resounding defeat, he retreated with his army.

Cao Cao in turn laid an ambush in the Anzhongshan Mountain, and defeated the troops of Zhang Xiu and Liu Biao.

At that time, news was reported to Cao Cao that Yuan Shao would invade Xudu. Cao Cao lost his cool and immediately gave an order to retreat. Rejecting Jia Xu's advice, Liu Biao and Zhang Xiu gave chase to Cao's army but were defeated by him. Later, Jia Xu asked them to again pursue Cao. As a result, they were victorious.

Seeing Cao's army had returned, Yuan Shao gave up his

attack on Xudu and instead attacked Sun Ce. Cao Cao also planned to launch an assault on Lu Bu and wrote to Liu Bei to invite him to join the assault. Learning about this, Lu Bu sent troops to besiege Xiaopei. Liu Bei hurriedly sent messengers to ask Cao Cao for help.

Lu Bu utterly defeated Cao's army at a place about 15 km from downtown Xuzhou and then occupied Xiaopei. All the kin of Liu Bei fell into the hands of Lu Bu. Separated from Guan Yu and Zhang Fei, Liu Bei rushed to Xuchang to seek refuge with Cao Cao.

Since Chen Gui and his son were cooperating with Cao Cao from within Xuzhou, Cao Cao was quickly able to occupy Xuzhou and Xiaopei. Lu Bu managed to escape with his family and his adviser Chen Gong to Xiapi.

Cao's army laid siege to Xiapi. Chen Gong advised Lu Bu to resist Cao Cao. However, worried about the safety of his family, Lu of the downtown to fight the enemy.

The concubines of Lu Bu drank wine with him to relieve his stress all day long. Chen Gong tried to persuade Lu Bu again, but again he rejected the counsel. Chen Gong raised his head and sighed, saying "We will die without a burial place."

Hou Cheng, a major general under Lu Bu, was all but killed by Lu Bu because he violated the his superior's order. All the generals and soldiers secretly hated Lu Bu. Hou Cheng, Song Xian and Wei Xu and so on prepared to rebel. Hou Cheng stole the beloved horse, Red Hare of Lu Bu and sent it to Cao Cao.

Cao Cao attacked the town for many days in succession. Lu Bu was exhausted and fell asleep on his chair on the top of the rampart. Song Xian and Wei Xu stole the trident halberd of Lu Bu and tied him up with ropes. They let Cao's army enter the town.

Soldiers escorted Lu Bu and Chen Gong to Cao Cao and Liu

Bei. Cao Cao killed Chen Gong. Lu Bu begged Liu Bei for mercy, but Cao Cao still killed Lu Bu.

Zhang Liao, a subordinate of Lu Bu lambasted Cao Cao. Cao wanted to kill him, but Guan Yu knelt before Cao Cao and begged for leniency for Zhang Liao. Cao Cao saw Zhang Liao was a brave fighter and set him free. Zhang Liao was extremely grateful and surrendered to Cao Cao. And then he was given the rank of Imperial Commander.

CHAPTER   6

Discussing Heroes While Sipping Wine

After Cao Cao killed Lu Bu, he led his army back to Xudu. He introduced Liu Bei to Emperor Xian. The emperor asked people to check his pedigree and then recognized Liu Bei as his uncle.

Cao Cao invited Emperor Xian to go hunting. Suddenly, a deer ran out from the brambles. Emperor Xian shot three arrows in succession but didn't hit it. He then asked Cao Cao to shoot it. Cao used the bow and arrow of Emperor Xian to shoot and kill the deer. The civil and military officials thought it was the emperor who shot it and shouted, "Long live the Emperor!" Cao Cao didn't pay any attention to the emperor. Guan Yu noticed this. With sword in hand, Guan Yu rode forth to try to cut down Cao but he was blocked by Liu Bei.

After Emperor Xian returned to the palace, he couldn't help weeping when he thought of the peremptoriness of Cao Cao during the hunt. Fu Wan, Empress Fu's father said Dong Cheng, the Emperor's Uncle, could get rid of Cao Cao. Hence, Emperor Xian drew up a decree, writing it in his own blood which he drew by biting his finger. He gave the document to Empress Fu to sew into the purple lining of her girdle. He then gave the girdle to

Dong Cheng.

When Dong Cheng left the palace, Cao Cao was waiting there. He asked a warrior to untie the girdle of Dong Cheng because he had some suspicion about it. Dong Cheng said in a panic to Cao Cao that, "If you like it, you can take it." Cao looked over every inch of it most carefully but discovered nothing unusual. So he returned it to Dong Cheng.

Dong had the secret decree of the emperor. He then swore an oath of alliance with ministers Wang Zifu, Zhong Ji, Wu Shuo, Wu Zilan, Ma Teng and Liu Bei by smearing their mouths with the blood of a sacrificial animal to do away with Cao Cao and to forever support the Han Dynasty.

Afraid that Cao Cao might suspect him, Liu Bei didn't leave from the side door. He only devoted himself to gardening,

planting vegetables, and watering them in the back garden. Guan Yu and Zhang Fei ventured to remonstrate with him for taking up such an occupation when more urgent matters needed attention. Liu Bei said he would find a way.

One day, Guan Yu and Zhang Fei went to the suburbs to practice shooting arrows. Liu Bei was watering the vegetables in the garden alone. Cao Cao sent Xu

Chu and Zhang Liao to invite Liu Bei to drink wine. When Cao Cao asked Liu Bei who were the greatest heroes of the day, Liu Bei pretended to be not aware of the proper answer, guessing one person after another. Cao Cao said "The only heroes in the world are you and I." Liu Bei gasped, and his spoon and chopsticks rattled to the floor.

Now just at that moment a storm began to rage with a tremendous peal of thunder. Liu Bei pretended to be afraid of thunder, thus glossing over the real fact, that it was the words he had heard that had so startled him. Then, Cao Cao didn't doubt him any more.

Yuan Shao killed Gongsun Zan, so Yuan Shu wanted to send the Imperial Jade Seal to him. Liu Bei asked Cao Cao for an army of 50,000 soldiers on the pretext of heading off Yuan Shu and took the chance to get away from Xudu. Cao also sent Generals Zhu Ling and Lu Zhao with Liu Bei.

Liu Bei defeated Yuan Shu. Yuan Shu was killed with a lot of blood spewing from his mouth. The Imperial Jade Seal fell into the hands of Cao Cao again.

Liu Bei returned to Xuzhou and asked Zhu Ling and Lu Zhao to go back to Xudu to report to Cao Cao. Cao was angry about this and secretly ordered Che Zhou, the defending general of Xuzhou, to kill Liu Bei. Guan Yu beheaded

Che Zhou, so Xuzhou was governed by Liu Bei again.

Cao Cao sent 200,000 troops divided into five groups to attack Xuzhou. Liu Bei asked Zheng Xuan to write to Yuan Shao for help.

Yuan Shao dispatched 300,000 troops to rescue Liu Bei. Yuan Shao asked Chen Lin, who was in charge of drafting writs to write an official denunciation of Cao Cao to publicize his crimes.

At that time, Cao Cao was taken ill. After reading the article of Chen Lin, he began to sweat all over and his illness was unexpectedly cured. He led an army to Liyang to meet Yuan Shao's army head-on and asked Liu Dai and Wang Zhong to lead an army to feign an attack on Liu Bei.

The armies of Cao Cao and Yuan Shao met in Liyang. Since the army of Cao was comparatively small, Cao used defence as a means of attack. Though Yuan had a huge army, he was overcautious and his army was not united. Yuan didn't attack Cao. The two armies were locked in a stalemate for two months. Finally, Cao's army withdrew.

Liu Dai and Wang Zhong were not enemies of Guan Yu and were captured. However, Liu Bei set them free and asked them to go back to Xudu and speak for Liu Bei in front of Cao Cao.

In line with the suggestion of an adviser called Sun Qian, Liu Bei sent troops to defend Xiapi and Xiaopei to support each other and guard against Cao Cao. Guan Yu defended Xiapi, Sun Qian guarded Xuzhou and Liu Bei defended Xiaopei with the help of Zhang Fei.

Cao Cao called on Zhang Xiu and Liu Biao to surrender. Zhang Xiu was hesitating between supporting Cao and Yuan. The military counsellor Jia Xu said, "Yuan Shao even can't even get on with his brother, not to mention others." Hence, Zhang Xiu decided to seek refuge with Cao Cao. Cao, disregarding his past grudges, treated Zhang Xiu and Jia Xu with courtesy.

Cao Cao asked Kong Rong to summon Liu Biao to surrender, but Kong recommended Mi Heng. When Cao Cao called in Mi Heng, Mi said the military officers and advisers under Cao Cao were not worth a cent and boasted that he could make his prince the rival of Kings Yao and Shun (two ideal kings from legend) and he himself could compare in virtue with Confucius and Yan Hui (two great philosophers). Cao Cao thought him too arrogant and demoted him to the position of drummer.

The following day, Cao Cao held a banquet and many guests were invited. He asked Mi Heng to play the drum to add to the fun. Mi took off all his clothes and cursed Cao Cao while beating the drum.

Cao didn't blame Mi Heng and asked him to summon Liu Biao to surrender and said to him that he would appoint him as a major official if he succeeded in doing it. Mi didn't write but Cao Cao asked people to compel him to write.

When Mi Heng saw Liu Biao, he jeered at Liu again. Liu Biao knew that Cao Cao wanted to kill Mi Heng, so he asked Mi Heng to meet Huang Zu. Since Huang was a military officer, he killed Mi Heng after hearing Mi's silly taunts.

CHAPTER 7

Riding on a Solitary Journey

In the year of 200 or the fifth year of the Jian'an Period, Cao Cao became the prime minister, and became even more brazen in his disrespect for the emperor. After Dong Cheng saw the emperor's decree hidden there was nothing he could do against Cao Cao, and he came down with an illness due to his indignation and anxiety. The Emperor Xian asked the imperial physician Ji Ping to cure his illness. Ji Ping decided to do away with Cao Cao after seeing the secret decree of the emperor. Dong and Ji discussed the best stratagy to deal with Cao Cao.

Unexpectedly, the walls had ears. Qin Qingtong, a servant of Dong Cheng, was heavily flogged 40 times by order of Dong because he had had a dubious relationship with a concubine of Dong. So he bore a grudge against Dong. After hearing the matter, he informed against Dong Cheng and Ji Ping to Cao Cao.

Cao Cao pretended to be ill and asked Ji Ping to treat him. Ji Ping concocted some medicine and sent it to Cao Cao, but Cao

asked Ji to taste it first. Ji Ping knew that their plot had been exposed. He tried his best to pour the poison into the mouth of Cao, but he was pushed away by the stronger man. The bowl of medicine fell on the ground. The poison in the medicine even made the bricks crack.

Cao Cao forced Ji Ping to reveal his accomplice. Ji refused to obey, and shouted many curses at Cao Cao. Cao Cao asked people to cut off his fingers and tongue. However, Ji Ping committed suicide by smashing his head against the stone steps.

Cao Cao put Dong Cheng, Wang Zifu, Wu Zilan and Zhong Ji to death. He also killed Dong Cheng's daughter the Imperial Concubine Dong who was five months pregnant. The emperor and empress begged for leniency but to no avail.

Knowing Liu Bei had also participated in their machinations, Cao Cao led 200,000 soldiers to Xuzhou from five different directions to attack Liu Bei.

Liu Bei sent his adviser Sun Qian to ask Yuan Shao for help. However, Yuan Shao's youngest son was on the verge of death due to illness, so Yuan was unwilling to send troops,. He offered Liu Bei refuge with him if he needed it.

Cao Cao's troops arrived outside the city wall; Liu Bei was at the end of his wits. Adopting the suggestion of Zhang Fei, Liu Bei went to attack Cao's battalion, but fell into Cao Cao's ambush. Liu Bei and Zhang Fei got separated. Liu Bei and his party went to Yuan Shao for shelter; Zhang Fei escaped to Mangdangshan Hill.

Yuan Shao led his subordinates 15 km outside the town limits to welcome Liu Bei.

Cao Cao attacked and occupied Xuzhou and Xiapi. Guan Yu protected the families of Liu Bei and was besieged by Cao's troops on a nearby hill.

Zhang Liao climbed up the hill to persuade Guan Yu to surrender to Cao Cao. Guan Yu thought it over and finally agreed to surrender on three conditions: he said he was surrendering to the Han Dynasty instead of to Cao Cao; he should be allowed to protect the two wives of Liu Bei and be granted a sufficient stipend; and once the whereabouts of Liu Bei became known, he would go to look for him.

Zhang Liao told Guan Yu's conditions to Cao Cao, who agreed eventually. Guan Yu protected the two wives of Liu Bei while following Cao Cao to Xudu. On the way, Cao Cao deliberately asked Guan Yu to stay in the same room as Liu Bei's two wives. Guan Yu held one candle in one hand and a sword in another hand, and stood guard throughout the night. Cao Cao admired Guan very much.

Cao Cao invited Guan Yu to dinner fairly frequently and sent beauties and numerous treasures to Guan Yu. However, Guan Yu asked the beauties to attend to the wives of Liu Bei and gave the treasures to the two wives of Liu Bei for safekeeping.

Cao Cao also sent the steed Red Hare to Guan Yu. Guan Yu thanked Cao again and again. Cao Cao felt it was a little strange and asked him why he hadn't thanked him before. Guan Yu said with the swift horse, he would find it easier to locate Liu Bei. Cao Cao was not happy.

When Yuan Shao launched an attack on Cao Cao, Cao Cao led 50,000 troops to meet the enemy head-on. Yan Liang, at the vanguard of Yuan Shao's army, was very brave and managed to kill Cao's generals Song Xian and Wei Xu. An adviser called Cheng Yu suggested Cao Cao dispatch Guan Yu to take on Yan Liang so as to make Yuan Shao hate Guan Yu and kill Liu Bei.

To express his gratitude for Cao Cao's kind treatment of him, Guan Yu killed Yan Liang and in the following day, killed another major general called Wen Chou. Cao Cao won an overwhelming victory.

After hearing the news, Yuan Shao asked his men to tie up Liu Bei. Liu Bei said, "Cao Cao deliberately asked Guan Yu to kill your two generals to irritate you and make you kill me. I will write a letter to Guan Yu immediately to ask him to give himself up to you. What do you think?" Yuan Shao was very pleased and didn't kill Liu Bei.

Seeing the letter from Liu Bei, Guan Yu bade farewell to Cao Cao, but Cao Cao avoided meeting him on purpose. Guan Yu left all the treasure and beauties sent to him by Cao Cao behind and hung up his great seal of the Lord of Hanshou. Leaving a letter to Cao Cao, he went to look for Liu Bei with the two wives of Liu Bei.

Cao Cao thought he had complied with Guan Yu's conditions, so he hurried to see Guan Yu off. Guan Yu was afraid that Cao Cao might have some final trick, and so he fetched the robe of brocade sent by Cao Cao to him with his sword on his horse and put it on. Cao Cao's subordinates thought Guan Yu was very impolite and they wanted to kill him but Cao Cao wouldn't let them.

Guan Yu came to the Donglingguan Pass with the two wives of Liu Bei. The defending general Kong Xiu blocked Guan Yu with the excuse that he hadn't seen the writ of Cao Cao. Kong was killed by Guan Yu.

The procurator of Luoyang Han Fu also blocked Guan Yu's way. Meng Tan also challenged Guan Yu but was chopped into two halves by Guan. Han Fu shot Guan Yu with an arrow in the left arm. Guan Yu pulled out the arrow with his mouth and then attacked Han Fu and killed him.

When Guan Yu arrived at Sishuiguan Pass, the defending general Bian Xi set an ambush, placing two hundred armed men in the State Guardian Temple. He let fall a cup as signal, and the hidden soldiers jumped out ready for the kill. One of the monks in the temple, whose name was Pujing, or Universal Purity, turned out to be from Guan's home area. He told Guan Yu about Bian Xi's ambush. Guan Yu managed to kill Bian Xi.

Guan Yu arrived at Xingyang. The governor of the district Wang Zhi was a relative of Han Fu. He wanted to kill Guan Yu to avenge the death of Han Fu. Hence, he prepared to set fire to where Guan Yu was staying. Hu Ban, a subordinate of Wang Zhi, informed Guan Yu of the plan. Guan Yu hurried off. Wang Zhi gave chase but was killed by Guan.

Guan Yu reached a ferry on the Yellow River. The commander of the ferry, Qin Qi, blocked Guan Yu's way but he was also killed by Guan Yu. Crossing the Yellow River, they reached the domain of Yuan Shao and met Sun Qian. Sun Qian told Guan Yu that Liu Bei was gone to Runan and asked Guan Yu to take his two wives there.

Guan Yu and Sun Qian crossed the Yellow River again and headed for Runan. Xia Houdun, a subordinate of Cao Cao, led an army and caught up with Guan Yu, where they fought a fierce battle. At that time, Zhang Liao arrived and delivered Cao Cao's orders, which allowed Guan Yu and his party to leave.

Guan Yu proceeded. On the way, he drew in a valiant general called Zhou Cang. When Guan Yu arrived in Gucheng, Zhang Fei who was occupying the town thought Guan Yu had surrendered to Cao Cao and didn't regard Guan Yu as his elder brother any more. He brandished his spear and thrust at Guan Yu.

At that time, Cai Yang, a subordinate general of Cao Cao, came to avenge the death of his nephew Qin Qi. Zhang Fei asked Guan Yu to slay Cai Yang before he had finished three rolls of the drum and then he would take Guan Yu as his brother. Guan Yu beheaded Cai Yang before Zhang finished even the first roll of the drum.

Zhang Fei became aware of what Guan Yu had suffered on the way, and he started crying loudly. He knelt down in front of Guan Yu to offer his apologies. Liu Bei went to the residence of Yuan Shao in Hebei. Guan Yu and Sun Qian also hurried to Hebei and met Liu Bei at Guanjiazhuang. The two brothers hugged each other and cried their eyes out. Guan Yu took Guan Ping as his adopted son.

Liu Bei was afraid that Yuan Shao might chase them, and thus he hastened to Gucheng which was defended by Zhang Fei. When they passed by the Woniushan Mountain, they met Zhao Yun, who went along with them to Gucheng.

Liu Bei was reunited with his two younger brothers and their force gained Zhao Yun, Guan Ping and Zhou Cang. Hence, they decided to slaughter cattle and sheep to celebrate their reunion. Considering that Gucheng was too small, Liu Bei led the army to camp at Runan. His army was reinforced as he plotted his future plans.

CHAPTER 8

Fighting at Guandu

At that time, the force of Sun Ce in the South Land grew day by day. In 200 AD, Xu Gong, the governor of Dongjun saw Sun Ce meant to attack Xudu. He wrote a letter to inform Cao Cao of this. Unexpectedly, the letter fell into the hands of Sun Ce. Enraged, Sun Ce killed Xu Gong.

One day, Sun Ce went hunting on a mountain. As he pursued a deer alone, he was attacked by three supporters of Xu Gong and was hit by a poisonous arrow. He was on the verge of death. The doctor persuaded him to rest quietly for 100 days to recuperate so that he could survive.

Sun Ce was impetuous. Hearing that Guo Jia, an adviser of Cao Cao, had criticized him, he exploded with anger and resolved to send troops to attack Cao Cao. He swore he would occupy Xuchang.

When Sun Ce was treating Chen Zhen, the envoy of Yuan Shao, his major commanders went downstairs to call on Yu Ji, a Taoist in the South Land. He was known as an immortal. Wherever he arrived, the local people burned incense to worship him like a god.

Sun Ce blew a fuse, execrating the evil Taoist for fooling the masses and ordering his soldiers to kill Yu Ji. Sun Ce's illness became worse due to worry and anger. He even often imagined he saw the soul of Yu Ji while in a trance. Soon after, he died at the age of 26 of the wound caused by the poisonous arrow.

Sun Quan succeeded his elder brother Sun Ce. With the support of Zhou Yu and Lu Su in the South Land, Sun Quan's force became stronger.

Thus, Cao Cao ordered the emperor to appoint Sun Quan as a general and the governor of Kuaiji. Yuan Shao got terribly angry after hearing of this. He dispatched 700,000 troops to attack Cao Cao.

Cao Cao was lacking in troops and provisions. He wanted to fight a quick decisive battle, and so he ordered Zhang Liao to meet the enemy head-on. Cao Hong led 3,000 handpicked troops to rush into the enemy lines. Yuan Shao's army shot swarms of arrows, and defeated Cao Cao's army. Cao Cao's army held their position until finally retreating to Guandu.

Adviser Xu You suggested Yuan Shao send an army to attack Xudu thus taking advantage of this victory, and converging on Cao Cao. Yuan Shao didn't adopt the suggestion. On the contrary, he suspected that Xu You was in league with Cao Cao.

Xu You saw Yuan Shao didn't accept his counsel and worse, soon after, his son and nephew were put into prison. He had to go to Cao Cao for help that night. Cao Cao hurried to welcome him in his bare feet. He prostrated himself before Xu You. Xu advised Cao to attack Wuchao and to burn the provisions of Yuan Shao's army.

Cao Cao's army launched a night attack on Wuchao and burned all their enemy's provisions and materials. The morale of Yuan Shao's army was sapped. Yuan's army, originally totaling 700,000 soldiers, suffered complete defeat and fled. Only some 800 soldiers were left.

When Cao Cao was going through the books and letters left by Yuan Shao, he discovered that many letters were written between his subordinates and Yuan Shao. His advisers suggested Cao Cao kill these men, but Cao didn't agree and burned all the letters as if it had never happened.

When Yuan Shao attacked Cao Cao, Yuan's adviser Tian Feng presented a memorial from prison to Yuan Shao to discourage Yuan from attacking Cao. Yuan Shao returned after his failure. A jailor congratulated Tian Feng, saying Yuan would set him free for sure. Tian Feng smiled and said, "My destined hour is coming." At that time, the person who was sent by Yuan Shao to kill Tian Feng came. Tian knew the score and cut his own throat in the prison.

Yuan Shao returned to Jizhou. His eldest son Yuan Tan led 50,000 soldiers there from Qingzhou; his second son Yuan Xi led 60,000 troops there from Youzhou; and his nephew Gao Gan also led 50,000 soldiers there. Yuan Shao integrated the three forces and fought Cao Cao again.

The troops of Cao Cao were stationed on the river. Several local elders offered wine and food to Cao Cao, and Cao was extremely moved. Cao ordered the whole army not to injure one dog or chicken of the common people; any violator would be immediately beheaded.

Cao Cao and his commanders discussed strategies for defeating the enemy. His adviser Cheng Yu put forward the scheme of "the ambush from ten sides." Finally, Yuan Shao was defeated and escaped back to Jizhou, crying with his three sons.

Liu Bei took advantage of the fact that Cao Cao was fighting fiercely with Yuan Shao. There were no troops in Xudu and so he led his army to attack Xudu. Unexpectedly, Cao Cao's troops had returned, but they were exhausted, and thus were defeated by Liu Bei's army.

Cao's army defended the battalion but wouldn't go out to fight. When Liu Bei was wondering what to do, he received a report that his provisions had been plundered by Cao's army and Runan had also been occupied by Cao's army. Liu Bei was greatly surprised and withdrew in the night. On the way, he fell into Cao Cao's ambush. Liu Bei's army fought bravely with Cao's army and finally escaped and went to Liu Biao for help.

Cao's army didn't pursue Liu Bei but instead returned to Xudu. In the spring of the following year, Cao Cao led his army to Guandu to attack Yuan Shao. At that time, Yuan Shao was very ill, so he asked his third son Yuan Shang to confront the enemy. In three bouts, Yuan Shang was finally defeated by Zhang Liao.

Seeing Yuan Shang returning after his defeat, Yuan Shao died of haematemesis. He asked Yuan Shang to take power after him. Yuan Shao's wife who was surnamed Liu killed the five concubines of Yuan Shao and Yuan Shang put all the families of the five concubines to death.

Yuan Shao's son led an army to defend Jizhou which Cao Cao's army had failed to occupy. Adviser Guo Jia persuaded Cao Cao not to interfere in the killing of the three sons of Yuan Shao. Cao agreed and led his army in an attack on Liu Biao.

Soon, the three sons of Yuan Shao killed each other in their struggle over the succession. The first son Yuan Tan adopted the scheme of Guo Tu, with a view to killing Yuan Shang using Cao's army. He pretended to surrender to Cao Cao.

Cao Cao received Yuan Tan and led his army to besiege

Jizhou. Yuan Shang asked Shen Pei to defend Jizhou and himself stationed his forces outside the town in order to cooperate with Shen Pei. Cao Cao didn't have a good strategy on how to break through the town's defences, so the two armies were deadlocked.

Xu You offered some advice to Cao Cao. Cao's army diverted the waters of the Zhanghe River into the town. In addition, there was no grain left in the town, so Yuan's army was trapped.

Yuan Shao's old commander Xin Pi lifted up the great seal and clothes of Yuan Shang with his spear in order to summon the defending soldiers of the town to surrender. Shen Pei was enraged by this and he had over 80 members of Xin Pi's family killed and he threw their heads over the city wall. Xin Pi cried his eyes out.

Shen Pei's nephew Shen Rong was a good friend of Xin Pi. He opened the west gate of the town, so Jizhou fell into the hands of Cao Cao.

The armed men pushed Chen Lin in front of Cao Cao. Cao questioned Chen asking him, "It's ok that you wrote article to curse me. But why did you disgrace my father and grandfather?" Cao's subordinates persuaded Cao to kill Chen Lin. However, Cao Cao knew Chen was a talent, and so he instead asked Chen to take charge of his army's writs.

When Cao Cao arrived in Jizhou, Xu You said to Cao Cao, "Without me, how could you enter Jizhou?" Cao Cao was left in convulsions. Grand General Xu Chu saw Xu You was overstepping his mark and killed him. When he carried Xu You's head to Cao Cao, Cao was extremely unhappy with Xu Chu's conduct and asked his men to give Xu You a grand burial.

Cao Cao's army pursued Yuan Tan to Nanpi. Yuan Tan asked the people in the town to join in the battle. In the battle, Yuan Tan was killed by Cao Hong.

Cao Cao asked the people to hang the head of Yuan Tan on

the gate of the town and ordered that anyone who cried for him would be beheaded. The commander of Qingzhou Wang Xiu cried under the wall of the town. Cao Cao had great admiration for the loyal people of Jizhou. He didn't kill Wang Xiu but promoted him to a very important position.

Yuan Xi and Yuan Shang escaped to Wuhuan in the middle of the desert. Adviser Guo Jia suggested Cao Cao pursue them.

In 207 AD, Cao's army decimated Yuan Xi and Yuan Shang on the White Wolf Mountain. Yuan Xi and Yuan Shang led several thousand of their cavalry to Liaodong in northeast China. Cao Cao thought the victory he gained was just a fluke, and thus he encouraging his advisers to make bold suggestions.

Guo Jia, the adviser who Cao Cao respected most died in the desert due to climate sickness. Cao Cao cried sadly. Guo Jia left a letter to Cao, persuading him not to attack Liaodong.

Cao Cao followed Guo's advice. Soon, Gongsun Kang in Liaodong feared that Yuan Xi and Yuan Shang would invade his domain and so he killed them and offered their heads to Cao Cao. Then, Cao Cao withdrew back to Xudu.

CHAPTER 9

Recommending Zhuge Liang

Cao Cao got a bronze bird. Officials said that it was a felicitous omen. Cao Cao ordered forthwith the building of a lofty tower to celebrate the find, and, in accordance with his son Cao Zhi's suggestion, the side towers were named Jade Dragon Tower on the left and Golden Phoenix Tower on the right.

Liu Biao sent Liu Bei to Jiangxia to undertake an expedition against Zhang Wu and Chen Sun. He returned victorious. Zhao Yun captured the horse of Zhang Wu and presented it to Liu Bei.

Liu Bei presented the horse to Liu Biao. Kuai Yue, a general of Liu Biao, saw it and said, "This horse has tear tracks running down from its eyes and a white blaze on its forehead. It is called a Dilu horse, and it is a danger to his master. That is why Zhang Wu was killed. I advise you not to ride it." Hearing this, Liu Biao returned it to Liu Bei.

Hearing what Lady Cai had said, Liu Biao ordered Liu Bei to garrison Xinye with his troops. When he left Jingzhou City, he noticed in the gate one of the secretaries of Liu Biao named

Yi Ji gesturing to him frantically. He said, "You should not ride that horse. That horse is a Dilu horse and invariably brings disaster to its owner" "A person's life is governed by fate and how can a horse interfere with that?" replied Liu Bei. Yi Ji had no reply.

The arrival of Liu Bei in Xinye was a matter of rejoicing to all the

inhabitants, and the whole administration was reformed. In the spring of AD 207, Liu Bei's wife, Lady Gan, gave birth to a son who was named Liu Shan.

Liu Biao wanted to pass over the younger candidate for the succession, so he inquired about Liu Bei's opinions. Liu Bei said, "All experience proves that to set aside the elder for the younger is to take the way of confusion. If you fear the power of the Cai faction, then gradually reduce its power and influence." Lady Cai was behind the screen when the matter was talked over, and she had great resentment against Liu Bei for what he had said. She determined to kill Liu Bei.

Lady Cai took counsel with her kinsman Cai Mao, as they plotted to remove Liu Bei. Now Liu Bei sat in his lodging reading by the light of a single candle till about the third watch, when he prepared to retire to bed. He was startled by a knock at his door and in came Yi Ji, who had heard word of the plot against his new master and had come in the darkness to warn him. He urged a speedy departure.

Cai Mao planned to kill Liu Bei at the Full Harvest Festival at Xiangyang. Yi Ji told this to Liu Bei. Liu Bei hastened to make his escape. The guards at the gate ran off to report to Cai Mao, who quickly went in pursuit with five hundred soldiers. Before Liu Bei had gone far there his way was blocked by a rushing river. It was the very wide and wild-rushing Tan Torrent. Liu Bei cried out furiously, "Dilu, Dilu, why betray me?" Whereupon the good steed suddenly reared up and leapt over the water and, with one tremendous leap, was on the western bank.

Liu Bei had narrowly escaped from grave danger. A cowherd conducted Liu Bei to consult the Water-Mirror. Suddenly the sound of a lute most skillfully played came to his ear. It was being played by the Water-Mirror Sima Hui. He said to Liu Bei, "If you

could find either the Sleeping Dragon or the Blooming Phoenix, you could restore order to the empire." Liu asked, "Where are they? What are they?" When Liu Bei persisted with his questions, the Water Mirror said that they would talk over these things tomorrow.

Liu Bei was shown to a chamber opening off the main room and went to bed. But he could not forget the words of his host, so he lay there restlessly far into the night. Liu Bei listened with great joy for he thought this visitor was certainly one of the two he was advised to look for. Liu Bei would have shown himself then and there, but he thought that would look strange. So he waited till daylight, he knew that the person had been in service of a wise lord. When Liu Bei asked his name, his host only replied, "Good, good!"

On reentering the city, Liu Bei met a person in the street wearing a hempen turban, a cotton robe tied with a black girdle, and black shoes. He came along singing a song, saying that he was a great sage waiting for his lord. He thought surely this must be one of the people the Water Mirror spoke of. He dismounted, spoke to the singer, and invited him into his residence. Then when they were seated, he asked the stranger's name. He said that his name was Shan Fu and that he had long wanted to meet Liu Bei. Hearing this, Liu Bei was very happy.

Liu Bei admired the talents of Shan Fu. Thereupon Shan Fu was made Commanding Adviser of the army, and carried out training with the soldiers each day.

Cao Cao sent Cao Ren to attack Xinye, who made an arrangement called 'The Eight Docked Gates.' Shan Fu broke the arrangement while dispatching troops to attack Fankou. The defeated Cao Ren escaped to Fankou, which had been captured by Guan Yu.

The Fankou Magistrate Liu Mi received Liu Bei as a guest in his own house and held banquets for him and treated him exceedingly well. In the retinue of the Magistrate, Liu Bei saw a very handsome and distinguished looking young man, who was Liu Mi's nephew, Kou Feng. Liu Bei had taken a great liking to the lad and proposed to adopt him. Guan Yu who was doubtful of the wisdom of adopting another son, asked him since he already had a son, why he thought it was necessary to adopt another.

Cao Cao's defeated generals had returned, and their leader found out that it was Shan Fu who had laid Liu Bei's plans. Cheng Yu said, "His real name is Xu Shu and he comes from Yingchuan. Shan Fu is merely an assumed name." Cao Cao summoned Xu Shu's mother to the capital, ordering her to write and summon her son.

Xu's mother, was a brave woman. She did not write to Xu Shu, but rather reproached Cao Cao and even picked up the inkstone to try to hit him. This so enraged Cao Cao that he forgot the need for caution and summarily sentenced the old woman to death. His adviser Cheng Yu, however, convinced him of the folly of this course of action.

Cheng Yu learned the old woman's handwriting so that he could forge a letter to her son. He dispatched the letter to Xinye.

On receiving the letter Xu Shu immediately went to seek out his chief and say farewell. Liu Bei prepared a banquet at Daisy Pavilion in honour of Xu Shu's departure.

Liu Bei stood gazing after Xu Shu and his retniue, watching it slowly disappear. Suddenly they saw Xu Shu galloping back. Liu Bei was very glad and thought that Xu Shu had changed his mind. Instead Xu Shu recommended Zhuge Liang to Liu Bei and said "The Blooming-Phoenix is Pang Tong of Xiangyang, and The Sleeping-Dragon is Zhuge Liang."

Xu Shu hastened to the capital. Seeing him, his mother suddenly grew very angry and concerned and cried out why he had been fooled by Cao Cao's forged letter. After weeping for some time, Lady Xun hanged herself. Xu Shu would never work for Cao Cao.

Liu Bei prepared gifts and went to Longzhong to pay a visit to Zhuge Liang. Liu Bei knocked at the rough door of the cottage. A youth appeared and told Liu Bei, "The Master left this morning very early. And it is uncertain when he will return." Liu Bei was very disappointed.

Some days after they returned to Xinye, Liu Bei heard that Zhuge Liang had come back. Therefore, he prepared to visit him again. Braving the snow, together with Guan Yu and Zhang Fei, he hastened there. They met his younger brother, Zhuge Jun, who said that only yesterday he had arranged to go on an outing with a friend. Liu Bei borrowed paper and ink, and left a note for Zhuge Liang.

Liu Bei was just taking his leave and coming out, when he saw the serving lad waving his hand and calling out, "The old Master is coming" Liu Bei thought that Here at last was the famous Sleeping Dragon, and hastily went up to greet him. However Zhuge Jun pointed out that that was not his brother but rather his father-in-law Huang Chenyan."

After returning again to Xinye the time slipped away till spring was near. Liu Bei cast lots to find a propitious day to make another journey in search of Zhuge Liang. The day being selected, he fasted for three days and then changed his dress ready for the visit. Guan Yu advised him not to go while Zhang Fei wanted to bring Zhuge Liang in with a hempen rope. Liu Bei was very angry and the other two had no choice but to follow him.

Soon the three stood at the door and they knocked. The serving lad came out and asked their business. The lad said that Zhuge was asleep. Liu Bei hastened to stop him from waking Zhuge Liang. Liu Bei bade his two brothers wait at the door quietly, and he himself entered with careful steps.

After some time Zhuge Liang woke up. This proved to Zhuge Liang the sincerity of Liu Bei's desire to meet with him. He invited Liu Bei into his cottage and brought out a map. He advised that Jingzhou be taken first as a base, the Western Land of Rivers next as an imperial foundation of. Being thus firmly established, Liu Bei could then lay plans for the attainment of the whole empire. Hearing this, Liu Bei's respect for this strategist soared.

Liu Bei invited Zhuge Liang to join his trusted circle. The tears rolled down unchecked onto the lapel and sleeves of Liu Bei's robes. This proved to Zhuge Liang the sincerity of Liu Bei's offer. Zhuge Liang accepted happily.

Zhuge Liang was made Commanding Adviser of the army and given the office seal, as Commander of the army.

CHAPTER 10

Burning of Xinye

Sun Quan obtained the assistance of many poeple of ability both in peace and war including Zhou Yu and Lu Su, and his forces greatly expanded. A large fleet of seven thousand battleships was in the Great River ready for service. Sun Quan appointed Zhou Yu to be the Supreme Admiral and Commander-in-Chief over all military forces.

Cao Cao had broken the power of Yuan Shao. At that time he sent a messenger to the South Lands ordering Sun Quan to send his son to court to serve in the retinue of the Emperor. His mother, Lady Wu, sent for Zhou Yu and Zhang Zhao and asked their advice. Zhou Yu thought that by sending a hostage to Cao Cao would force them to support them and give him power over them. So Sun Quan dismissed the messenger but did not send his son.

Sun Quan's younger brother, Sun Yi, was Governor of Dangyang. He was a hard man and much given to drink and, when under the influence, could be very harsh to his people, regularly ordering floggings. Two of his officers, the military Inspector Gui Lan and Secretary Dai Yuan, took into their confidence one Bian Hong, of the Governor's escort, and the three plotted to kill their master at a great assembly of officials at Dangyang during the banqueting. The faithless guardsman followed his master at dusk as the gathering was dispersing, and stabbed him with a dagger. The two prime movers at once seized Bian Hong and beheaded him in the market place.

Gui Lan was taken with the beauty of the dead Governor's wife and tried to force her to marry him. Lady Xu pretended to accept his offer but secretly sent for two of her husband's old generals, Sun Gao and Fu Ying. The drunken Gui Lan, incapable of resistance, was murdered with daggers. Next Lady Xu invited Dai Yuan to a supper, and he was slain in similar fashion.

Very soon her brother-in-law came with an army, and

hearing the story of the deeds of the two generals from the widow, gave them the command of the forces at Dangyang. When Sun Quan left, he took with him his brother's widow to his own home to pass the remainder of her days.

In the spring of AD 207, Gan Ning, one of the leaders of Huang Zu, offered to surrender. Sun Quan himself commanded the main army of one hundred thousand troops to attack Huang Zu, who was defeated. Huang Zu was shot to death by Gan Ning when trying to escape.

After Sun Quan broke the resistance of Huang Zu, Liu Biao sent for Liu Bei to Jingzhou for a meeting. Liu Biao was getting old and weak, and hoped that Liu Bei would be able to manage affairs in this region. But Liu Bei would not agree.

Zhuge Liang asked why he declined this offer of power over the region. He said that he could not take advantage of Liu Biao's weakness. "A perfectly kind and gracious lord," sighed Zhuge Liang.

Cao Cao sent Xiahou Dun one hundred thousand troops to make an expedition against Xinye. Xun Yu said, "Liu Bei is a famous warrior, and he has lately taken to himself as his Counsellor Zhuge Liang. Caution is needed." Xiahou Dun replied, "Liu Bei is a mean rat. I will certainly take him prisoner."

When he heard that Xiahou Dun was leading an army of one hundred thousand troops against them, Zhang Fei said to his brother, Guan Yu, "We will get this famous Zhuge Liang to go and fight them." Just at that moment they were summoned to Liu Bei, who asked their advice. "Why not send the 'Water' Brother?" said Zhang Fei. Liu Bei criticized Zhang Fei, "For strategy I rely on Zhuge Liang; but for action I put my faith in you, my brothers. Are you going to fail me?"

Fearing that Liu Bei's brothers would not obey him, Zhuge

Liang requested Liu Bei to give him a seal of office and a sword of authority. So Liu Bei gave him both. Armed with these insignias of power, Zhuge Liang assembled the officers to receive their orders. Guan Yu said, "All of us are to go out to face the enemy, but I have not yet heard what you are going to do." "I am going to guard the city," Zhuge Liang said. Zhang Fei burst into laughter.

Xiahou Dun had no respect at all for the enemy and rode forward at great speed. They were led into Bowang Gorge. Then a great shout was heard behind him. A rushing noise came from the reeds and great tongues of flame shot up here and there. These flames spread and soon the fire was all around them, fanned by a strong wind. Xiahou Dun's troops were thrown into confusion and trampled on each other. Xiahou Dun dashed through the fire and smoke to escape.

As Guan Yu and Zhang Fei rode homeward they had to admit that "Zhuge Liang is really a fine strategist!" Before long they saw Zhuge Liang. Guan Yu and Zhang Fei dismounted and bowed before him.

Liu Bei knew that Cao Cao would come again with an even stronger force. Zhuge Liang said that Liu Biao was ill and was failing fast, so this was the time to make the region his base where they could ensure their safety against Cao Cao. "You speak well, but Liu Biao has shown me great kindness, and I cannot bear to do him an ill turn," said Liu Bei. "If you do

not take this opportunity, you will regret it for ever," said Zhuge Liang.

When Xiahou Dun leading the defeated soldiers returned to the capital, he presented himself to his master Cao Cao and asked to be executed. But his master pardoned him. New orders were issued by Cao Cao to prepare an army of five hundred thousand troops, divided into five divisions of ten legions each, with the aim of sweeping the south clean.

One of his Ministers, Kong Rong, thought Cao Cao should not undertake this unjustifiable expedition. One of the clients of the Imperial Inspector Chi Lu, whom Kong Rong had always treated contemptuously and disdainfully, happened to hear this and carried the tale to Cao Cao. Chi Lu's tale angered Cao Cao, who ordered the arrest and execution of the high minister and his family.

About this time the Imperial Protector of Jingzhou became seriously ill, and he summoned Liu Bei to his chamber. Liu Biao entrusted his children to Liu Bei's guardianship. He begged Liu Bei to administer the region after his death.

Eventually Liu Biao died. Then the widow and her supporters took counsel together and forged a will and testament conferring the lordship of Jingzhou on the second son Liu Zong. No notice of the death was sent to Liu Qi, the first son, or to Liu Bei, the uncle. So the younger son was placed in his father's seat, and the Cai clan shared among them the whole military authority of the region. Lady Cai and her son took up their residence in Xiangyang so as to be out of the reach of the rightful heir and his uncle.

Then startling news of the approach of Cao Cao's great army arrived. Fu Xuan, Kuai Yue and others wanted to surrender to Cao Cao. Liu Zong disagreed, but Lady Cai supported the surrender.

The letter of surrender was composed and entrusted to one Song Zhong to convey secretly to Cao Cao, offering the whole region to him.

The messenger tried to escape observation, but was captured and taken to be questioned by Guan Yu. Then he was carried off to Xinye and made to retell his story to Liu Bei who was angry and concerned at the news. Yi Ji advised Liu Bei to go to Xiangyang as if he was going to attend the mourning ceremonies. Then he could draw out Liu Zong from the city to welcome him. Then he could seize him, slay his entire supporting party, and take over the region. Liu did not agree. He decided to abandon Xinye and move to Fankou, thus evading Cao Cao's forces.

Then notices were posted on all gates to the effect that all the people, without exception, were to follow their ruler at once to the new city in order to escape danger. Zhuge Liang gave directions to move forces to confront Cao's men. Zhuge Liang and Liu Bei went away to an elevated position from where they could watch what happened and await reports of victory.

The red flags were to move left and the blue to move right to confuse the enemy so that Xu Chu's men would be afraid to advance further and would camp at Magpie Tail Slope. Then he heard from the hills the sound of musical instruments and, looking up, saw on the hill top two umbrellas surrounded by many banners. There sat Liu Bei and Zhuge Liang quietly drinking and watching the proceedings. Angry at their perceived coolness, Xu Chu sought for a way up the mountain, but huge logs of wood and great stones were thrown down, and he was driven back.

Then Cao Ren arrived and ordered an attack on Xinye so that he would have a place to rest in. They marched to the walls and found the gates wide open. They entered and found a deserted city. No one could be seen anywhere. After the first watch the wind began to blow. Soon after the gate guards reported that a fire had started. A great hubbub of shouting sprung up behind them, and Zhao Yun's troops came up and attacked.

Cao Ren's men directed their way to the White River, joyfully remembering that the river was shallow and easily fordable. And they went down into the stream and drank their fill, the humans shouting and the horses neighing. About the fourth watch, Guan Yu heard downstream the sounds of soldiers and horses and at once ordered the breaking of the dam. The water rushed down in a torrent and overwhelmed the soldiers in the bed of the river. Many were swept away and drowned.

Presently Cao Ren and his troops reached the Boling Ferry in Boling. Here, where they thought there would be safe, they found their way barred. With great shouts suddenly being heard, they were intercepted by Zhang Fei. A great battle broke out.

Zhuge Liang anticipated that they could not defend Fankou, so he had requested Liu Bei to take Xiangyang. All the people were willing to follow the Prince even to death. They started at once, some lamenting, some weeping, the young helping the aged, parents leading their children, the strong soldiers carrying the women. "Why was I ever born," said Liu Bei, "to be the cause of all this misery to the people?" He made to leap into the river,

but they held him back and wouldn't let him.

When Xiangyang came into view, they saw many flags flying on the walls and that the moat was protected by barbed barriers. Liu Zong's general Wei Yan opened the gate to let in Liu Bei. Seeing the conflict inside Xiangyang, Liu Bei did not wish to enter the city. Zhuge Liang came up with a plan, and advised Liu Bei to take Jiang Ling, an important strategic town, as a good place to settle for the moment.

Liu Bei's followers numbered more than a hundred thousand, and they slowly walked to Jiangling. When they were just about to be overtaken, the generals of Liu Bei advised him to leave the people to their fate for a time and press on at greater speed to Jiangling. But Liu Bei refused, saying, "The success of every great enterprise depends upon the people; how can I abandon these people who have freely joined me?"

Meanwhile Cao Cao was at Fankou. In AD 208, he summoned Liu Zong, but Liu Zong was too afraid to answer his call. Then Cai Mao and Zhang Yun went to Fankou to see Cao Cao. Cao Cao conferred upon Cai Mao the title of Lord Who Controls the South, and Supreme Admiral of the Naval Force; and Zhang Yun was made his Vice Admiral and given the title of Lord Who Brings Obedience. He asked them to communicate to Liu Zong that Liu Biao's son would be made Perpetual Imperial Protector of Jingzhou in succession to his late father.

Liu Zong's mother crossed the river to welcome Cao Cao, who conferred upon Liu Zong the title of Imperial Protector of Qingzhou in the north. Liu Zong was greatly frightened and had to proceed to his region forthwith. Cao Cao sent Yue Jin to put Liu Zong and his mother to death.

CHAPTER 11

Fight at the Long Slope Bridge

Being told that soldiers and the people led by Liu Bei could move forward only three or four miles daily, Cao Cao chose five thousand of his most trusted horsemen and sent them in pursuit of the cavalcade, ordering them to overtake the convoy with a day and a night.

Liu Bei hoped that Zhuge Liang would go to Jingzhou to try to persuade Liu Qi, the elder son of Liu Biao, with his troops to offer help. Liu Bei led his soldiers and people to camp just outside Dangyang. In the middle of the fourth watch, Cao Cao's men appeared and launched a fierce onslaught. In the midst of the crisis Zhang Fei apppeared, and heroically managed to rescue his brother, and bring him away to Long Slope Bridge.

Now Zhao Yun, after battling the enemy from the fourth watch till daylight, could see no sign of his lord and, moreover, had dire fears that he had also lost his lord's family. Zhao Yun found Lady Mi seriously wounded beside an old well behind the

broken wall of a burned house. She begged Zhao Yun to take Liu Shan and escape. She turned over and threw herself into the old well.

Zhao Yun pushed over the wall to fill the well, thus making a grave for the lady. Then he loosened his armor, and placed the child by his breast. This done he slung his spear and remounted, and fought his way out of the conflict. Zhao Yun was approaching the bridge where he saw Zhang Fei standing ready for the fray. "Help me, Zhang Fei!" he cried and crossed the bridge.

When he came to Liu Bei, Zhao Yun handed over Liu Shan. He dismounted and couldn't stop weeping. The tears also came to Liu Bei's eyes when he saw his faithful commander. Liu Bei took the child but threw it aside angrily, saying, "To preserve this suckling I very nearly lost a great commander!" Zhao Yun picked up the child again and, still weeping, said, "Were I to be ground to powder, I still could never express my gratitude."

There he was seated on his battle steed, guarding the bridge. They also saw great clouds of dust rising above the trees and concluded they would definitely fall into an ambush if they ventured across the bridge. So they halted the pursuit, and did not dare to advance further, lest they should become victims of another ruse inspired by Zhuge Liang. Turning to his followers, Cao Cao said, "Guan Yu has said that his brother Zhang Fei was the sort of man who would go through an army of a hundred legions to take the head of its commander in chief, and would

do it easily. Now here lies this terror in front of us, and we must be careful." This great noise had scarcely begun when one of Cao Cao's staff, Xiahou Jie, fell from his horse terror-stricken, paralyzed with fear.

Zhang Fei saw this weakness and disorder in the enemy but he dared not go in pursuit. Instead he ordered his men to destroy the bridge.

This done he went to report to Liu Bei and told him of the destruction of the bridge. Liu Bei said, "The destruction of the bridge will bring him in pursuit." So orders were given to march, and they went by a bye-road which led diagonally to Hanyang and Minyang.

Now Cao Cao issued his orders to his army saying, "Every general must do whatever possible to press on." In consequence every leader bade those under him to hasten forward. They were pressing on at great speed when suddenly a body of soldiers appeared from the hills and a voice cried, "I will wait for longer." As soon as Guan Yu appeared, Cao Cao stopped Zhuge Liang! Without any more ado he ordered a full retreat.

Guan Yu wanted to act as a guard for his elder brother on his way to Jiangjin. The troops hadn't gone far on the boats before they saw Liu Qi leading reinforcement. Subsequently, in the southwest there appeared a line of fighting ships sailing up before a fair wind led by Zhuge Liang. Liu Qi wanted his uncle to stay a while in Jiangxia till the army was thoroughly organised. Then he could move onto Xiakou.

Seeing Liu Bei retreating to Jiangxia, Cao Cao used Xun You's ruse. He sent letters to Sun Quan, urging him to join him in an attack on Liu Bei, while he himself prepared his army, horse and foot and boats. The attack was to be by land and water at the same time. The fleet advanced up the river in two lines. On the west the line extended to Jingxia, on the east to Qichun. The stockades stretched for one hundred miles.

The story of Cao Cao's movements and successes had reached Sun Quan, then camped at Chaisang. He assembled his strategists to decide on the best defensive scheme. Lu Su said, "Jingzhou is contiguous to our borders. It is strong and its people are rich. It is the sort of country that an emperor or a king should covet. Liu Biao's recent death offers an excuse for me to be sent to convey condolence and thus I can spy out the actual situation.

Zhuge Liang hoped that Sun Quan and Cao Cao would end up fighting each other. Lu Su invited Zhuge Liang to cross the River to see Sun Quan.

In the boat on the way to Chaisang, Lu Su said to his companion, "When you see my master, do not reveal the truth about the magnitude of Cao Cao's army." Zhuge Liang said that there was no need to remind him of that.

After Sun Quan recieved the letter from Cao Cao proposing a joint attack upon Liu Bei, he called in all his civil and military officials for a meeting. Many civil officials including Zhang Zhao advocated surrendering to Cao Cao. Suan Quan deferred making a decision.

Outside he took Lu Su by the hand, and asked for Lu Su's opinion. Lu Su said, "A common person might submit; you cannot." Sun Quan agreed with Lu's view. "I have brought back with me Zhuge Liang, the younger brother of our Zhuge Jin. If you question him, he can explain the situation clearly," Lu Su added.

The other officers now began to have some fear of this influential man. Suddenly Huang Gai appeared from outside and angrily shouted, "You all sit there talking talking talking while our archenemy Cao Cao is nearing our borders. Instead of discussing how to oppose Cao Cao, you are all wrangling and disputing." He turned to address Zhuge Liang, and said, "There is a saying that though something may be gained by talk, there is more to be got by silence. Why not give my lord the advantage of your valuable advice instead of wasting time talking with this crowd."

As Huang Gai and Lu Su led the guest toward their master's apartments, Zhuge Liang glanced up at his host. He noted the dignified commanding air of the man and thought to himself, "Certainly in appearance this is no common man. He is one that could be incited perhaps, but not persuaded. "Zhuge Liang said that including cavalry and soldiers, on land and sea, Cao Cao had a million strong force and that there were more than a thousand capable and experienced leaders; maybe as many as two thousand. Lu Su was much disturbed and turned pale. He looked at the bold speaker, but Zhuge Liang did not return his gaze.

Sun Quan asked Zhuge Liang what he should do. Zhuge Liang said, "I advise you to count your forces and decide whether they are sufficient to venture forth to confront Cao Cao without delay. If you cannot, then follow the advice of your councilors. "Sun Quan asked him why Liu Bei would not yield. He replied that it was necessary to remember that Liu Bei was from a Dynastic Family, besides being a man of great renown. Every one looks up to him. His lack of success is simply the will of Heaven, but manifestly he cannot bow the knee to any one. Feeling that according to Zhuge Liang, he could not match Liu Bei, Sun Quan rose and went to the inner room.

Lu Su was annoyed and reproached Zhuge Liang for his direct way of talking to Sun Quan, saying, "Luckily for you, my lord is too tolerant to rebuke you to your face, for you spoke to him in a tone most inappropriate."

Zhuge Liang threw back his head and laughed. "What a sensitive fellow you are!" he cried. "I know how Cao Cao can be destroyed, but he didn't ask me; so I said nothing."

Both host and guest retired to the inner room where wine was served. People continued their discussions. Zhuge Liang analyzed the weakness of Cao Cao's forces and strategy and talked about Sun and Liu's possible joint resistance against Cao. Sun Quan was overjoyed and decided to prepare for a joint attack on Cao Cao.

Unexpectedly, the doubts of Zhang Rang and others again surged up in the mind of Sun Quan. He recalled the dying message of Sun Ce—"for internal matters consult Zhang Zhao; for external policy, Zhou Yu."

CHAPTER 12

Zhuge Liang Debates with Scholars

Zhou Yu had been training his naval forces on Poyang Lake when he heard of the approach of Cao Cao's forces and had started for Chaisang immediately. As he and Lu Su were close friends, the latter went to welcome him and told him of all that had happened. Zhou Yu asked Lu Su to rest assured and to go and beg Zhuge Liang to come to see him.

First came Zhang Zhao, Zhang Hong, Gu Yong, and Bu Zhi to represent their factions to find out what might be afoot. Zhou Yu asked, "Are you all unanimous in your opinions?" "We are perfectly unanimous," said Zhang Zhao. Zhou Yu said, "The fact is I have also desired to surrender for a long time. I beg you to leave me now, and tomorrow we will see our master, and I shall convince him."

Very soon came the military party led by Cheng Pu, Huang Gai, and Han Dang. They said that they would rather die than surrender. Zhou Yu said, "My desire also is to decide matters with Cao Cao on the battlefield. How can we think of submission? Now I pray you retire, generals, and when I see our lord, I will settle his doubts."

About evening time, Lu Su and Zhuge Liang came, and Zhou Yu went out to the main gate to receive them. Zhou Yu spoke: "We cannot oppose Cao Cao when he acts at the command of the Emperor. However, he is very strong, and to attack him is a serious risk. In my opinion, opposition will mean certain defeat and, since submission means peace, I have decided to advise our lord to write and offer surrender." The two wrangled for a long time, while Zhuge Liang sat smiling with his arms folded.

Presently Zhou Yu asked, "Why do you smile thus, Master?" And Zhuge Liang replied, "I am thinking of your opponent Lu Su, who knows nothing of the affairs of the day. There is another way to do this, and a cheaper one. If Cao Cao got only these two

persons behind him, his hordes and legions would just drop their weapons, roll up their banners, and silently vanish away." He added, "Cao Cao built a pavilion on the River Zhang; it was to be named the Bronze Bird Tower. He wanted to get these two very famous beauties from Wu, surnamed Qiao. Given these two, Cao Cao would retreat troops." Zhou Yu cried out, "You old rebel; this insult is too outrageous!" Zhou Yu listened to the end but then suddenly jumped up in a tremendous rage.

"You do not know, Sir," replied Zhou Yu. "These two women of the Qiao family you mention, the Elder Qiao is the widow of Sun Ce, our late ruler, and the Younger Qiao is my wife!" Zhuge Liang feigned the greatest astonishment and said that he had no idea! Zhou Yu replied sincerely, "What I said just now was to see how you stood. I left Poyang Lake with the intention of attacking the north, and nothing can change that intention, not even a sword at my breast or an ax on my neck. But I trust you will lend the strength of your arm, and we will smite Cao Cao together." Zhuge Liang happily agreed.

Next day at dawn Sun Quan went to the council chamber, where his officials, civil and military, were already assembled. After presenting an analysis of the favourable conditions for Wu against Cao Cao's army, Zhou Yu said, "Thy servant will fight a decisive battle, and shrink not from any sacrifice. General, do not hesitate." Sun Quan drew the sword that hung at his side and slashed off a corner of the table in front of him, exclaiming, "Let any other person mention surrender, and he shall be served just as this table."

Then he handed the sword to Zhou Yu, at the same time commissioning him as Commander-in-Chief and Supreme Admiral, Cheng Pu was made Vice Admiral. Lu Su was also nominated Assistant Commander. In conclusion Sun Quan said, "With this sword you may slay any officer who disobeys your commands."

Next morning at dawn, Zhou Yu went to his camp and took his seat in the council tent. The armed guards took up their stations to the right and left, and the officers ranged themselves in lines to listen to their orders. He ordered a division of the troops into five parts, and they all set out immediately to camp at the meeting of the three Rivers.

Zhou Yu invited Lu and Zhuge Liang to the meeting of the three Rivers. Zhou Yu entrusted the task of cutting off supplies to Zhuge Liang and his colleagues Guan Yu, Zhang Fei, and Zhao Yun. He knew that Zhou Yu hoped to set Liu's troops against Cao Cao. He could not refuse; therefore Zhuge Liang accepted the task with alacrity.

Lu Su left and went to see Zhuge Liang to find out if he suspected anything. Lu Su found him looking quite unconcerned preparing the soldiers to march. Unable to let Zhuge Liang go without a warning, however, Lu Su asked plaintively whether this expedition would succeed. Zhuge Liang laughingly replied, "I am an adept at all sorts of fighting, on foot, horse, and chariot on land and on sea. There is no doubting my success. I am not like you and your friend, who can only move in one direction."

Lu Su carried this story to Zhou Yu, which only alienated him even more against Zhuge Liang. He himself wanted to go to the Iron Pile Mountains to cut off supplies. Zhuge Liang said, "Zhou Yu only wanted me to go on this expedition because he wanted Cao Cao to kill me. Now is the critical moment, and Marquis Sun Quan and my master must act in harmony if we are to succeed. If each one tries to harm the other, the whole scheme will fail." Lu Su carried this story to Zhou Yu. Zhou Yu sighed, "This man is far too clever; he defeats me ten to one. He will have to be done away with or my country will suffer."

Zhuge Liang had gone to Wu some time previously, and no word had come from him, so Liu Bei sent Mi Zhu to go to find out what was happening in the name of rewarding the troops. Accepting the gifts, Zhou Yu expressed the hope that Mi Zhu could go back to ask Liu Bei to cross the River and make a joint move against Cao's men, thus sentencing Liu Bei and Zhuge Liang to certain death.

In order to launch a joint attack upon Cao Cao's men, Liu Bei had to move forward. He let Guan Yu come with him while Zhang Fei and Zhao Yun kept guard. Zhou Yu sent for the executioners and placed them in hiding between the outer and inner tents, and picked up a cup ready to remove Liu Bei. This was the signal agreed upon. But at that moment Zhou Yu saw so fierce a look upon the face of the trusty henchman who stood, sword in hand, behind his guest. He hesitated.

When Liu Bei went back to the boat after the banquet, he found Zhuge Liang waiting in the boat. Liu Bei was exceedingly pleased, but Zhuge Liang told him of the great danger he was in. Liu Bei just understood. Zhuge Liang demanded that Liu Bei on the twentieth day of the eleventh month, send Zhao Yun with a small ship to the south bank to wait for him. He said to be sure there was no mistake. With that, Zhuge Liang pressed him to go.

Zhou Yu was angry at his hesitation in killing Liu Bei, when suddenly a messenger was announced with a letter from Cao Cao. Zhou Yu ordered them to bring him in and took the letter. But when he saw the greeting, "The First Minister of Han to Commander-in-Chief Zhou Yu," He fell into a frenzy of rage, tore the letter to fragments, and threw them on the ground. The messengers were slain to show their dignity and independence.

Finding that the unhappy bearer of the letter had been decapitated, and his head sent back to Cao Cao, Cao Cao went as hastily as possible to the meeting of the three rivers.

Cao Cao's soldiers, being mostly from the dry plains of the north, did not know how to fight effectually on water, and the southern ships had the battle all their own way. Cao Cao ordered the Supreme Admiral Cai Mao, the Vice Admiral Zhang Yun, and others of the Jingzhou officers who had joined his side, to train the sea-based troops day and night.

When night fell, Zhou Yu went up to the summit of one of the hills and looked out over the long line of bright lights stretching toward the west, showing the extent of the enemy's camp. Next day Zhou Yu decided that he would go in person to

find out the strength of the enemy. Seeing that everything was most admirable and hearing that Cai Mao and Zhang Yun were in command of the troops, he thought, "I must find some means of removing them."

Cao Cao was told that Zhou Yu had discovered the camps of his water-based troops, so he called in his generals for a meeting. Jiang Gan, one of his counselors in the camp said that Zhou Yu and he were fellow students and friends and that he would go over and persuade him to surrender.

CHAPTER 13

Battle of Chibi in AD 208

hou Yu left the tent to meet Jiang Gan, and said "You have wandered far and suffered much in this task of emissary in Cao Cao's cause." Jiang Gan said "I came to visit you for the sake of old times." Seeing Zhou Yu didn't believe him, Jiang Gan was about to leave. Zhou Yu took Jiang Gan by the arm, said, "I feared you might be coming on his behalf to try to persuade me. But if this is not your intention, you need not go away so hastily." Zhou Yu ordered servants to prepare a banquet and he introduced his officers to Jiang Gan.

Zhou Yu said to them, "Jiang Gan is an old fellow student of mine, and we are pledged friends. Though he has arrived here from the north, he is no artful pleader. This day we speak only of friendship and we shan't discuss military affairs." Then Zhou Yu took off his sword and handed it to Taishi Ci, saying "This day we meet only as friends and speak only of friendship, and if any one begins a discussion of the questions at issue between Cao Cao and our country, just slay him." Jiang Gan didn't dare to say a word.

When all were half drunk, Zhou Yu, laying hold of Jiang Gan's hand, led him outside the tent, asking him to have a look at the battalion, grain and forage. Zhou Yu pretended to be quite intoxicated and said "A man of the time, I have found a proper lord to serve. He listens to my words and follows my plans. We share the same fair or evil fortune. Even when persuaders' words pour forth like a rushing river, their tongues are as a sharp sword. It is impossible to move men such as me." Zhou Yu burst into a loud laugh as he finished, and Jiang Gan's face became clay-colored and he remained silent.

Zhou Yu then led his guest back into the tent, and again they fell to drinking. He pointed to the others at table and said to Jiang Gan, "These are all the best and bravest of the land of the south; one might even call this a 'Meeting of Heroes.'" Zhou Yu even gave an exhibition of sword play and sang till the lamps had been lit. Zhou Yu.

When Zhou Yu emitted uncouth grunts and groans in his sleep, Jiang Gan rose and saw on the table a heap of papers, and he looked at them furtively, and saw they were letters. Among them he saw one marked as coming from Cai Mao and Zhang Yun. Jiang hid the letter in his pocket. Then, he blew out the light and went to the couch again. However, Jiang found it hard to fall asleep.

During the fourth watch, some one came in, saying "General!" Zhou Yu started awake and walked out of the tent with the man to talk in low voices. Jiang Gan listened intently. He heard the man say that Cai Mao and Zhang Yun were not yet in a position to carry out their plan. But he couldn't make out what fol lowed.

Jiang Gan thought he would never be able to escape after day broke if he didn't escape immediately. He hastened back to Cao Cao's camp and gave the letter to Cao Cao. Cao Cao was very angry and had Cai Mao and Zhang Yun executed. By that time Cao Cao had thought over the matter, and it dawned upon him that he had been tricked. He was extremely guilty.

After hearing that Cai Mao and Zhang Yun had been beheaded, Zhou Yu asked Lu Su to meet with Zhuge Liang to see whether he knew anything of it. Zhuge Liang said, "Cai Mao and Zhang Yun are gone and your country is freed from the grave anxiety caused by Cao Cao's navy." Zhuge Liang also persuaded Lu Su not to tell what he had said to Zhou Yu for fear that Zhou Yu would seek some chance to do him harm.

Lu Su promised; nevertheless he went straight to Zhou Yu and related the whole thing just as it happened. The following day, Zhou Yu asked Zhuge Liang to make a hundred thousand arrows within ten days or face being beheaded. Zhuge Liang said, "Let me have three days." Zhou Yu asked Lu Su to make sure the workers delayed as much as they could so as to give him an excuse to kill Zhuge Liang.

Zhuge Liang asked Lu Su to lend him twenty vessels, each manned by thirty people. He also lashed blue cotton screens and bundles of straw to the sides of the boats. He also said to Lu Su that he must on no account let Zhou Yu know, or his scheme would not work. Lu Su consented in confusion and this time he kept his word.

At midnight on the third day, the night proved very foggy

and the mist was very thick along the river. Zhuge Liang sent a private message asking Lu Su to come to his boat to pick up the arrows. The twenty boats were fastened together by long ropes and had moved over to the north bank. When they were about to reach Cao Cao's naval camp, Zhuge Liang gave orders to beat the drums and shout loudly. Cao Cao thought he was under attack. He ordered his soldiers to fire their arrows, all of which hit the jackstraws. When the fog dispersed, Zhuge Liang had got over one hundred thousand arrows.

Zhuge Liang went back to the tent of Zhou Yu to report on his completion of the mission. Zhu Yu hosted a banquet in honour of Zhuge Liang. He said to Zhuge Liang, "I have thought of a plan, but I am not sure if it will work. I should be very happy if you would give me your opinion." Zhuge Liang said, "Do not say what your plan is, and each of us will write in the palm of his hand and see whether our opinions agree." Then they sat together on the same bench, and each showed his hand to the other. They both burst out laughing, for both had written the same word "fire".

Cao Cao had expended a forest of arrows for no vain and was much irritated in consequence. Xun You suggested Cao Cao sending some one who should pretend to surrender to Zhou Yu so as to assassinate him. Cao Cao decided to try this plan, and he sent two younger brothers of Cai Mao, Cai Zhong and Cai He, to surrender to the South Land.

Zhou Yu saw the two people coming without their families, and he knew their desertion was only pretense. He kept them at arms length but greatly rewarded them. Then he ordered them to join Gan Ning in the vanguard of the fighting but asked Gan Ning to keep a careful watch over them.

That night, when Zhou Yu was in his tent, Huang Gai came in privately, saying he was willing to feign desertion to Cao Cao. They talked for a while and then Huang Gai left. The next day, Zhou Yu called all the officers together to his tent to discuss official business. Huang Gai said loudly that he wanted to surrender to Cao Cao. Zhou Yu asked the lictors to deal the culprit one hundred blows. Huang Gai's back was cut in many places, and the blood flowed in streams.

Huang Gai's good friend Kan Ze was deeply moved and was willing to present Huang Gai's surrender letter to Cao Cao.

Kan Ze disguised himself as an old fisherman and sent the letter to Cao Cao. Cao Cao didn't believe Kan Ze and wanted to put him to death. At the critical moment, someone came with the secret letter of Cai Zhong and Cai He and handed it to Cao Cao. Then, Cao Cao then believed Kan Ze and asked him to go back to the land of the south to be a double agent.

However, Cao Cao still wanted entirely convinced and he sent Jiang Gan to cross the river to nose around to try to find out the real situation.

Knowing Jiang Gan had arrived, Zhou Yu was pleased because he thought his stratagem had succeeded. When Zhou Yu saw Jiang Gan, Zhou Yu put on an angry face and said, "My friend, why did you treat me so badly? You plundered my private letters and caused all my plans to miscarry. Now what have you come for? Certainly, it is not out of kindness to me." Zhou Yu sent Jiang Gan to a hut in the Western Hills to rest for a few days. Jiang Gan had no choice but to agree.

When Jiang Gan found himself in the lonely hut, he was very depressed and so he took a walk behind the hut. Suddenly, he heard a person playing a flute. He knocked at the door and knew it was Pang Tong, a Master known as Blooming Phoenix. He asked why Pang lived in such a lonely place. Pang said, "That fellow Zhou Yu is too conceited to allow that any one else has any talent but him, and so I live here quietly." Jiang Gan advised him to enter Cao Cao's service and Pang agreed. Thus, they crossed the river and returned back to Cao Cao's camp.

When Cao Cao heard that the newcomer was Master Blooming Phoenix, he went to meet him personally. He invited Pang Tong to tour their camp. Pang praised Cao Cao and offered some advice—join up all the ships, large and small, stern to stern with iron chains and spread boards across them so that there would be no fear of the wind and the waves and the rising and falling tides. Cao Cao asked his people to do it at once.

Pang Tong also said he would go back to induce some other great talents from the land of the south to come over to Cao Cao and take their families along with him. Cao Cao agreed. When Pang Tong was crossing the river, he was seized by someone who said, "You are very bold. Huang Gai is planning to use the 'personal injury ruse', and Kan Ze has presented the letter of pretended desertion. You have proffered the fatal scheme of chaining the ships together lest the flames may not completely destroy them!" Upon turning to look at the man, Pang Tong saw it was Xu Shu, an old friend. Xu Shu asked Pang how he could escape from the disaster of war. Pang Tong shared with him an idea.

Xu Shu acted according to the idea. He mischievously spread certain rumors in the camp that Han Sui and Ma Teng were marching from Xiliang to attack the capital Xudu. Xu Shu said to Cao Cao he would like to lead an army to guard the San Pass and Cao Cao agreed with him. Thus, Xu Shu escaped from Cao's camp.

Cao Cao's anxiety diminished after he had thus sent away Xu Shu. Seeing the southern expedition was about to succeed, Cao Cao was jubilant. He prepared a great banquet on the boats, with music, and invited all his leaders. After a while, Cao Cao started to mock Zhou Yu, Liu Bei and Zhuge Liang and said after he got the South Lands, he would ask Elder Qiao and the Younger Qiao of the South Lands to rejoice in his declining years.

All the officers flattered him in chorus. Cao Cao became even more intoxicated. Setting up his spear in the prow of the ship, he began to chant a poem in high spirits.

The following day, Cao Cao watched his navy from the

General's Terrace and was delighted with their maneuvers. Cheng Yu and Xun You said to Cao Cao, "The ships are firmly attached to each other with iron chains, but you should prepare for an attack by fire so that they can separate in order to avoid it." Cao Cao laughed, saying "Any one using fire depends upon the wind. This is now winter and only west winds blow. You will get neither east nor south winds. I am on the northwest, and the enemy is on the southeast bank. If they use fire, they will destroy themselves."

Zhou Yu watched his own and the enemy ships out on the river. Then an extra violent blast of wind came by. A corner of his own flag flicked Zhou Yu on the cheek, and suddenly a thought flashed through his mind—everything is ready except for the east wind. Suddenly Zhou Yu uttered a loud cry, staggered, and fell backward unconscious.

Zhou Yu lay senseless in bed. Lu Su anxiously went to see Zhuge Liang to talk it over. "I can cure the general," said Zhuge Liang laughing. Lu Su begged Zhuge Liang to quickly come to see the sick man.

Zhou Yu bade his servants help him to a sitting position, and Zhuge Liang entered. "I have not seen you for days," said Zhuge Liang. "How could I guess that you were unwell?" "How can any one feel secure? We are constantly the playthings of luck, good or bad." "Yes; Heaven's winds and clouds are not to be measured. No one can reckon their comings and goings, can they?" Zhou Yu turned pale. Zhuge Liang continued, "You need cooling medicine to dissipate the sense of oppression you feel." Zhou Yu asked him for the prescription.

Zhuge Liang got out his writing materials, sent away the servants, and then wrote a few words "To burn out the fleet Of Cao Cao, you have all you need except for winds from the east." Zhou Yu asked him how to get the east wind. Zhuge Liang asked

Zhou Yu to build an Altar of the Seven Stars. He would work a spell to procure a strong southeast gale for three days and three nights to defeat Cao Cao. Hearing that, Zhou Yu completely recovered.

After the Altar of the Seven Stars was completed, Zhuge Liang, with his hair disheveled and in his bare feet, robed himself as a Taoist and began to procure the east wind.

Towards the third watch, the sound of a strange movement arose in the air.

Zhou Yu was pleased, but suddenly thought that the man had power over the heavens and authority over the earth and he couldn't be allowed to live to be a danger to the lands of the south. He immediately sent two of the generals of his guard, Ding Feng and Xu Sheng, to slay Zhuge Liang. But they found no Zhuge Liang there.

Ding Feng and Xu Sheng hurried to give chase to Zhuge Liang on the river, seeing him in distance. Seeing Xu Sheng came, Zhuge Liang said loudly, "Return and tell the General to make good use of his soldiers. I know all about his plans, and that Zhou Yu would not let me go and that he wants to kill me. That is why Zhao Yun was waiting for me. You had better not come nearer." But Xu Sheng maintained the pursuit. Zhao Yun shot his bow and the arrow whizzed overhead cutting the rope that held up the sail of Xu Sheng's boat. Then, Zhao Yun's boat hoisted its sail, and the fair wind speedily carried it out of sight.

Ding Feng and Xu Sheng returned to camp and told their master about the preparations that Zhuge Liang had made to ensure his safety. Zhou Yu was indeed puzzled at the depth of his rival's insight, "I shall have no peace day or night while he lives."

Immediately after Zhuge Liang returned to Xiakou, he moved the forces to block and attack Cao Cao's army. All this time

Guan Yu had been silently waiting his return, but Zhuge Liang said not one word to him. He asked Zhuge Liang why. Zhuge Liang said he was afraid that Guan Yu might let Cao Cao pass. Guan Yu wrote a formal undertaking and gave the document to Zhuge Liang to guarantee that he wouldn't let Cao Cao pass. Finally, Zhuge Liang agreed to trust him. He sent Guan Yu to lay an ambush with Guan Ping and Zhou Cang at the Huarong Road.

Huang Gai prepared 20 fire boats filled with reeds and firewood as well as fish oil and sulfur. At the third watch of the evening, the twenty boats were sent towards Cao Cao's camp. When Cao Cao realized the danger, it was too late. The boats were all aflame, and with the strong wind, soon gained speed and burst on Cao Cao's camp like fiery arrows. Soon, it seemed as if the universe was filled with flame.

Gan Ning, unfurling the banner of Cao Cao's army, led an army to set fire to the grain depot in the Black Forest. At once, the river and bank were all on fire. Cao Cao and Zhang Liao, with a small party of horsemen, fled through the burning forest and rushed to the Black Forest.

Cao Cao escaped to the Black Forest. Seeing the thickly crowded trees all about him, and the steep hills and narrow passes, Cao Cao threw up his head and laughed, saying "I am only laughing at the stupidity of Zhou Yu and the ignorance of Zhuge Liang. If they had only set an ambush there, as I would have done, why, there would be no escape." Cao Cao had scarcely finished speaking when from the side dashed in a batallion of troops, with Zhao Yun at the vanguard. Cao Cao nearly fell off his horse he was so startled.

Cao Cao ordered Xu Huang and Zhang He to engage the ambushers, and he himself rode off into the smoke and fire. By the time Hulu Valley was reached, his soldiers were almost starving and could march no more; their horses too were worn out. Cao Cao asked soldiers to stop and prepare some food. He began to laugh out loud again, saying "I am laughing again at the ignorance of the same two men. If I were in their place, and conducting their campaign, I should have set another ambush here, to set upon us when we were tired out. Then, even if we escaped with our lives, we should suffer very severely." Just at that moment behind them rose a great yell, as Zhang Fei appeared with a good number of troops.

The soldiers were terrified at the sight of the terrible warrior Zhang Fei. Xu Chu, mounted on a bare-backed horse, rode up to engage him, and Zhang Liao and Xu Huang galloped to his aid, while Cao Cao made off at top speed. At the crossroads, the soldiers asked Cao Cao for instructions on the direction they should take. Cao Cao had heard that the high road was usually quiet and there were several columns of smoke rising from the hills along the bye road which was narrow and difficult to set an ambush on. So, Cao Cao bade take the bye road.

When they pressed on, the path became moderately level. Cao Cao broke out once again into loud laughter. The officers and soldiers knew that Cao Cao was laughing at Zhuge Liang and Zhou Yu again. Cao Cao had not finished his speech this time when the explosion of a firecracker broke the silence, and a company of troops appeared barring the way. The leader was Guan Yu.

The soldiers were exhausted and their horses spent, and they had no strength to fight any more. Cheng Yu suggested Cao Cao go and beg Guan Yu for leniency. Cao Cao agreed to try. Seeing the soldiers of Cao Cao lacking clothing and armor and so tattered and disordered, Guan Yu breathed a deep sigh and pulled at the bridle of his steed and turned away, letting them pass.

The military order suddenly occurred again to Guan Yu. He turned to look back and uttered a great shout. Cao Cao's soldiers jumped off their horses and knelt on the ground crying for mercy. Guan Yu had great pity for them. He let all of them pass.

Having escaped this danger, Cao Cao hastened to leave the valley. When Cao Ren came to aid Cao Cao, he had only 27 horsemen. Cao Cao cried aloud. The officers asked him why. Cao Cao said, "I am thinking of my friend Guo Jia; had he been alive, he would not have let me suffer this loss." This harsh reproach shamed his advisers.

After having allowed the escape of Cao Cao, Guan Yu found his way back to headquarters. Zhuge Liang called in the lictors and told them to take away Guan Yu and put him to death. Liu Bei personally begged his counsellor to forgive Guan Yu, saying Guan Yu had been responsible for many major victories in the past. So the sentence was remitted.

CHAPTER 14

Seizing Nanjun Town

Zhou Yu felt very happy about his great success in defeating Cao Cao. He mustered his officers and called in his soldiers, with a view to attacking and capturing Nanjun. Sun Qian arrived with congratulations and presents from Liu Bei. Hearing that Liu Bei was encamped at Youkou, at the mouth of the River You, Zhou Yu knew that Liu Bei also wanted to capture Nanjun, so he was quite angry. He went to negotiate with Liu Bei using the excuse of thanking him for his help in defeating Cao Cao.

Liu Bei asked Zhuge Liang why Zhou Yu should come to render thanks in person. Zhuge Liang said he had come in connection with Nanjun and talked over possible countermeasures with Liu Bei. They drew up their warships on the river and ranged their soldiers along the banks and asked Zhao Yun to welcome Zhou Yu.

When the arrival of Zhou Yu was formally announced, Zhao Yun went to welcome him and Liu Bei held a banquet in his honour. When they mentioned the matter of capturing Nanjun, Liu Bei said Cao Ren had previously overseen the region and he was hard to cope with, but Zhou Yu said, "Well, if we do not take it then, Sir, you may have it."

Zhou Yu put Jiang Qin in command of his vanguard, with Xu Sheng and Ding Feng as assistants. They quickly captured Yiling and then moved to attack Nanjun. Cao Ren was anxious and opened a letter of guidance from Cao Cao. In accordance with the plan in the letter, the whole army moved out of the city, but they left behind the banners on the walls.

In the following day, the army of the South Lands attacked the city, but Cao Ren and Cao Hong pretended to flee. The army of the South Land continued to pursue them. Zhou Yu, seeing the city gates standing wide open and no guards upon the walls, ordered the raiding of the city. Unexpectedly, the archers and crossbowmen let fly, and arrows flew forth in a sudden fierce shower. Zhou Yu managed to pull up in time, but turning to escape, he was wounded on the left side and rescued by his subordinates. Cao Ren and Cao Hong led the troops back from different directions, and the battle went badly against the soldiers of Zhou Yu.

Zhou Yu was hit by a poisonous arrow. The army physician said to him, "You, General, must keep quiet and free from any irritation, because this will cause the wound to reopen." Cao Ren, knowing that Zhou Yu was severely wounded, ordered his soldiers to shout curses every day. Zhou Yu was terribly indignant and couldn't stop himself from engaging once again with the opponent. Before the two armies crossed swords, Zhou Yu suddenly uttered a loud cry, and he fell to the ground with blood gushing from his mouth. His men managed to take him back to his tent safely.

Soon after the army of the South Lands returned to their camp, they dressed in the symbols of mourning, giving the message that Zhou Yu was dead. Pleased at this news, Cao Ren at once began to arrange to make a night attack on the camp. However, he played into the hands of Zhou Yu, who of course was not dead, and only escaped after a severe defeat.

Zhou Yu and his army then made their way to Nanjun where they were startled to see flags on the walls and every sign of occupation. Before they had recovered from their surprise, there appeared a figure who cried, "Pardon, General; I have orders from the Directing Instructor to take this city. I am Zhao Yun of Changshan." Zhou Yu was fiercely angry and gave orders to assault the city, but the defenders sent down flight after flight of arrows, and his troops could not get near the ramparts.

In the meantime he decided to send Gan Ning with a force of several thousand to capture Jingzhou City, and Ling Tong

with another army to take Xiangyang. But even as these orders were being given, the scouts came in hurriedly to report that Zhuge Liang, had suddenly forged a military commission, and had induced the guards of Jingzhou and Xiangyang to both leave; whereupon Zhang Fei occupied Jingzhou and Guan Yu seized Xiangyang. Zhou Yu uttered a great cry, for at that moment his wound had suddenly burst open. He fell to the ground with blood gushing from his mouth.

Several days later, Zhou Yu planned to attack Nanjun, but was prevented by Lu Su who said, "Let me go and see Liu Bei and talk reason to him. If I cannot arrive at an understanding, then attack at once."

Lu Su met Liu Bei and Zhuge Liang, and told them that the South Lands had spent much treasure and military force beating back the army of Cao Cao, so Jingzhou with its nine territories ought to be ceded to the South Lands. Zhuge Liang said, "These places have never belonged to the South Lands, but were part of the patrimony of Liu Biao, and though he is dead, his son remains. Should not the uncle assist the nephew to recover his own lands? How could my master do otherwise?" Lu Su said not a word; he was too much taken aback. However, he recovered himself presently and said if Liu Qi died, Jingzhou and Xiangyang should be returned to the South Lands.

Lu Su hastened back to his own camp and gave Zhou Yu an account of his mission. Zhou Yu was greatly irritated again. At that moment, Sun Quan ordered Zhou Yu to go to Hefei to help him. Zhou Yu had to withdraw troops.

Liu Bei was exceedingly well satisfied with the new possessions in this new region and readily gave the green light to the plan forwarded by Ma Liang to attack Lingling and Guiyang. Zhao Yun and Zhang Fei vied to be given responsibility for the mission to attack Gui Yang. They were told to decide the issue by drawing lots, and Zhao Yun drew the winning lot and immediately pledged to take Guiyang with only 3,000 soldiers.

The governor of Guiyang, Zhao Fan, intended to surrender because he was afraid of the army of Liu Bei. However, his officers Chen Ying and Bao Long were determined to confront the invaders and turn them back. Later, Chen Ying was taken captive by Zhao Yun and Zhao Fan opened the city gates in surrender.

Zhao Fan held a banquet for Zhao Yun and swore brotherhood with him. Zhao Fan asked his sister-in-law who had lost her husband to offer a cup of wine to Zhao Yun, with a view to perhaps offering her in marriage. Zhao Yun was very angry. He raised his fist and knocked Zhao Fan down. Then he strode out of the place, mounted, and rode out of the city.

Zhao Fan plotted with Chen Ying and Bao Long about how they could murder Zhao Yun. However, their plot was discovered by Zhao Yun, who killed Chen Ying and Bao Long and took Zhao Fan captive.

When Liu Bei and Zhuge Liang arrived in Guiyang, Zhao Fan related the history of the proposed marriage to them. Both Liu Bei and Zhuge Liang thought it a fine idea, but Zhao Yun didn't agree. Liu Bei praised Zhao Yun as an honorable man.

When Zhang Fei attacked Wuling, the Governor of Wuling, Jin Xuan by name, closed his ears to his main adviser Gong Zhi who tried to persuade him to surrender to Zhang Fei. Zhang Fei shouted in a voice of thunder. Poor Jin Xuan was seized with panic, turned pale and could not go on. He turned his steed and fled. At the city wall, the fugitives were greeted by a shower of arrows from their own wall. Greatly frightened, Jin Xuan looked up to see what this meant, and there was Gong Zhi, who had opposed him. An arrow wounded Jin Xuan in the face. Gong Zhi then went out and made a formal submission.

Guan Yu proposed an attack on Changsha. Zhuge Liang said the Governor of Changsha, Han Xuan, had a certain general named Huang Zhong who was a man to be feared and a deadly accurate archer and suggested Guan Yu take a larger number of troops. However, Guan Yu wouldn't listen, and only take five hundred swordsmen.

Guan Yu and Huang Zhong fought a hundred and more bouts, and neither seemed any nearer victory. The next day, Guan Yu suddenly wheeled round his horse and fled from his fight with Huang Zhong. Of course Huang Zhong gave chase. However, Huang Zhong's steed stumbled and threw him. Guan Yu didn't kill him and asked him to change horses so they could fight again.

In the battle the following day, Huang Zhong fled as if he was about to be overcome. Guan Yu pursued him. Huang Zhong took his bow and fired his bow twice. One of the arrows hit the base of Guan Yu's helmet. Guan Yu understood that his opponent was giving him this warning in gratitude for sparing him the previous day. Both withdrew.

Han Xuan saw all clearly from the city wall. He said Huang Zhong had collaborated with the enemy and would kill Huang Zhong. However, Huang was rescued by Wei Yan, who killed Han Xuan and offered the city to Guan Yu.

Liu Bei and Zhuge Liang held a celebration in honour of Guan Yu. Huang Zhong pleaded illness and wouldn't go to meet them. Liu Bei went in person to Huang Zhong's house and inquired after him, whereupon Huang Zhong came forth and yielded formally.

Zhuge Liang said Wei Yan was a most disloyal man to eat a man's bread and then slay him and he felt he was most wrong to live on his land and offer his territory to another; he would certainly turn against his new master. So Zhuge Liang issued the order to put Wei Yan to death and prevent him from doing future harm. Liu Bei stopped him at once. Zhuge Liang said to Wei Yan, "Do not let a single thought stray elsewhere, or I will have your head by fair means or foul."

Liu Bei and his army returned to Jingzhou. The name of Youkou was changed to Gongan. He enlarged the army and collected grain and money, with a view to accomplishing his undertaking.

CHAPTER 15

Sweet Dew Temple

Sun Quan fought fiercely with Cao Cao's generals Zhang Liao, Li Dian and Yue Jin. Sun Quan's subordinate Song Qian was killed by Yue Jin. Sun Quan was rescued by Cheng Pu.

Taishi Ci, a general under Sun Quan, launched a moonlight attack upon Cao Cao's camp. Unexpectedly, he was defeated by Zhang Liao. He was hit by an arrow and died. Losing two major generals, Sun Quan withdrew his troops.

Soon, Liu Qi died of illness. The South Lands sent Lu Su to get Jingzhou back. Zhuge Liang advised Liu Bei to write a memorial, saying if Liu Bei got the western region, then Jingzhou would be given up to the South Lands.

Lu Su returned and reported to Zhou Yu who said Zhuge Liang had eaten his own words. At that moment, a scout came to report that Lady Gan, the wife of Liu Bei, had died. An idea came to Zhou Yu's mind after hearing this.

Zhou Yu wrote to Sun Quan to send an intermediary to arrange for his sister to wed Liu Bei at her family home and thus they could entice Liu Bei to Nanxu and then detain him and demand Jingzhou as ransom. Zhou Yu asked Lu Su to send the letter to Sun Quan.

Having read that letter, Sun Quan was very pleased and sent Lu Fan to Jingzhou as an intermediary. When Lu Fan talked with Liu Bei about the proposal, Zhuge Liang was listening behind the screen. Liu Bei hesitated and wouldn't dare agree. He asked Lu Fan to stay and promised to give him a reply the following day.

Zhuge Liang persuaded Liu Bei to accept the proposal. However, Liu Bei was worried Zhou Yu might slay him, so he was unwilling to take a risk and go to the South Lands. Zhuge Liang laughed and said, "Let Zhou Yu employ all his ruses; do you think he can get the better of me? Let me act for you, and his calculations will always fall short of his intended mark. Once Sun Quan's sister is in your power, there will be no fear about

Jingzhou." Zhuge Liang asked Sun Qian to go to the South Lands to finalise the engagement.

In the tenth month of the 14th year of the Rebuilt Tranquillity (209 AD), Liu Bei, escorted by Zhao Yun, Sun Qian and five hundred soldiers, went to Nanxu by boat to receive his new bride. Before his departure, Zhuge Liang called in Zhao Yun, and gave him three silken bags holding three schemes and asked him to act as they directed at whatever critical moment should arise.

They arrived and the ships were anchored. This done, the time had come for the first of the silken bags to be opened. And so it was; and thereupon Zhao Yun gave each of his five hundred guards instructions, and they went their several ways, scattering over the city buying all sorts of things, as they said, for the wedding of Liu Bei to the daughter of the Sun House. Next Zhao Yun told Liu Bei what he was to do: pay a visit first to the State Patriarch Qiao, who was the father-in-law of Sun Ce and of Zhou Yu, and to tell him about the marriage.

The State Patriarch Qiao went to the Dowager Marchioness, mother of Sun Quan, to congratulate her on the happy event. But Dowager Marchioness knew nothing about the event. She at once summoned her son and also sent her servants into town to see what was going on. Her servants returned and affirmed the truth of it.

The Dowager Marchioness was terribly taken aback and

upset so that when Sun Quan arrived, he found his mother beating her breast and weeping bitterly. Sun Quan said there was no truth to it and that it was just one of Zhou Yu's ruses to get hold of Jingzhou. But the Dowager was in a rage and vented her wrath by abusing Sun Quan and Zhou Yu. She said to Sun Quan, "Arrange for me to get a look at him tomorrow at the Sweet Dew Temple. If he displeases me, you may do what you want with him."

Sun Quan had to do as his mother said, but prepared an ambush of swordsmen in the Sweet Dew Temple ready to act depending on the Dowager's attitude. Unexpectedly, the Dowager Marchioness was delighted with the appearance of Liu Bei, and she said, "Liu Bei is an ideal son-in-law for me!" Sun Quan, instead of killing him, had to hold a banquet for Liu Bei.

Zhao Yun came in and said to his master that there were a lot of armed ruffians hidden away in the temple. Thereupon Liu Bei knelt at the feet of the Dowager and asked her to save him. The Dowager scolded her son sharply but Sun Quan blamed Jia Hua. The Dowager ordered him put to death. Both Liu Bei and the State Patriarch Qiao interceded for Jia Hua, and thus she only ordered the general out of her presence.

Strolling out of the banquet room into the temple grounds, Liu Bei came to a boulder. Drawing his sword he looked up to heaven and prayed, saying, "If I am to return to Jingzhou to achieve my ambition to become a chief ruler, then allow me to cleave this boulder asunder with my sword." Raising his sword he smote the boulder. Sparks flew in all directions, and the boulder lay split in twain.

Liu Bei and Sun Quan walked on, looking at the high land and the rolling river spread out in a glorious panorama before their eyes. In the midst of the waves appeared a tiny leaf of a boat riding over the waves as if all was perfect calm. "The northern people are riders and the southern people are sailors;

it is quite true," sighed Liu Bei. Sun Quan hearing this remark took it as a slight upon his horsemanship. Bidding his servants bring up his steed, Sun Quan leaped into the saddle and set off, full gallop, down the hill. Liu Bei also jumped upon his horse to ride after Sun Quan. The two steeds stood side by side on the declivity, the riders flourishing their whips and laughing.

In response to the request of Liu Bei, the State Patriarch Qiao asked the Dowager to marry her daughter to Liu Bei as soon as possible. The Dowager chose a day for the celebration of the wedding.

Liu Bei entered the nuptial apartment. To his extreme surprise, Liu Bei found the chambers furnished with spears and swords, while every waiting-maid was wearing a sword. The bridegroom turned pale. Lady Sun laughed, saying, "Afraid of a few weapons after half a life time spent in slaughter!" But she ordered the removal of the weapons and bade the maids take off their swords while they were at work.

Seeing the situation, Sun Quan decided to try Zhou Yu's plan, letting Liu Bei enjoy himself as a prisoner of luxury. Indeed Liu Bei was soon so immersed in sensuous pleasure that he gave no thought to return.

Zhao Yun went to meet Liu Bei after seeing the second bag, saying, "Today early Zhuge Liang sent a messenger to say that Cao Cao was trying to avenge his last defeat and was leading five hundred thousand troops to attack Jingzhou, which was thus in great danger. And he wished you to return." Liu Bei said he understood and asked Zhao Yun to leave first.

The conversation between Liu Bei and Zhao Yun was heard by Lady Sun. After hearing Liu Bei's worries, Lady Sun decided to follow Liu Bei when he returned to Jingzhou. They decided to go away on New Year's Day using the excuse of making a sacrifice on the river bank.

On New Year's Day, Liu Bei and Lady Sun, with the protection of Zhao Yun, left Nanxu for the river bank.

That day, at the New Year banquet, Sun Quan drank freely with the officers so that he had to be helped to his chamber. When Sun Quan heard the story, it was the next day. Sun Quan urgently ordered Chen Wu and Pan Zhang to pursue Liu Bei and Lady Sun at top speed. Cheng Pu said they didn't dare lay hands on Lady Sun. Sun Quan drew his sword and called up Jiang Qin and Zhou Tai and asked them to bring back the heads of Lady Sun and Liu Bei.

Just as Liu Bei and Lady Sun reached the confines of Chaisang, a force was in hot pursuit. Zhao Yun opened the bag and handed it to Liu Bei. As soon as Liu Bei had seen the contents, he hastened to Lady Sun's carriage and told her about the plots of Zhou Yu and Sun Quan and asked her to rescue him.

Lady Sun rolled up her curtains and launched into a torrent of abuse directed at Xu Sheng, Ding Feng, Chen Wu and Pan Zhang. They gave way and retreated leaving the road open.

When Jiang Qin and Zhou Tai arrived, the carriage had gone ahead a good distance. Jiang Qin asked Xu Sheng and Ding Feng to go to tell Zhou Yu to send fast boats to pursue Liu Bei by river while Jiang Qin himself followed on the bank.

When Liu Bei and his party arrived at Liulangpu, they saw the enemy coming nearer and nearer. Then as things began to look most desperate, he saw a line of some twenty boats all in the act of setting sail. After Liu Bei and Lady Sun boarded a ship, they realised all the businessmen on board were soldiers from Jingzhou. Liu Bei rejoiced at the sudden happy turn of affairs. Before long the four pursuing leaders reached the bank, but the boats had already sailed.

At that time, there appeared a huge fleet of war ships, sailing under the flag of Zhou Yu. Zhou Yu himself was there in command of the fleet. Zhuge Liang ordered the boats to row over to the north bank, and the party disembarked. Zhou Yu also landed. But from out of a gully dashed a troop of swordsmen led by Guan Yu, Zhou Yu was astonished and was unprepared to do anything but flee. As he came to the river and was going down into his ship, the soldiers of Liu Bei on the bank jeered at him and shouted, "General Zhou Yu has given Uncle Liu Bei a wife and has lost his soldiers." Zhou Yu was so annoyed that he fainted in a swoon.

Just as Sun Quan and Zhou Yu was about to send an army to attack Jingzhou, Zhang Zhao said it could not be done. Gu Yong supported Zhang Zhao, saying to Sun Quan, "The plan is to secure the friendship of Liu Bei by memorializing that he be

made Imperial Protector of Jingzhou. This will make Cao Cao afraid to send any army against the South Lands. At the same time it will raise kindly feelings in the heart of Liu Bei and win his support. You will be able to find some one who will provoke a quarrel between Cao Cao and Liu Bei and set them against each other, and that will be your

opportunity. In this way you will succeed." Sun Quan agreed and sent Hua Xin to Xudu.

CHAPTER 16

Provoking Zhou Yu Three Times

At that time, Cao Cao was celebrating the completion of the Bronze Bird Tower at Yejun. He invited a vast assembly to celebrate its inauguration with banquets and rejoicing. For the military officers an archery competition was arranged, and one of his attendants brought forth a robe of red crimson Sichuan silk as a prize. This was suspended from one of the drooping branches of a willow tree, beneath which was the target. The military officers were keen to show their skills.

After the military officers had competed in the mounted archery competition, Cao Cao asked the civil officers to offer some complimentary odes to commemorate the completion of the Bronze Bird Tower. Cao Cao enthusiastically also composed a poem.

Suddenly, it was announced that the Marquis of Wu had sent Hua Xin as an envoy there. After seeing the memorial presented by Hua Xin, Cao Cao discussed it with his advisers, fermenting plans to set Sun Quan and Liu Bei against one another. He presented a memorial assigning Zhou Yu and Cheng Pu to the governorships of Nanjun and Jiangxia, and Hua Xin was retained at the capital in a ministerial post.

Having taken over his command, Zhou Yu thought of nothing but the revenge he contemplated and, to bring matters to a head, he wrote to Sun Quan asking him to send Lu Su and renew demands for the rendition of Jingzhou. Lu Su, however, had to go to Jingzhou.

When Lu Su came to Jingzhou, Liu Bei began to cry following the plan of Zhuge

Liang. Zhuge Liang said, "And if Liu Bei gives up this place before he has another, where can he rest? Yet, while he retains this place it seems to shame you. This thing is hard on both sides, and that is why he weeps so bitterly." In this way, Zhuge Liang asked Lu Su to entreat Sun Quan to let them stay there a little longer.

Lu Su reported to Zhou Yu. But Zhou Yu stamped his foot with rage and said, "My friend, you have been fooled again." He said to Lu Su, "Do not go to see our master but return to Jingzhou. Since Liu Bei has qualms about attacking the west, we will do it for him. Thus, the South Lands will send an army under this pretext. What we will really do is go to Jingzhou, and we shall catch him unawares. The road to the west runs through his city, and we will call upon him for supplies. He will come out to thank the army, and we will assassinate him thereby gaining our revenge."

Lu Su came to Jingzhou again, and said that Zhou Yu had determined to take the western country on the Imperial Uncle's behalf and, that done, Jingzhou could be exchanged for it without further delay. Liu Bei saluted happily and said, "This is due to your friendly efforts on our behalf. When the brave army arrives, we shall certainly come out to meet them and entertain the soldiers." Lu Su felt great satisfaction and was quite happy at his success; he took his leave and went homeward.

Zhou Yu led fifty thousand troops to Jingzhou. When Zhou Yu was approaching Jingzhou, he saw two white flags flying on the city walls but no sign of life. He navigated his ship to shore, and he himself landed on the bank, where he mounted a horse and led 20 cavalry troops to look over the city walls.

Immediately was heard the thud of a club, and the wall came alive with thousands of troops. And from the tower came out Zhao Yun who said, "The Directing Instructor knows that you are trying the ruse of 'Borrowing a Road to Destroy the Host.' And so he stationed me here." At this Zhou Yu turned his horse as if to retreat. Just then his scouts came up to report: "Armed bands are moving toward us from all four sides, led by Guan Yu, Zhang Fei, Huang Zhong, and Wei Yan." At these tidings Zhou Yu's excitement became so intense that he fell to the ground with a great cry, and his old wound reopened. Then he was carried to his boat.

It only added to his rage and mortification to be told that Liu Bei and Zhuge Liang could be seen on the top of one of the hills apparently feasting and enjoying some music. He lay grinding his teeth in vexation, saying "They say I shall never be able to get Yizhou! But I will; I swear I will." Zhou Yu ordered his army to go forward towards Yizhou, and they got to Baqiu. There they stopped, for the scouts reported large forces under Liu Bei's generals—Liu Feng and Guan Ping—barring the route via the Great River.

This failure did not make the Commander-in-Chief any calmer. About this time a letter from Zhuge Liang arrived, saying: "Since our parting at Chaisang I have thought of you often. Now comes to me a report that you desire to take the Western Land of Rivers, which I regret to say I consider impossible. Now if you undertake a long expedition, will Cao Cao not seize the occasion to fall upon the South Lands and grind it to powder." The letter made Zhou Yu feel very upset and he began to vomit blood. He knew his end was at hand. He called for paper and ink and wrote to the Marquis of Wu to recommend Lu Su as his successor. Before his death, he sighed heavily, "God,

since thou made Zhou Yu, why did thou also create Zhuge Liang?" Soon after he passed away; he was only thirty-six.

Sun Quan wept aloud at the sad tidings of Zhou Yu's death. In accordance with the will of Zhou Yu, he appointed Lu Su as the Commander-in-Chief.

Zhuge Liang went to the South Lands to mourn Zhou Yu. He knelt before the bier and read the threnody. The sacrifice finished, Zhuge Liang bowed to the ground and wept with his tears gushing forth in floods. Lu Su was particularly affected by this display of feelings and thought, "Plainly Zhuge Liang loved Zhou Yu very much, but Zhou Yu in life was not broadminded enough and did everything he could to do Zhuge Liang to death."

Just as Zhuge Liang was leaving, his arm was clutched by a person in Taoist dress who said with a smile, "You exasperated to death the man whose body lies up there with three successive tricks; to come here as a mourner is an open insult to the South Lands." At first Zhuge Liang did not recognize the speaker, but very soon he saw it was no other than Pang Tong. Then Zhuge Liang laughed in his turn, and they two hand in hand went down to the ship, where they talked animatedly for a long time. Before leaving, Zhuge Liang gave his friend a letter, asking Pang Tong to come to Jingzhou and help Liu Bei.

Lu Su was not satisfied that he was the fittest successor to his late chief and recommended Pang Tong to Sun Quan. Whereupon Pang Tong was invited to the Palace and introduced, Sun Quan was disappointed with the man's appearance, which was indeed extraordinary. In addition, Pang Tong disparaged Zhou Yu with an arrogant speech. Sun Quan refused to consider him.

Pang Tong went to throw in his lot with Liu Bei. However, when he saw Liu Bei, he didn't produce his letter from Zhuge Liang. His lack of courtesy and ugly face did not please Liu Bei, who only appointed him as a chief in Leiyang County. But when Pang Tong arrived at his post, he paid no attention to business at all; he gave himself up entirely to dissipation.

So Liu Bei sent Zhang Fei to the county with orders to make a general inspection of the whole county. They went to the magistracy, took their seats in the hall of justice, and summoned the Magistrate before them. He came with dress all disordered and still under the influence of wine. Zhang Fei criticized him for throwing the affairs of the county into disorder. Thereupon Pang Tong bade the clerks bring in all the arrears and he would settle them at once. By midday all of the cases were disposed of, and all the arrears of the hundred days were settled and decided. Zhang Fei was astonished at the man's ability, rose from his seat, and crossed over, saying, "You are indeed a marvel, Master." Pang Tong then drew forth Zhuge Liang's letter of recommendation.

Zhang Fei left the magistracy and returned to Liu Bei to whom he related what had happened and gave the letter to Liu Bei. Then Liu Bei lost no time, but sent Zhang Fei off to the northeast to request Pang Tong to come to Jingzhou City. When he arrived, Liu Bei went out to meet him and at the foot of the steps asked pardon for his mistake. Then he appointed Pang Tong as Vice Directing Instructor and General.

CHAPTER 17

Xiliang Troops Rebel

Cao Cao was told of Liu Bei's increasingly strong force, and he was determined to embark on a military expedition against Liu Bei. But, he feared Ma Teng from Xiliang would attack the capitain his absence. He summoned Ma Teng to the capital in the hope of getting rid of him. Ma Teng led troops to the capital and camped seven miles from Xuchang, wishing to wait for an opportunity to kill Cao Cao.

Cao Cao sent Huang Kui to try to deceive Ma Teng into coming in immediately for an audience with the Emperor so that he could kill him. Huang had always nourished resentment against Cao Cao. He told Ma Teng of Cao Cao's conspiracy, and advised him to assassinate Cao Cao when he came to review the army.

However, Huang Kui told all this to his concubine, Li Chunxiang. And it happened that she was having an affair with his wife's younger brother, Miao Ze, who much desired to marry her. Li Chunxiang of course told her paramour, who told Cao Cao.

Thus Cao Cao pretended to review the troops, but had placed his soldiers in ambush, so that when Ma Teng pounced, he was captured and beheaded. Then Cao Cao bade the executioners to also put both Miao Ze and the woman Li Chunxiang to death.

In AD 211, Cao Cao decided to set out on his expedition to the south. But then came the disquieting news of the military preparations of Liu Bei, whose objective was said to be the west. An expeditionary force of three hundred thousand troops set out for Hefei.

Sun Quan soon heard of the move and ordered Lu Su to write at once to Liu Bei to ask for his help. Zhuge Liang wrote a reply, telling Lu Su to lay aside all anxiety He also asked Liu Bei to write a letter to Ma Chao, asking Ma Chao to march through the pass so as to avenge his father.

Reading Liu Bei's letter, Ma Chao mustered his troops to the capital Xuchang seeking revenge. Han Sui and Ma Teng were sworn brothers. So Han Sui had eight divisions under eight commanders and, together with Ma Chao, they marched to Chang'an.

The Xiliang soldiers fought bravely and smashed into enemy territory just like splitting bamboo. Soon, they were on the point of capturing Chang'an. Cao Cao was alarmed and sent Cao Hong and Xu Huang to lead troops to Tong Pass to support Zhong Yao. He ordered them to hold the Pass at all costs for ten days, or they would pay for the loss with their heads.

Zhong Yao and others confined themselves to defending their position. Ma Chao appeared every day and shouted shameful things about the three generations of Cao Cao's family. Cao Hong was enraged at the daily insults and would have led the defenders out to fight had not his colleague restrained him. Thus it continued till the ninth day. Then the defenders saw that their enemies had turned all their horses loose and were lolling about on the grass and sleeping as if quite fatigued. Thereupon Cao Hong led a lightning attack. However it was a trap and as the drums rolled two huge battalions

of troops led by Ma Chao and Pang De came out from behind the hills. Cao Hong's troops were defeated and fled in disorder. Tong Pass was captured by Ma Chao.

Cao Cao led his main army and advanced to the Tong Pass. Because Cao Hong had lost the Pass on the ninth day, Cao Cao ordered Cao Hong to be put to death according to military law. But his brother officers begged that he might be pardoned, and as he had confessed his mistakes, he was allowed to go free and unpunished.

Cao Cao ordered an attack on the Pass. Ma Chao was a great fighter and defeated a dozen of Cao Cao's generals. The Xiliang troops overwhelmed Cao Cao's forces, and Ma Chao, Pang De, and Ma Dai rode forward to try to capture Cao Cao. When they came close, he hastily tore off his red robe, threw it away, cut off some of his beard, wrapped the corner of a flag about his neck and face and fled.

As Cao Cao fwas fleeing in terror, unexpectedly, he saw Ma Chao quite close. The whip dropped from Cao Cao's hand as he saw his enemy coming closer and closer. But just as Ma Chao was readying his spear for a thrust, Cao Cao slipped behind a tree, changing the direction of his flight and so escaped, while Ma Chao struck the tree with his spear. Cao Hong then suddenly appeared and saved Cao Cao's life.

Cao Cao wished to cross the River Wei and cut off Ma Chao's retreat. Cao Cao and his guards took up station on the south bank to watch the crossing. They saw Ma Chao coming. This terrified them and they made a rush to get into

their boats. The yelling of the troops and the neighing of the horses of the approaching army came nearer and nearer. Xu Chu took Cao Cao on his back and leapt on board. And so Cao Cao escaped.

The next day, Ma Chao and Xu Chu fought over a hundred bouts, with neither gaining the advantage. Suddenly Xu Chu galloped back to his own side, stripped off his armor, showing his magnificent muscles and, naked as he was, leapt again into the saddle and rode out to continue the battle. The contest was renewed, and a hundred more encounters took place, still without victory to either side. Fearing the loss of Xu Chu, Cao Cao ordered the beating of gongs to signal a retreat.

Ma Chao was brave but not very astute, so Cao Cao tried to sow suspicion between Han Sui and Ma Chao. Ma Chao was taken in as expected as he already felt suspicious of Han Sui. To guard his own interests, Han Sui decided to go over to the Prime Minister's side. Hearing of this, Ma Chao killed two of Han Sui's generals, and cut off his left hand.

Cao Cao's troops poured in from all sides and took the opportunity to attack Ma Chao. With few troops left, Ma Chao, together with Pang De and Ma Dai, traveled toward Lintao, a city in today's Gansu Province.

Cao Cao had defeated Ma Chao, and so his prestige and importance increased greatly. So the army returned to the Capital Xuchang where it was welcomed by the Emperor in his state chariot.

CHAPTER 18

Zhang Song Offers a Map to Liu Bei

After Ma Chao had been defeated, tens of thousand of his defeated Xiliang soldiers fled to Hanzhong and joined Zhang Lu's army. Fearing that Cao Cao would invade Hanzhong, Zhang Lu desired the title of Prince of Hanning. His subordinates advised him to take possession of the Western Land of Rivers first and thus make his desire a reality as soon as possible. So he decided to raise an army to march to the Western Land of Rivers.

When Liu Zhang received news from his commander of Zhang Lu's movements, his heart sank within him in fear, and he hastily called in his advisers. Zhang Song, who belonged to Yizhou in today's Sichuan Province and held the small office of Supernumerary Charioteer, proposed that if they could get Cao Cao to march an army against Hanzhong, that would keep Zhang Lu occupied so that they would be left alone. Liu Zhang appointed Zhang Song as his emissary. He took gold and pearls and other treasure to Xuchang. Zhang Song in the meantime secretly began copying maps and plans of the west country.

The mean appearance of the emissary had prejudiced Cao Cao from the outset; and when Cao Cao heard the emissary's blunt words, he suddenly shook out his sleeves, rose and left the hall.

Perceiving the ridicule in Zhang Song's speech, Yang Xiu, Chief of the Secretariat of the Prime Minister, invited him to go to the library where they could talk more freely. Then Yang Xiu brought a book The New Book of Cao Cao written by Cao Cao and showed this to his guest.

Zhang Song said that it was written by some obscure person at the time of the Warring States and that every child in Yizhou knew this by heart. Then he repeated the whole book, word for word, from beginning to end. Yang Xiu was very surprised and he thought he was marvelous.

By and by Yang Xiu went to see Cao Cao to tell him of how Zhang Song was able to recite word for word The New Book of Cao Cao. Cao Cao thought, "it only shows that the ancients and I were in secret sympathy." However, Cao Cao ordered the book to be torn up and burned. The next day, Cao Cao ordered that Zhang Song be brought to the western parade ground to let him see what their army looked like.

Cao Cao called up Zhang Song and, pointing to his army, asked whether he had ever seen such fine bold fellows in Yizhou? Zhang Song said, "We never see this kind of military parade in Yizhou; we govern the people by righteousness." He added, "I knew it when you attacked Lu Bu at Puyang; and when you fought Zhang Xiu at Wancheng; and when you met Zhou Yu at the Red Cliffs; and when in Huarong Valley you encountered Guan Yu; and on that day when you cut off your beard and threw away your robe at Tong Pass; and when you hid in a boat to escape the arrows on the River Wei. On all these occasions, no one could stand against you." It made Cao Cao very angry to be thus ridiculed with his past misfortunes. Zhang Song was ordered to be beaten and thrown out.

Zhang Song made for Jingzhou so that he could see what manner of man Liu Bei was. He had reached the boundaries of Jingzhou when he was met by Zhao Yun and led to the nearest posthouse. Guan Yu also came to offer him a banquet to refresh him after his long and toilsome journey. Zhang Song felt that Liu Bei was a generous and liberal leader.

Next day, Liu Bei himself, with an escort, and his two chief advisers—Zhuge Liang and Pang Tong—welcomed Zhang Song. The next three days were spent in banqueting. Zhang Song said that he was willing to serve as Liu Bei's planted agent. He did his best to persuade Liu Bei to take Yizhou and offered him the maps of the country. He also recommended his two friends—Fa Zheng and Meng Da—to Liu Bei, saying that they should be put in very important positions.

After arriving back in Yizhou, Zhang Song persuaded Liu Zhang to send Fa Zheng to Jingzhou as an emissary. Meng Da would follow in due course with an army to welcome Liu Bei. Huang Quan and Wang Lei advised Liu Zhang not to follow this course of action on many occasions lest he would be killed by Liu Bei. Liu Zhang closed his ears to them.

Liu Bei ordered Zhuge Liang and his three best generals—Guan Yu, Zhang Fei, and Zhao Yun—to defend Jingzhou, while he himself led Pang Tong, and his two generals Huang Zhong and Wei Yan into the west. The Imperial Protector proposed to go out in person to welcome Liu Bei. Huang Quan seized hold of the Imperial Protector's robe with his teeth to try to stop him. Liu Zhang angrily shook off his robe and rose from his seat, but Huang Quan still held on till two of his teeth fell out.

When Liu Zhang was about to leave the gates of Yizhou, Secretary Wang Lei suspended himself, head downwards, from the city gates to try to dissuade him. Liu Zhang closed his ears to him again. At this Wang Lei gave a great cry, severed the rope, falling to the ground dead.

Then Fa Zheng secretly showed Pang Tong a letter from Zhang Song advocating the assassination of Liu Zhang near the place of welcome. Pang Tong set Wei Yan's sword-play to work and took advantage of the confusion to try to kill Liu Zhang.

Finding that Wei Yan had bad intentions, Zhang Ren, a general of Liu Zhang, also displayed his skill at the same time to protect Liu Zhang. Seeing that, Liu Bei promptly drew his sword and cried, "Anyone who does not discard his sword will be beheaded." They all threw away their swords.

The news came that Zhang Lu was about to invade the Western Land of Rivers at the Jiameng Pass. Thereupon the Imperial Protector begged Liu Bei to go and defend it. Liu Bei consented and left immediately with his own troops.

Knowing that Liu Bei and his army were in the Western Land of Rivers, Sun Quan wished to seize the opportunity to attack Jingzhou. Dowager Marchioness feared that if the two states engaged, Liu Bei would kill her daughter. She did not approve the plan. Zhang Zhao wrote a secret letter, chose a trusty man and sent him to give it to Princess Sun, saying that her mother was dangerously ill, so she should rush home and bring

with her the only son of Liu Bei. Liu Bei would be glad enough to exchange Jingzhou for his son. It was decided that Zhou Shan set out along the river route for the city of Jingzhou disguised as an ordinary trader.

Lady Sun read that her mother was near death, and Liu Bei was far away on military service. Fearing others would try to stop her, she took Liu Shan with her, and left.

Zhao Yun was told of Lady Sun's sudden departure, and dashed down to the river bank like a whirlwind, and took a small boat to try to intercept her.

After a long pursuit, Zhao Yun caught up. He went down into the body of the ship. Then he took the boy from her arms, but the vessel had gone as far as the center of the River. He was quite unable to get the vessel in toward the shore. Just then Zhang Fei came along by boat, boarded the vessel and slew Zhou Shan. Taking the child with them, Zhang Fei and Zhao Yun left the vessel, and the five ships of the South Lands continued their voyage down stream.

Seeing that his sister has returned home, he planned to attack Jingzhou. But before they could decide upon any plan, their deliberations were suddenly cut short by the news that Cao Cao was coming down upon the South Lands with four hundred thousand troops, burning to avenge his defeat at the Red Cliffs. Sun Quan was alarmed. Complying with Lu Meng's proposal, he sent soldiers to build ramparts at the River Ruxu as a defensive protection against Cao Cao.

High Counselor Dong Zhao proposed in a memorial to the Throne that the title of Duke of Wei should be conferred upon Cao Cao and that the Nine Dignities also be added. High Adviser Xun Yu suggested to Cao Cao that he should remain loyal and humble. He took it to mean that Xun Yu would no longer aid him or help him in his plans. Xun Yu received one day a box much like a box that would normally hold candies. It was addressed in Cao Cao's own handwriting. Opening it, Xun Yu found nothing inside. He understood from this that Cao Cao wished him dead. He took poison and died.

In the winter of AD 212, Cao Cao decided to send an army to conquer the South Lands. Not knowing where Sun Quan had stationed his troops, Cao Cao led his army to the river to watch the enemy and deploy his troops accordingly. Suddenly, a firecracker exploded and a number of ships appeared and came flying toward him, while a force moved out of the River Ruxu. Cao Cao's soldiers at once retreated 25 miles in great haste.

So the two armies remained facing each other for a whole month, fighting occasional skirmishes and battles in which victory fell sometimes to the one and sometimes to the other. And so it went on till the new year, and the spring rains filled the watercourses to overflowing, and the soldiers were wading in deep mud. Their sufferings were extreme. After receiving a letter from Sun Quan proposing a ceasefire, Cao Cao issued orders to retreat.

CHAPTER 19

Liu Bei Takes the Protectorship of Yizhou
in AD 212—214

When he received the news of Cao Cao's threatened attack upon Wu, Liu Bei was troubled about the region of Jingzhou. He urged Liu Zhang to lend veterans and a plentiful supply of food. Liu Zhang actually decided to send only four thousand worn out soldiers and a paltry supply of grain. Liu Bei was furious. Pang Tong had three schemes ready in his mind, for Liu Bei might choose. He chose the second scheme.

So a letter was written by Liu Bei to Liu Zhang saying that he had to go back to Jingzhou. He wished to take the opportunity to kill Yang Huai and Gao Pei, two generals of the Western Land of Rivers guarding the River Fu Pass. Thinking that the real desire of Liu Bei was to return to Jingzhou, Zhang Song then also composed a letter to Liu Bei. While he was looking about for a trusty person to take it, his brother Zhang Su, who was the Governor of Guanghan, came to see him. Zhang Song hid the letter in his sleeve while he talked with his brother. Wine was brought in and, as the two brothers chatted, the letter dropped to the floor unnoticed by Zhang Song. Zhang Su picked it up, opened it and read it. At his earliest convenience he laid the whole matter before the Imperial Protector. Liu Zhang issued orders to arrest Zhang Song and behead him and all his household in the market place.

The two generals of the Western Land of Rivers, Yang Huai and Gao Pei, also wished to find an opportunity to kill Liu Bei. When Liu Bei was about to go back to the Fu River Pass, the generals went to Liu Bei's tent to kill him on the pretext of paying a farewell visit. As a result, they were both beheaded by Liu Feng and Guan Ping. Liu Bei captured the River Fu Pass.

When Imperial Protector Liu Zhang heard of the doings of his relative and guest, on the same night he sent without delay a force to hold Luocheng, which was at the very throat of the road he needed to take. Liu Bei sent Huang Zhong and Wei Yan to attack the two camps established twenty miles away from Luocheng. Huang Zhong and Wei Yan fought closely and captured the two camps.

Liu Zhang sent his eldest son, Liu Xun, and his brother-in-law Wu Yi to go to defend Luocheng. Wu Yi planned to inundate the Fujiang river banks, flood their camp, and drown Liu Bei and his army with him. Peng Zhu, a hero of Shu, told Liu Bei about this, and Liu Bei sent troops to defeat the troops who were about to inundate the banks.

Pang Tong desired to win glory by capturing Luocheng. He demanded that Liu Bei advance along the high road while he himself advanced by road. When they were setting out, suddenly Pang Tong's horse shied and stumbled, throwing him off. Liu Bei let him ride his "Dilu" horse.

Pang Tong led his troops to the forest and asked if any knew the name of that place. When he was told that this was called 'The Fallen Phoenix Slope', Pang Tong shuddered and decided to retire. But as he gave the order, arrows began to fly toward him thick as swarming locusts. And there, wounded by many arrows, poor Pang Tong died.

Alternately fighting and marching, the army of Liu Bei strove hard to reach the River Fu Pass. One of the fugitives from the army finally reached the River Fu Pass and told Liu Bei of the sad news of Pang Tong—both man and horse mortally wounded. Liu Bei turned his face to the west and mourned bitterly. From then on, Liu Bei set his troops to guard the Pass most vigilantly, waiting for the arrival of Director Instructor Zhuge Liang after Guan Ping was sent to Jingzhou by night.

After reading the letter of Liu Bei, he ordered Guan Yu to undertake the defense of Jingzhou. He gave him his advice in a few words: "North, fight Cao Cao; south, ally with Sun Quan." Zhang Fei, with ten thousand troops, was sent to fight his way into the country west of Bazhou and Luocheng, and he was to go with all speed. Zhao Yun was to lead a force up the Great River and make a junction at Luocheng. Zhuge Liang, with Jiang Rong, Jiang Wan, and his own body of fifteen thousand troops, would follow.

So when Zhang Fei's troops drew near the county of Bazhou, the Governor Yan Yan refused to come out from behind the walls till he hoped hunger would vanquish their enemies. That night Zhang Fei sat in his tent trying to think of some means to overcome the enemy. Foiled again, a plan began to form

behind his bushy eyebrows. That very night he ordered food be readied during the second watch, and the army moved out during the third, pretending to bypass the county of Bazhou. Hearing this, Yan Yan placed his troops in ambush on the small road, hoping to intercept Zhang Fei as he passed. Zhang Fei had a soldier dressed and made to resemble him escort the army provisions and pass first, while he came near the rear. The two leaders engaged. Yan Yan was taken prisoner, and in a moment was fast bound with cords.

Yan Yan faced death unflinchingly. Zhang Fei admired him, dressed him in new garments and led him to a high seat. When Yan Yan was seated, Zhang Fei made a low bow. Yan Yan was overcome with this kindness and forthwith surrendered.

Zhuge Liang wrote to inform Liu Bei that he had made Luocheng the rendezvous for the various armies. Complying with Huang Zhong's proposal, Liu Bei raised troops to attack Luocheng. However, Zhang Ren, a famous general of Shu area (today's Sichuan Province), plotted against him and launched a surprise attack upon them. Liu's troops were defeated. Liu Bei fled to the hills. Zhang Ren followed and soon came very close to Liu Bei. As Liu Bei fingered his whip he felt that the odds were much against him. Just then Zhang Fei and Yan Yan appeared and saved him from possible death.

Zhuge Liang assembled with Liu Bei and Zhang Fei. Zhuge Liang had planned an ambush on all sides and captured Zhang Ren. The prisoner was irreconcilable and kept up a stream of furious abuse. So at last the order was given for his execution.

Fa Zheng wrote a letter to Imperial Protector Liu Zhang, trying to persuade him to surrender. The letter angered Liu Zhang, who tore the letter to pieces and drove the bearer of the letter from his presence. He then sent an army under the leadership of Fei Guan, his wife's brother, to reinforce Mianzhu. Complying with a proposal of his advisor, he sent Huang Quan to Hanzhong, to get aid from Zhang Lu in his fight against Liu Bei.

By then Ma Chao had conquered portions of Longxi. After his long campaign, only Jicheng remained uncaptured. The Governor of Jicheng, Wei Kang, had sent many urgent appeals for help to Xiahou Yuan, who is a general of Cao Cao, however, he would do nothing without his master's order. He wanted to surrender. However, Military Advisor Yang Fu wept and earnestly opposed this.

Wei Kang still opened the city gates and bowed his head in submission. After entering the city, Ma Chao thought that Wei Kang had only yielded now as a last resort. Whereupon he put to death Wei Kang and all his family, he also appointed Yang Fu as his military advisor.

On the pretext of going to Licheng to see his aunt, Yang Fu asked her to persuade his maternal cousin, General Jiang Xu, Commander of Licheng, to dispatch troops to attack Ma Chao. Not daring to defy his mother's order, Jiang Xu had to act.

Then Ma Chao marched his force, together with Pang De and Ma Dai, to Licheng, and the troops under Jiang Xu and Yang Fu went out to confront them. There suddenly appeared a third force under Xiahou Yuan, who had just received orders from Cao Cao to move against Ma Chao. Three attacks at once were too much for Ma Chao, and he fled, his forces in utter confusion. Having escaped from their pursuers, Ma Chao and his few followers decided to make for Hanzhong and offer their services to Governor Zhang Lu.

Knowing that Ma Chao was extraordinarily brave, Zhang Lu thought to cement their friendship by giving Ma Chao a daughter as a wife. But this displeased one of his generals, Yang Bo. Whereupon Ma Chao was very annoyed and sought to kill Yang Bo. At this time Huang Quan bearing the letter of Liu Zhang of Yizhou arrived in Hanzhong, to seek troops from Zhang Lu. Ma Chao came forward and said that he would lead an army to take the Jiameng Pass and capture Liu Bei. This offer was accepted joyfully by Zhang Lu.

To take Chengdu, the center city of Yizhou, Mianzhu had to

be captured first. Expert at commanding troops, Li Yan, a general defending Mianzhu, would not be overcome by mere force. Zhuge Liang ordered that Li Yan be led into the hills by means of a clever ruse. Having no way out, Li Yan got off his horse, threw aside his armor, and offered submission to Liu Bei. Li Yan persuaded Fei Guan to open the city gates and yield to Liu Bei. Mianzhu was thus captured by Liu Bei.

While Liu Bei set out his forces to take Chengdu, a messenger came in haste to tell of Mao Chao's attack upon the Jiameng Pass. Zhuge Liang said to Liu Bei that nobody could stand up to him, unless they could get Guan Yu from Jingzhou. This angered Zhang Fei who immediately pledged in writing that he would overcome Mao Chao. Wei Yan was allowed to go with five hundred light horse in advance of Zhang Fei. Knowing that Zhang Fei was rude and rash, Zhuge Liang, together with Liu Bei, marched third.

As soon as Zhang Fei arrived at Jiameng Pass, the fight between him and Ma Chao began and continued for 200 bouts. Neither could gain the advantage. Then they changed horses and refought. At dark, they lit many thousands of torches till it seemed as light as day, and the two great generals went again to fight. They fought another hundred bouts. Neither had the advantage.

Early next day the Directing Instructor arrived. Finding that Liu Bei admired Ma Chao, he planned to send Sun Qian secretly to see Yang Song, an advisor of Zhang Lu, and give him gold and silver and so win his support.

Sun Qian was quickly led into the presence of Zhang Lu by Yang Song. Sun Qian said that Liu Bei could personally ask the Throne to confer on him the title of 'Prince of Hanzhong.' Zhang Lu assented. He sent orders to Ma Chao to cease fighting. Ma Chao refused to cease fighting till he had been successful. Yang Song spread rumours to the effect that "Ma Chao will not withdraw his soldiers because he contemplates rebellion. Thus Ma Chao was helpless and could see no way out of the difficulty.

Zhuge Liang ordered Li Hui, an old friend of Ma Chao, to go to his camp to persuade him to surrender. Li Hui used his silver tongue to convince Ma Chao of the wisdom of the course thus recommended. Ma Chao slew Yang Bo. Taking with him the head of his victim, Ma Chao came to tender his submission to Liu Bei.

Liu Bei detached a force to go to capture Chengdu. Finding that the game was up, Liu Zhang ordered the gates opened and surrendered. Afterwards Liu Bei led his troops into the city. The people gave Liu Bei a cordial welcome. Liu Bei took over the protectorship of Yizhou.

CHAPTER 20

Guan Yu Goes to a Feast Alone

Hearing that Ma Chao was brave and bold, Guan Yu asked Guan Ping to send a letter to Liu Bei, saying that he wanted to go to the Western Lands of the River to compete with Ma Chao. Zhuge Liang wrote back, saying, "He might be brave and bold,, but he is far from your standard, O Lord of the Beautiful Beard." Guan Yu smiled as he read the letter. "The Instructor knows me thoroughly," said he to himself.

The successes of Liu Bei in the west had been duly noted by Sun Quan, who ordered the seizure of Zhuge Jin's family and sent him west to see Zhuge Liang and make Zhuge Liang persuade Liu Bei to return to Jingzhou so as to save his family

The two brothers went to visit Liu Bei. At this point Zhuge Liang prostrated himself weeping at his lord's feet and prayed his lord to give back the region. But Liu Bei refused. He seemed obdurate, but Zhuge Liang persisted in his entreaty. Liu Bei had to say, "The Instructor pleads for it, so I will give up three territories—Changsha, Lingling, and Guiyang." Zhuge Jin was happy, but did not know that it was all in fact a plan thought up by Zhuge Liang.

Zhuge Jin, having got Liu Bei's letter, took his leave and went straightaway to Jingzhou. He asked for an interview with Guan Yu, and asked him to hand over these three territories. Reading the letter of Liu Bei, given by the emissary, Guan Yu, who had earlier received the letter from Zhuge Liang, was furious and said, "Jingzhou is a portion of the Han domain, so how can any part be given to another? When a leader is in the field, he receives no orders, not even those of his prince. Although you have brought letters from my brother, yet will I not yield these territories."

Zhuge Jin hastily returned to Chengdu to see his brother. But Zhuge Liang had gone away upon a journey. However, he saw Liu Bei and related what had happened. Liu Bei advised Zhuge Jin to return home for the present. Zhuge Jin had no choice but to accept this reply and carry the unsatisfactory news to his master, who was greatly annoyed and asked Lu Su what to do. Lu Su designed a plan, inviting Guan Yu to a banquet at Lukou to try to persuade him. If he still remained obstinate, some assassins should be ready to slay him.

Guan Yu decided to cross the River to go to the feast the next day. Lu Su had the assassins hidden in the camp and placed Lu Meng and Gan Ning and their troops in ambush by the riverside. At noon, Guan Yu took a boat and landed.

Guan Yu was led to the banquet chamber for the wine. Guan Yu rose in his place, and took his sword from his sword-bearer Zhou Cang. The mighty sword in his right hand, Guan Yu laid hold of Lu Su with his left and, simulating intoxication, said, "You have kindly invited me today, Sir, but do not say anything about Jingzhou, for I am so drunk that I may forget our old friendship. Some other day I hope to invite you to Jingzhou, and then we will talk about that matter."

Lu Meng and Gan Ning dared not act and so made no move

lest they should bring about the doom of Lu Su. They looked on helplessly as Guan Yu got on board, and went back to Jingzhou. Sun Quan, in his wrath, was in favour of sending every available soldier at once against Jingzhou. But just as this crisis was reaching a head there came news that Cao Cao was raising a huge army with the intention of attacking the South Lands.

Making no move against Jingzhou, he sent all available troops from Hefei and Ruxu toward the north to repel Cao Cao.

Cao Cao planned to march south. One of his military advisers, Fu Gan, sent a memorial against the scheme: he claimed it was more fitting to increase the authority of the civil government, to lay aside arms and to cease from war and spend the time training the soldiers until the times were be favorable. After reading this, Cao Cao put aside thoughts of an expedition against the south. Instead, he established schools and set himself to attract and promote people of ability.

Seeing Cao Cao's increasing power and influence, Emperor Xian feared that he had ambitions for the throne. He plotted with Empress Fu, and asked Empress Fu's father Fu Wan to slay Cao Cao. A eunuch named Mu Shun was willing to convey this secret letter to Fu Wan despite the danger.

Cao Cao had numerous spies and so heard of the letters. So he waited at the palace gate for Mu Shun to come out. Nothing was found in his hat, but when it was given back Mu Shun who was alarmed put it on with both hands. There was something suspicious about this movement, and Cao Cao bade the searchers examine his hair. Therein the letter of Fu Wan was found.

Cao put Fu Wan and all his family to death. He also took away the seal of the Empress Fu. He ordered the executioners to beat her till she died. Her two sons were also executed.

In the first month of the twentieth year of Rebuilt Tranquillity, Cao Cao demanded Emperor Xian establish his daughter Lady Cao as Empress. Emperor Xian dared not refuse. Therefore Lady Cao's name was inscribed on the dynastic rolls as Empress.

Cao Cao called in his civil and military officials for a meeting about how they could subdue Liu Bei and Sun Quan. Xiahou Dun gave his opinion, saying that the two rivals should be left until Zhang Lu of Hanzhong has been subdued. A great army that could overcome Zhang Lu would then be ready to attack the Western Land of Rivers. The advice struck a chord with Cao Cao's own idea, and so he prepared an expedition to the west.

As soon as he arrived at the Yangping Pass, Cao Cao saw the dangerous and evil nature of the place. And as he knew nothing of the roads and was fearful of an ambush, and so dared not march. For fifty days his army and that of Yang Ang, general of of Zhang Lu, held each other at bay without engaging. After many attacks, Cao Cao could not capture the Yangping Pass. Later Cao Cao killed Yang Ang with the help of a clever ruse so that the Yangping Pass was finally captured. Then he brought up his army, and marched straightaway to Nanzheng.

Cao Cao's troops were attacking Nanzheng. Zhang Lu ordered Pang De, a bold general from Xiliang who had previously served under Ma Chao, to defend Nanzheng. Now Cao Cao, remembering Pang De's boldness at the battle of River Wei Bridge, wanted to win this warrior for himself. He bribed Yang Song to slander Pang De to his master so as to weaken Pang De's position.

Zhang Lu swallowed the bait really. He ordered Pang De to win a victory in a battle next day; otherwise his head would be taken according to military law. Cao Cao rode his horse to the top of a hill so as to lure Pang De in.

But Pang De boldly faced his escort and rode up the hill. He and his followers rode headlong into ditches and pits that had been specially dug. Out flew Cao Cao's troops with ropes and hooks, and Pang De was taken prisoner. Pang De surrendered to Cao Cao.

After occupying Nanzheng, Cao Cao's large army advanced to Bazhong. Having no way out, Zhang Lu gave in. Cao Cao treated him with great kindness and consoled him with the title of General Who Guards the South. Other surrendered generals were also awarded titles. Yang Song was condemned to public execution. From then on, Hanzhong was under the jurisdiction of Cao Cao.

When the Eastern Land of Rivers was quite subdued, First Secretary Sima Yi and Lie Ye suggested that Cao Cao should try to take and capture the Western Land of Rivers. Cao Cao sighed, "There is no end; human want has no limit; now that I have Hanzhong, I must take Yizhou." He decided to take no action.

CHAPTER 21

War at Ruxu

To prevent Cao Cao from attacking the Western Land of Rivers, Zhuge Liang demanded that his lord make an alliance with Wu. He suggested that the three territories of Jingzhou "Changsha, Jiangxia, and Guiyang" should first be restored to Wu and then the whole of the Jingzhou Region after they took the Eastern Land of Rivers. In return Wu would attack Hefei. Liu Bei approved, and sent Yi Ji to Wu.

Seeing Sun Quan, Yi Jie presented him with letters and prepared gifts and explained the benefit of allying against Cao Cao. Since Cao Cao was away from Hanzhong, Sun Quan thought it would be a good opportunity to seize the opportunity and attack Hefei. He made a promise to ally with Liu Bei and immediately dispatched troops to attack Hefei.

Sun Quan won victory in the first battle and took Huancheng. The army set out for Hefei. Zhang Liao, a general defending Hefei, led his troops, together with Yue Jin and Li Dian to launch a three-pronged attack upon the Wu soldiers who were defeated at the Flageolet Ford. Sun Quan leapt his horse over the broken bridge and escaped danger.

Then Sun Quan led the remnants of his defeated army back to Ruxu and began to put his ships in order so that the army and navy might attack Hefei again in unison. Zhang Liao sent to Hanzhong for reinforcements. Seeing that they could not take the Western Land of Rivers for some time, Cao Cao broke up his camp and went toward Ruxu with all his commanders to reinforce Hefei.

Before Cao Cao's army had recovered from the long march, Gan Ning, a Wu general, leading only a hundred horse raided the enemy's camp. Gan Ning treated his soldiers to mutton and wine and ordered them to fight to the last. At the second watch, they quickly burst into Cao Cao's camp, dashed hither and thither, cutting and slashing, till Cao Cao's men were quite bewildered and frightened.

Next day, Zhang Liao launched another attack. Both armies fought on the river bank. Sun Quan dashed into Cao's army and was himself surrounded in turn and soon found himself in desperate straits. At this critical juncture, Zhou Tai fought his way to his master's side and, despite being severely wounded, rescued Sun Quan.

As a recompense for Zhou Tai's services in his rescue, Sun Quan prepared in his honor a great banquet, where Sun Quan himself offered Zhou Tai a goblet of wine. While the tears coursed down his cheeks, he said, "Twice you saved my life, careless of your own. What sort of a man should I be if I did not treat you as one of my own flesh and blood?" Then Sun Quan bade Zhou Tai to open his robe and exhibit his wounds for all the assembly to see. For every wound Sun Quan made him drink off a goblet of wine till he became thoroughly intoxicated. The other generals and soldiers were also very moved.

At the end of the month the two armies were both at Ruxu and neither had won victory. To avoid losing more soldiers, Sun Quan sued for peace. Cao Cao also saw that the South Lands was too strong to be overcome, and consented. He marched his army back to the Capital Xuchang.

In the fifth month of the twenty-first year of Rebuilt Tranquillity (216), Emperor Xian approved a great memorial signed by many officers and made Cao Cao Prince of Wei. Thrice Cao Cao with seeming modesty pretended to decline the honor, but thrice was his refusal rejected.

Finding his father wished his brother Cao Zhi to be named as heir, the eldest son, Cao Pi sought from the High Adviser Jia Xu a plan to secure his rights of primogeniture. Whenever the father went out on any military expedition, Cao Zhi wrote fulsome panegyrics. Then Jia Xu told Cao Pi to weep copiously when bidding his father farewell. After a long time, Cao Cao thought Cao Pi so sincerely filial that he declared his eldest son his heir.

Before long came the news that Lu Su of Wu had died of illness. Zhang Fei and Ma Chao led troops to attack Hanzhong. Cao Cao, with his main army, also marched there.

In the early months of AD 218, Geng Ji, Wei Huang, Jin and Ji Ping's sons Ji Mao and Ji Mu swore before Heaven to be loyal, and they smeared their lips with blood to show the sincerity of their oath to get rid of Cao Cao. They agreed to lead their people to begin their work at the second watch on the fifteenth day of the first month.

Besides, Jin was friendly with Wang Bi, the High Minister in command of the Imperial Guard, who was much given to wine. That night of the fifteenth day of the first month, the Commander of the Imperial Guards, Wang Bi, and his officers held a feast in their camp. Jin took advantage of this opportunity to steal into the camp from the rear and set fire to it. Seeing the fire, Geng Ji and Wei Huang led their troops there. Then the flames were leaping higher and higher.

Wang Bi fled to the house of Cao Xiu. Cao Xiu immediately led a thousand troops into the city. Xiahou Dun mustered his army and surrounded the city. The disturbance was put down just before dawn. The households of the five conspirators including Jin and Wei Huang were arrested and killed. Geng Ji shouted against Cao Cao before death, "Living we have failed to slay you, Cao Cao; dead we will be malicious spirits smiting rebels in all places!" Xiahou Dun carried out his chief's orders and sent the officials he had arrested to Yejun. There Cao Cao set up two flags, one red and one white, on the drill ground and sent all the officials to stand before the flags. He asked those who had tried to put out the fire to take their stand by the red flag, and those who had remained in their houses to go to the white flag. Then the order was given to kill all those by the red flag, saying that at that time they intended not to put out the flames but to aid the rebels.

Cao Hong went with an army into Hanzhong. Seeing that Ma Chao declined to come out to fight, he suspected some ruse, so he dared not advance rashly. His general Zhang He wished to go to Baxi to attack Zhang Fei. Fearing his carelessness, Cao Hong made him put his undertaking in writing, and then Zhang He marched to the attack.

The news soon reached Baxi. Zhang Fei gave five thousand troops to Lei Tong and let them lay an ambush in the hills in the area of Langzhong while he himself led out ten thousand troops to challenge Zhang He to single combat. With enemies on both sides, Zhang He managed to fight his way out and made his way back to his camp at Dangqu.

Zhang Fei made camp three miles off. Every day Zhang Fei went forth and offered battle, but Zhang He remained on the defensive. Zhang Fei sat in the tent day after day drinking till he became half drunk. And then, he would revile his opponent. However he would never go out to give battle.

Liu Bei was told that his brother was giving himself over to wine. He feared that Zhang Fei would maybe be defeated because of drinking. Zhuge Liang knew what Zhang Fei's aim was however, so he sent him fifty vessels of the best brew in Chengdu. Liu Bei opposed this plan. Zhuge Liang said, "But this is his plan to get the better of Zhang He." Liu Bei sent Wei Yan with the wine to the Frontier Army.

Zhang Fei told Wei Yan and Lei Tong each to take a thousand troops and lay ambush outside the camp, while he himself sat in the tent drinking, with two of the soldiers holding a boxing exhibition for his amusement. When Zhang He on the hill-top saw his opponent drinking, he thought that the defences would be weak. So Zhang He gave orders to prepare for a night attack on the enemy camp.

That night Zhang He took advantage of the darkness to steal down the side of the hill. He got quite close to the enemy camp and stood for a time looking at Zhang Fei sitting amid a blaze of lamps and drinking. Zhang He rushed at him and delivered a mighty thrust with his spear. It was a Zhang Fei made of straw. Zhang He thought he was trapped and turned his steed immediately. At that moment they were intercepted by Zhang Fei. The glare of fire out in the moutains of Dangqu told him of the seizure of his third camp by Zhang Fei's rear force. Nothing could be done, and Zhang He fought his way out of the trap, and fled to Wakou Pass.

Then Zhang Fei sent off Wei Yan to make a full frontal attack on the Pass, while he himself with five hundred light horse attacked from the rear by way of Mount Zitong. Zhang He escaped. He saw Cao Hong, and Cao Hong was so angry at his plight that he ordered the lictors to put Zhang He to death according to military rules. The other generals interceded. Cao Hong gave him command of another army and sent him to take Jiameng Pass and so perhaps redeem his past errors with some

meritorious service.

Being told of Zhang He's taking Jiameng Pass, Directing Instructor wished to get Zhang Fei from Langzhong to drive off Zhang He. The veteran General Huang Zhong cried out angrily that the Instructor was disrespecting them and that they would slay Zhang He. Directing Instructor ordered Veteran General Yan Yan together to fight Zhang He.

Despite being despised by Zhang He for their age, Huang Zhong and Yan Yan defeated Zhang He many times and captured supplies stored in Tiandangshan Mountain. When the news of victory arrived, Liu Bei took advantage of the favorable position and led his main army to attack Hanzhong. Huang Zhong volunteered to go to Dingjunshan Mountain and fight Xiahou Yuan. Zhuge Liang sent Fa Zheng to aid him.

CHAPTER 22

Dingjunshan Mountain

Being told of Liu Bei's leading his army to take Hanzhong, Cao Cao himself led an army of four hundred thousand troops on a punitive expedition against him.

As they moved through Tong Pass, Cao Cao passed by the Indigo Field, seeing the estate of the late Minister Cai Yong. Thinking on past events, he was greatly grieved. Cai Yong had been killed in previous years. His daughter Cai Yan had composed a ballad called "Eighteen Stanzas for the Mongolian Flute", which was very popular in the empire. Cao Cao sent a messenger with a thousand ounces of gold to ransom her from the frontier Hun State. She was married to Dong Si and from then on they lived in the Indigo Field.

Cao Cao dismounted and went into the estate. Cai Yan hastened to come out to welcome him. Seeing a rubbing of a tablet hanging on the wall, Cao Cao asked his hostess about it. Cai Yan said that it was a tablet of Cao E, or the fair Lady Cao which had been inscribed by Handan Chun in memory of an event when he was only thirteen. Eight large characters on the reverse of the stone had been written by her father, which read, "yellow silk, young wife, a daughter's child, pestle and mortar." Cao Cao asked her what they meant, and she said that she could not interpret them. He also turned to his staff and asked them. But no one could make any reply.

First Secretary Yang Xiu finally said he had fathomed the meaning. Cao Cao asked him not tell him yet and to let him think about it some more. Soon after they took leave of the lady and rode on. About 30 miles from the farm, the meaning suddenly dawned upon Cao Cao, and he let Yang Xiu explain. Yang Xiu said the characters meant "Decidedly fine and well told." Cao Cao was astonished at Yang Xiu's cleverness, and said that it was just what he had figured out. Those in the traveling party were in awe of

Yang Xiu's ingenuity and knowledge.

Xiahou Yuan had been defending Dingjunshan Mountain and had not gone on the attack. Reaching Nanzheng, Cao Cao ordered Xiahou Yuan to launch an attack on the enemy. Xiahou Yuan brought out his troops and attacked. The Shu general Chen Shi had no chance against them and was quickly taken prisoner. In the very first bout Huang Zhong captured Xiahou Shang. Next day both sides exchanged prisoners. From then on, Xiahou Yuan simply remained on the defensive and did not launch any attacks.

Overseer Fa Zheng was planning to take a steep hill just opposite and on the west of Dingjunshan Mountain. Knowing that from the top of that hill the whole of Cao Cao's army's position would be visible: their strength and their weakness, Xiahou Yuan really wanted to capture the hill. After the soldiers of Xiahou Yuan became weary and dispirited, Huang Zhong led his force down the slope. Xiahou Yuan was too surprised to defend himself. With a thundering shout, Huang Zhong raised his

sword and cleft Xiahou Yuan right between the head and shoulders so that he fell into two pieces. Huang Zhong took advantage and captured Dingjunshan Mountain.

Cao Cao led his army of two hundred thousand troops out against Dingjunshan Mountain to avenge Xiahou Yuan's death. He sent Zhang He to move their stores in Micangshan Mountain to the Northern Mountain near the River Han. Hearing the news,

Zhuge Liang ordered Huang Zhong and Zhao Yun to burn Cao's army's stores of grain and forage. Huang Zhong and Zhao Yun both strived to lead the way and they cast lots for who was to have that honour. The Veteran General won the prize.

That night, Huang Zhong and his general, Zhang Zhu, led their troops across the River Han to the foot of the hills. Cao's troops had taken precautions however, and Huang Zhong was surrounded. Noon came with no news of Huang Zhong. Therefore Zhao Yun took three thousand troops with him and went to his aid. He launched a fierce attack on the enemy, killing many of them and rescued his fellow warriors Huang Zhong and Zhang Zhu.

Cao Cao was filled with rage to see his troops falling away before Zhao Yun. He went in pursuit himself with his officers. Then Zhao Yun placed his archers and bowmen in a covered position outside, while he threw down all his weapons and flags and opened the gates. But he himself, alone, stood outside the gates of the camp. Cao Cao urged his army to march forward quicker. Then Zhao Yun gave the signal to his troops to come out of the moat, and the archers and bowmen opened fire. Zhao Yun and his troops dashed out. Cao Cao's troops were defeated and abandoned their stores of food and forage.

Cao Cao was coming down through the Xie Valley again to try to capture the River Han. He sent out Xu

Huang to lead the attack. Wang Ping, a native of Shu, was sent as second in command. In spite of the advice offered by Wang Ping, Xu Huang crossed the River Han and made camp. Xu Huang was badly defeated. Wang Ping crossed the river and surrendered to Zhao Yun. Wang Ping's defection made Cao Cao very angry. Cao Cao placed himself at the head of a force and tried to retake the bank of the river. The two armies stood on opposite sides of the waters of the river.

Zhuge Liang ordered Zhao Yun to organise five hundred troops, with drums and horns, in an ambush behind the hill. He ordered them to beat a long roll of the drums every night, all of which kept Cao Cao sleepless for the whole night. Cao Cao broke up his camp, marched his troops ten miles further back and pitched his camp. The troops of Shu then crossed the river and camped with the stream behind them. Liu Bei could not understand this. Zhuge Liang said, smiling, "Cao Cao is skilled in war, but still he finds it difficult to counter deceitful tricks."

Seeing Liu Bei thus encamped, Cao Cao wanted to provoke them. He invited Liu Bei to a parley, and they abused each other. Then the two armies fought an intense battle.

Defeated, the troops of Shu fled toward the river abandoning everything, even throwing aside their weapons, which littered the road. The soldiers of Cao Cao picked them up. As Cao Cao was about to retreat, Zhuge Liang gave the signal to attack. Immediately, several Shu armies pressed forward and Cao's troops were utterly defeated and fled.

Liu Bei and his main army followed them to Nanzheng. Soon it became known that their city of refuge was in the hands of Zhang Fei and Wei Yan. Disappointed and saddened, Cao Cao bade them march to Yangping Pass. Liu Bei asked Zhuge Liang why Cao Cao was exceedingly quick to see the trap set for him.

"He has always been of a suspicious nature," said Zhuge Liang, "and that has led to many failures on his part although he is a good leader of armies. I have defeated him by playing upon his doubts."

All armies made haste towards Yangping Pass. But the soldiers of Shu came right up to the walls of the Pass, and some burned the east gate while others shouted at the west. Others, again, burned the north gate while drums rolled at the south. Cao Cao was frightened and presently they left the Pass and fled again. Zhao Yun and Huang Zhong followed closely.

When Cao Cao fled to the Xie Valley, his second son, Cao Zhang came to help him to fight. Then the army was marched back again and pitched camp at the Xie Valley.

One day, while he was anxiously trying to decide what to do, his cook sent in some chicken broth. He noticed in the broth some chicken tendons. He was still deep in thought when Xiahou Dun entered his tent to ask the watchword for that night. Cao Cao at once involuntarily replied, "Chicken tendon."

When First Secretary Yang Xiu saw the order that the watchword was "chicken tendon", he told all his people to pack up their belongings ready for the march. Xiahou Dun sent for Yang Xiu and asked why he had packed up. Yang Xiu replied, "'Chicken tendons' are tasteless things to eat, and yet it is a pity to waste them. You will certainly see the Prince of Wei retreat before long." The word was passed, and other generals and soldiers also packed up their belongings ready for departure.

Cao Cao's mind was too perturbed for sleep. That night he got up, and wandered through the camp. When he got to Xiahou Dun's tents, he saw everything packed and ready for a move. Much surprised, he made his way back to his own tent and sent for him and asked him why he had packed. Xiahou Dun told him what Yang Xiu had said. Cao Cao felt that Yang Xiu was a man of acute and ingenious mind, but sometimes inclined to show off and that his lack of restraint over his tongue was sometimes damaging. So he was beheaded on a charge of damaging the morale of the army.

Next he issued an order to advance the next day. A soldier came flying in to say that the rear and center camps had been seized by Ma Chao. Cao Cao drew his sword and took up station on the top of a hill from where he could survey the field. Wei Yan fitted an arrow to his bow, and shot and wounded Cao Cao on the lip. The arrow knocked out two of his front teeth. He was saved by Pang De and returned to camp. He gave the order to retreat.

It was after this that the general body of the officers decided to urge Liu Bei to assume the title of Emperor, but he refused. "My lord," said Zhuge Liang, "you have made rectitude your motto all your life. If you really object to this most honored title, then, since you have Jingzhou, Yizhou, and Hanzhong, take temporarily the title of 'Prince of Hanzhong.'" As there seemed no other option, Liu Bei listened and complied.

In the seventh month of AD 219, Liu Bei ascended an altar set up at Mianyang, and received the salutes and congratulations of all his officers as the Prince of Hanzhong. And his son Liu Shan was nominated as his heir-apparent. Xu Jing was given the title of Royal Guardian; Fa Zheng that of Chair of the Secretariat. Zhuge Liang was reappointed Directing Instructor of the Forces.

CHAPTER 23

Guan Yu Drowns the Enemy Troops

Now that Liu Bei called himself the new Prince of Hanzhong, Cao Cao was greatly vexed. So he issued orders for the whole force of the state to go out against the two Lands of Rivers to wage fierce war with the new Prince of Hanzhong. First Secretary Sima Yi persuaded him to send some able communicator with a letter to the state of Wu to persuade the Marquis to send an army to recover Jingzhou. That would draw away all the armies of Shu, and then he could send his armies to Hanzhong. The scheme pleased Cao Cao. He at once drew up a letter and sent it with Man Chong.

Having read Cao Cao's letter, Sun Quan discussed the matter with his council of advisers. Zhuge Jin said, "I hear that Guan Yu has a daughter. Let me go to ask for her in marriage on behalf of your heir. If Guan Yu agrees, then we can arrange with him to attack Cao Cao. If Guan Yu refuses, then let us aid Cao Cao in an attack on Jingzhou." Sun Quan took this advice.

Guan Yu had always despised Sun Quan. When Zhuge Jin put forward the proposal, the warrior flared up and said, "How can a tiger's daughter marry with a dog's whelp? Were it not for your brother, I would take your head. Say no more!" Guan Yu called his servants to throw out the hapless messenger.

Sun Quan was furious, and decided to aid Cao Cao in a joint attack upon Jingzhou. Cao Cao made Cao Ren attack Jingzhou by land, while the Wu forces would attack from water.

At that time his spies told him of the treaty between Cao Cao and Sun Quan, and their designs upon Jingzhou, and he hastily called in Zhuge Liang to ask what should be done. Zhuge Liang said, "First send a special messenger to Guan Yu with his new title, telling him to capture Fankou, which will so dampen the ardor of the enemy that they will abandon their plan." Therefore Liu Bei sent Fei Shi, a minister from his Board of War, to take word of the new title to Guan Yu.

Guan Yu went out of the city to receive Fei Shi. Guan Yu expressed complaints about Huang Zhong's being conferred one of the Five Tiger Generals. After repeated persuasion, Guan Yu then humbly received the seal.

Wishing to march to Fankou, Guan Yu appointed Fu Shiren and Mi Fang Leaders of the Vanguard to take the first army out of the city into camp. He found that the two generals had also been feasting, and a fire had started behind their tent. A spark fell into some explosives, and the conflagration spread and destroyed the whole camp and all that was in it. Guan Yu sentenced them both to death. However, Fei Shi interceded for them. So the two officers received forty blows each and were not allowed to lead the van.

Guan Yu managed to capture Xiangyang, and Cao Cao's troops retreated to Fankou. Fearing that Sun Quan would attack Jingzhou, the Marching General, Wang Fu, advised Guan Yu to order Zhao Lei to guard the city. Despite realising that Wang Fu's advice was reasonable, Guan Yu still sent Pan Jun who was jealous and selfish to perform the task.

Being told that Xiangyang had fallen and that Fankou was in imminent danger of falling, Cao Cao sent Yu Jin to reinforce Fankou. Pang De volunteered to lead the van. Because Pang De had once been under the command of Ma Chao, Cao Cao was afraid that he would work for his own interests. Pang De took off his head dress and prostrated himself, bitter tears rolling down his cheeks. Cao Cao finally agreed.

Then Pang De took his leave and returned to his house, where he ordered a coffin made. He claimed that he would fight to the end with Guan Yu. When the army marched, the coffin was carried behind. Pang De hastened to Fankou with all the pomp of war, his gongs clanging, his drums rolling as he marched.

Being told that Pang De was carrying a coffin, and had come to fight with him to the death, Guan Yu was determined to kill

Pang De. The first day, they fought over a hundred bouts, with no decisive conclusion. Next day, after fifty more bouts, Pang De reined in his horse, sheathed his sword, and fled. Guan Yu went in pursuit, but he was not nimble enough to avoid the arrow that was fired at him and he was wounded in the left arm.

Seeing the arrow had wounded Guan Yu's left arm, Pan De demanded Yu Jin take advantage of the moment to advance. Jealous of the glory that might accrue to his next in command Yu Jin urged caution and obedience to the command of the Prince of Wei. Yu Jin refused to move his army in spite of Pang De's repeated entreaties; moreover, Yu Jin led the army to a new camp behind the hills some three miles north of Fankou. There his own army prevented communication by the main road, while he sent Pang De into a valley in the rear so that Pang De could do nothing.

After his wound healed, Guan Yu went up to a high vantage point to reconnoiter. Guan Yu noted that the whole layout of the enemy seemed very slack in Fankou, and that the relief armies were camped in a valley named Zengkou Stream to the north, so he came up with the scheme to drown the soldiers of Wei.

A heavy downpour came on, lasting several days. Orders were given to move the Jingzhou troops to higher ground. Then he sent orders to open the dams and let the water out in order to flood Fankou. All the soldiers of Cao Cao were drowned. Yu Jin surrendered and Pang De was taken prisoner by Zhou Cang.

Guan Yu advised Pang De to surrender, but he would rather perish beneath the sword than surrender. He reviled his captors without pause until, losing patience at last, Guan Yu sent him to his death. The floodwaters were still high, and taking advantage of them, the troops of Jingzhou boarded boats to move toward Fankou.

The entire population, male and female, were mobilized by Cao Ren to carry mud and bricks to strengthen the city walls. Cao Ren remained on the defensive and refused to leave to give battle. Cao Ren, who was among his soldiers on the wall, saw that Guan Yu had no armor on, so he ordered his men to shoot. Guan Yu hastily reined in his horse and retreated, but an arrow struck him in the arm. He fell from his horse.

The arrow head had been poisoned. Guan Yu's right arm became discolored and swollen and useless. The other leaders persuaded Guan Yu to withdraw to Jingzhou, where his wound could be treated.

Guan Yu engaged in a game of chess with Ma Liang, although his arm was still very painful. But Guan Yu was determined to keep up appearances so as not to discourage his troops. Hearing of the wound sustained by the famous general, Hua Tuo specially came to try to offer treatment by scraping away the poison from the bone.

Huo Tuo wished to erect a post with a steel ring. He wanted to put Guan Yu's arm into the ring and then try to operate. The warrior extended his arm for the operation but insisted on continuing with his game, only drinking a cup of wine now and again, and his face betrayed no sign of pain. "I have spent my life in practice of medicine," said Hua Tuo, "but I have never seen such a patient as you, Sir. It is as if you are not from earth but rather from heaven."

Having captured Yu Jin and accomplished the death of Pang De, Guan Yu astonished Cao Cao so much that he wanted to remove his capital from Xuchang. Sima Yi persuaded Cao Cao to send a messenger into the state of Wu to foment disunity and hopefully cause Sun Quan to launch his armies against the armies of Guan Yu from the rear. In this way Fankou would be

relieved. In line with this plan, Cao Cao sent Xu Huang to lead his forces to the Yangling Slopes, where they halted to see if any support was forthcoming from the southeast.

CHAPTER 24

Guan Yu Retreats to Maicheng

Sun Quan fell in with Cao Cao's scheme as soon as he had read Cao Cao's letter. Then he placed the task of taking Jingzhou on Lu Meng's shoulders.

So Lu Meng took his leave and went back to Lukou. But soon scouts reported that Guan Yu had erected beacon towers at short distances apart all along the Great River, and that the army of Jingzhou was being prepared in a most efficient manner. Therefore he used the excuse of illness and stayed at home. The Marquis of Wu sent his son-in-law Lu Xun to inquire about Lu Meng's position. He also advised him to use the excuse of illness to resign his post.

In accordance with Cao Cao's plan, Sun Quan issued a command for Lu Meng to retire and go to Jianye to attend to the recovery of his health. He thereupon ordered Lu Xun to replace Lu Meng and gave him responsibility for the defence of the port. Lu Xun set about drawing up a letter to Guan Yu, which was couched in the most modest language. Guan Yu eased the defense of Jingzhou and sent half his troops to Jingzhou to assist in the siege of Fankou.

Sun Quan saw this reduced force in Jingzhou, and appointed Lu Meng to the position of sole command to attack Jingzhou. Lu Meng dressed a number of sailors in the plain white costumes of ordinary merchants and put them on board his vessels. He concealed his veterans in the compartments. Thus they deceived the beacon-keepers. At about the second watch the soldiers came out of hiding in the holds of the transports, occupied the beacon towers and got possession of Jingzhou.

Now when Fu Shiren heard of the capture of Jingzhou, he was glas for he had long harboured resentment against Guan Yu. So he went to Jingzhou to surrender to Sun Quan. Sun Quan sent him to Nanjun to induce his former colleague Mi Fang to join him in changing sides. Mi Fang also threw in his lot with Sun Quan,

Hearing that Jingzhou had fallen to Wu, Cao Cao's general Xu Huang who had stationed his troops at Yangling Slope, made an ingenious military move and took possession of Yancheng and Sizhong. Although defeated Guan Ping and the Shu got away and returned to their main camp. He went to his father and told him that Jingzhou was in the enemy's hands. Guan Yu could not believe it.

Xu Huang arrived. Though his wound had not healed yet, Guan Yu himself went into the battle and fought ten or more bouts with Xu Huang. Cao Ren, having heard of the arrival of reinforcing made a sortie from Fankou and was just about to attack to assist Xu Huang. The army of Jingzhou was attacked from either side by Xu and Cao, Guan Yu, with as many of his officers as could escape, fled in disorder.

Crossing the River Xiang, Guan Yu made for Xiangyang. Suddenly the scouts reported that Jingzhou had fallen and that the generals defending Gong'an and Nanjun had surrendered. The story filled Guan Yu with boundless rage. His wound reopened, and he fell into a swoon. Complying with Zhao Lei's proposal, he sent to Chengdu for help while returning to Jingzhou to try to recover that city.

The siege of Fankou being thus raised, Cao Cao did not pursue, but rather observed the engagement between Wu and Guan Yu. When Xu Huang returned, Cao Cao went out of the stockade to meet him and on the spot conferred on his commander the title of General Who Pacifies the South. Xu Huang was sent soon after to bolster the defense of Xiangyang along with Xiahou Shang.

Guan Yu found himself trapped on the road to Jingzhou with the army of Wu in front and the men of Wei coming up behind.

When he was told that Lu Meng had tried to affect his soldier's morale and that many generals and soldiers had deserted, he indignantly said, "If I cannot slay him while I live, I will after I am dead."

Guan Yu advanced to Jingzhou, constantly fighting with Wu soldiers on the way. When he entered a valley, Guan Yu was like a kernel in a nut, quite surrounded. Seeing that his soldiers' hearts were all discouraged, Guan Ping persuaded Guan Yu to camp at Maicheng and send Liao Hua to Shangyong to ask for help from Meng Da and Liu Feng.

Hearing Liao Hua's message about how assistance was urgently needed, Liu Feng wanted to go to Guan Yu's aid immediately. But Meng Da listed the wrongs committed by Guan Yu, and Liu Feng changed his mind. They were not willing to offer help. Seeing that it was no use weeping or begging, Liao Hua went at once to Chengdu.

Guan Yu was in a sorry plight. Wu sent Zhuge Jin to try to persuade him to surrender. But Guan Yu replied, quite calmly, saying, "The city may fall, and then perhaps I will die. Jade may be shattered, but its whiteness remains; bamboo may be burned, but its joints stand straight. My body may be broken, but my fame shall live in history. Say no more, but leave the city, I beg you. I will fight Sun Quan to the death." Zhuge Jin returned with no success.

Zhuge Jin told Sun Quan of Guan Yu's obstinacy and his rejection of all rational argument. Lu Meng said that he had an idea to capture Guan Yu. So Zhu Ran was sent to lay an ambush several miles north of Maicheng, and Pan Zhang was placed in command of an ambush to be laid near Linju. Generals and soldiers were sent to attack the city vigorously on all sides but one, leaving the north gate open for escape.

Guan Yu was unwilling to be stranded in Maicheng and wanted to escape into the Western Land of Rivers along a small path. Wang Fu advised him to go along the main road. The old warrior said that even though there might be an ambush, he was not afraid. Wang Fu would defend the city to the very last, so the two parted in tears.

Guan Yu, Guan Ping, and Zhao Lei marched out of the north gate of Maicheng with two hundred horses. Soon, out sprang troops led by Zhu Ran from all sides. Guan Yu dared not engage such a number, and fled in the direction of Linju. When he reached Zhuxi, a place with mountains on both sides, they were intercepted by another ambush led by Pan Zhang. In the disorder, Guan Yu's horse fell, and Guan Yu tumbled out of the saddle. In a moment Ma Zhong, the Marching General of Pan Zhang, took him prisoner.

Sun Quan admired Guan Yu so much on account of his great virtues that he tried to win him over to his side. Guan Yu opened his eyes wide and abused Sun Quan in a loud voice. After a long time thinking about it, Sun Quan finally had the father and son executed.

After being involved in plotting to kill Guan Yu, Lu Meng felt uneasy. One day, Sun Quan held a great feast at which Lu Meng was given the seat of honor. Lu Meng became somewhat deranged, called himself Guan Yu and said he wanted to kill Lu Meng for revenge. Thereupon Lu Meng fell over dead.

Zhang Zhao suggested a plan to divert this evil from the state of Wu. Sun Qun sent Guan Yu's head to Cao Cao to make it appear that Cao Cao was the prime cause of his destruction. Cao Cao saw through the ruse, so he made a wooden image of the remainder of the body and buried it accompanied with the rites appropriate for a great warrior and a minister of state.

When he heard of the terrible news of the death of the two Guans, Liu Bei uttered a great cry and fell down in a swoon.

For three days he refused all nourishment, and he wept so bitterly that his garments were soaked, and there were spots of blood all over them. He swore that he would avenge Guan Yu by marching to Wu. The Prince went outside the south gate to summon the spirit of his brother home, and made sacrifices and wept for a whole day for his dead warrior, his brother.

CHAPTER 25

Brothers Contend for the Throne

For a long time after Cao Cao buried Lord Guan, he saw him in his dreams every night. Cao Cao's suffered serious headaches as a result of these frightening experiences. Hua Tuo made a careful examination of Cao Cao, and told him, "Prince, your headaches are due to a malignant tumor within your brain. The tumor is too thick to get out. I propose to administer a dose of hashish, then open the skull casing and remove the thickened tumor. That would be the most radical cure." However, Cao Cao suspected that Hua Tuo wanted to kill him and told his lictors to put Hua Tuo in gaol.

A gaoler named Wu was kindly disposed towards Hua Tuo and saw to it that he was well fed. Hua Tuo knew Cao Cao would certainly kill him. He sent his Treatise of the Black Bag to the gaoler. After Hua Tuo died, the gaoler bought a coffin and had him buried.

Unexpectedly, the wife of the gaoler burned the book. The gaoler only managed to snatch away two unburned pages. The upshot of all this was that the learning in the Treatise of the Black Bag was lost to the world.

Meanwhile, Cao Cao's condition grew worse, and the uncertainty he felt about the intentions of his rivals severely aggravated his disease. An envoy was then announced who had come with letters from the state of Wu in which Sun Quan tried to persuade Cao Cao to become the emperor. Cao Cao said, "Is Sun Quan trying to put me in a furnace?"

Knowing that he would die soon, Cao Cao called in Cao

Hong and Sima Yi and some others to hear his last wishes. Cao Cao said to them, "Among my four sons, my second son, Cao Zhang is valiant, but imprudent; the third, Cao Zhi, is vain and unreliable; and the fourth, Cao Xiong, is a weakling and may not live long. My eldest, Cao Pi, is steady and serious; he is best suited to succeed me, and I look to you all to support him."

Then Cao Cao bade his servants bring him the Tibetan incense and fragrances that he burned every day, and he handed them out to his handmaids. And he said to them, "After my death you must diligently attend to your labors. You can make silken shoes to sell, and so earn your own living." Next he commanded that seventy-two sites for a tomb should be selected near Jiangwu, so that no one should know his actual burial place, lest his remains be dug up.

Cao Cao passed away in the first month of AD 220. He was sixty-six. His body was enclosed in a silver shell, and laid in a golden coffin and was sent at once to his home in Yejun. The eldest son Cao Pi wept bitter tears and went out with all his retinue to meet the procession and escort the body of his father home.

Cao Pi became the Prince of Wei. He thereupon took his seat in the palace and received the congratulations of all the court officials, during a great banquet. While the banquet was in progress, the news camethat Cao Zhang, the Lord of Yanling, was approaching from Chang'an with an army of one hundred thousand troops. The new Prince was in a state of consternation because he knew Cao Zhang was obstinate and determined and had considerable military skill. His High Minister Jia Kui came forward to persuade Cao Zhang to refrain from launching an attack.

Cao Zhang was finally persuaded. He entered the city alone. When the Cao brothers met, they fell into each other's arms and wept. Then Cao Zhang yielded command of all his army, and he was instructed to go back to Yanling. Cao Pi was now firmly established in AD 220.

Prime Minister Hua Xin petitioned Cao Pi, saying "Your two brothers did not attend the funeral of their father. Their conduct should be inquired into and punished." Cao Xiong hanged himself rather than be punished.

When the envoy of Cao Pi reached Linzi, Cao Zhi, was spending his time in dissipation, his usual companions being two brothers named Ding Zhengli and Ding Jingli, who had the nerve to deride Cao Pi. And then Cao Zhi, in a fit of anger, ordered his lictors to beat the chief envoy and throw him out.

This treatment of his messenger greatly angered Cao Pi, and he dispatched a force of three thousand Imperial Tiger Guards under Xu Chu to arrest his brother and all his immediate associates. Cao Pi put Ding Zhengli and Ding Jingli to death and imprisoned Cao Zhi.

Cao Pi's mother, Lady Bian, was alarmed at the severity of her son's new rule, and the suicide of her youngest son wounded her deeply. When she heard that Cao Zhi had been arrested and his comrades put to death, she left her palace and went to see her eldest son to try to intercede for Cao Zhi. Cao Pi said, "I have no intention of hurting him. But he needs to change his ways."

Cao Pi demanded that Cao Zhi compose a poem within the time taken to walk seven paces, or he would have him killed. Cao Zhi took seven paces and then recited a poem. This exhibition of skill amazed the Prince and the whole court.

Cao Pi thought he would try another test, so he bade his

brother improvise on the theme of their fraternal relationship, without using the words "brotherhood" or "brother". Without seeming to think at all, Cao Zhi rattled off this rhyme: "They were boiling beans on a beanstalk fire; A plaintive voice from the pot: Since we sprang from the selfsame root, why should you kill me with angry heat?" The allusion in these verses was not lost upon Cao Pi, and he shed a few silent tears. Cao Zhi was downgraded to the rank of Lord of Anxiang.

Liu Bei wanted to destroy Sun Quan in revenge for the death of Guan Yu. Liao Hua threw himself upon the earth, and pleaded with tears in his eyes, "Liu Feng and Meng Da were the true cause of the death of your brother and his adopted son; both these renegades deserve death." But Zhuge Liang offered wiser advice, "That is not the way; go slowly or you may stir up strife. Promote these two and separate them. After that you may arrest them."

Liu Bei raised Liu Feng to the Governorship of Mianzhu, and so separated the two miscreants. Knowing Liu Bei would kill him, Meng Da went to throw in his lot with Cao Pi immediately.

Zhuge Liang bade Liu Feng to capture Meng Da with an army of 50,000 soldiers. With the help of Xiahou Shang and Xu Huang, Meng Da defeated Liu Feng, who escaped back to Chengdu but was eventually beheaded by Liu Bei.

Cao Pi became even more impetuous than Cao Cao. Cao Pi promoted all his officers to high rank and readied an army numbering three hundred thousand. He marched them all over the southern territories and held enormous banquets in the county of Qiao in the old state of Pei, which was the land of his ancestors. As the grand army passed by, the aged villagers lined the roads offering gifts of wine, just as when the Founder of the Han had returned home to Pei.

Hua Xin, Jia Xu and Li Fu and others who had wanted to support Cao Pi claim to be emperor went to the Palace and proposed to Emperor Xian that he should abdicate and yield to the Prince of Wei, Cao Pi using the pretext of propitious signs. The Emperor wept aloud and retired to his private chamber.

Next morning they assembled in the court, but the Emperor did not appear. So they sent the palace officers to summon him. Still he would not show himself. Cao Hong and Cao Xiu, both armed, forced their way into the inner apartments and requested His Majesty to come to the Hall of Imperial Audience, and at last he had to yield. The Empress heaped great abuse on her brother Cao Pi for his treachery.

The Emperor, alarmed at the violence of the language of Hua Xin, shook out his sleeves and rose to leave. But Hua Xin rushed forward and seized the Emperor by the sleeve. The Emperor was in a state of abject terror, as he saw the whole court filling up with armed guards. In order not to be butchered, he had to give up the throne to the Prince.

Chen Qun was directed to draft the abdication manifesto. As soon as it was finished, Hua Xin took it to the palace and presented it, with the Imperial Hereditary Seal, in the name of the Emperor. However, Sima Yi suggested Cao Pi present a memorial twice modestly declining the succession in order to silence the criticism of the people.

Hua Xin also asked the Emperor Xian to set up a Terrace of Abdication and assemble the nobles, officers, and common people to witness the act of abdication. The Emperor had to consent. On the appointed day, Emperor Xian requested Cao Pi to ascend the terrace and receive his abdication. Thereupon the Emperor presented the seal, which Cao Pi received into his hands. In AD 220, the East Han government became that of the Great Wei. Then the new Emperor Pi conferred upon Emperor Xian the title of Duke of Shanyang, bidding him depart forthwith. Soon, he sent emissaries to poison the Emperor Xian.

CHAPTER 26

Setting the Camps Ablaze

Word these events reached Chengdu and caused great grief to the Prince of Hanzhong, when he heard that the Emperor had been put to death. He issued an order for mourning to be worn and instituted a series of sacrificial rites. The stress brought on an illness, so that he could not carry on the business of the court, which was left in the hands of Zhuge Liang.

Zhuge Liang and Xu Jing, and a large number of officials, presented a memorial requesting Liu Bei to assume the title of Emperor. But Liu Bei rejected it. Then Zhuge Liang pleaded illness and remained at home.

When Liu Bei went to see Zhuge Liang, outlined the damage done by Liu Bei refusing to proclaim himself emperor. Liu Bei finally agreed to assume the title of emperor.

Zhuge Liang arranged for the building of an altar in Chengdu. And when all was ready, Liu Bei went up to the altar and performed the appointed sacrifice. Zhuge Liang, in the name of all those assembled, presented the Imperial Seal. All the officials shouted, "Eternal life to the Emperor!" Liu Shan was declared Heir—Apparent. Zhuge Liang became Prime Minister, and Xu Jing, Imperial Guardian. This year was AD 220.

Liu Bei wanted to devote all of the forces of his kingdom to the destruction of the state of Wu to avenge the death of Guan Yu. Zhao Yun spoke against the plan, saying "The empire must come first." However, Zhao Yun's opinion was disregarded, and orders were sent forth to prepare an army to march against the Wu. The First Ruler also sent emissaries into the Five Valleys to seek the aid of fifty thousand tribesmen.

Many of the courtiers, headed by Zhuge Liang, also went to try to persuade Liu Bei to change his mind. The First Ruler was touched by the depth of his minister's concern and the sincerity of his counsel, and was just on the point of yielding when the arrival of Zhang Fei from Langzhong was announced. Zhang Fei, weeping bitterly, requested that Liu Bei immediately avenge the death of Guan Yu. Liu Bei agreed at once and dispatched troops.

As soon as Zhang Fei returned to his post, he issued orders that his soldiers should be ready to march in three days and a day of mourning was declared, with white uniforms and whitened arms. Just after the order appeared, two generals named Fan Jiang and Zhang Da came to their chief, saying "The time allowed is insufficient to make white flags and armors. Pray give us more time, General!" Zhang Fei wouldn't listen. He called in the lictors, had the two officers bound to trees, and ordered that each receive fifty lashes. After the flogging, he said, "Now you will be ready

tomorrow; if you are not, I will put you both to death as an example!"

Fan Jiang and Zhang Da were humiliated and filled with a sense of injustice against Zhang Fei. That night when they knew Zhang Fei was asleep on his couch intoxicated, they crept in and killed him. Having carried out their bloody deed, the two murderers hacked off his head and escaped towards the country of Wu without delay.

At that time, Liu Bei was on the march with his army. Hearing that Zhang Fei had been murdered, Liu Bei uttered a loud cry and fell down senseless in a swoon.

The next day, Zhang Bao, the son of Zhang Fei, and Guan Xing, the son of Guan Yu, came to meet Liu Bei, who clasped his two nephews to him, as tears rolled down his face.

Seeing that Liu Bei was so inconsolable, his officers went to seek out a hermit named Li Yi. The seer got paper and a brush and drew "soldiers, horses and weapons" again and again on many sheets of paper. Having done this, he suddenly tore them into fragments. Furthermore, he drew a picture of a tall man lying supine and another above him digging a grave. And over it all he wrote "White". After this he bowed and departed, leaving the First Ruler in a state of annoyance. After burning the paper, he ordered that the army advance at full speed.

Hearing that Liu Bei was personally leading a great army of more than seven hundred thousand to avenge the death of his brothers, Sun Quan hurriedly assembled his officers to advise on possible countermeasures. Zhuge Jin volunteered to meet Liu Bei to try to persuade the First Ruler to keep the peace.

Zhuge Jin saw Liu Bei and said to him that Sun Quan would like to return Jingzhou and Lady Sun, but Liu Bei was unwilling to accept these terms.

Sun Quan sent Zhao Zi to meet Cao Pi to ask him to attack Hanzhong to help the South Land raise the siege.

Cao Pi asked Zhao Zi some questions, and he answered fluently and courteously. Cao Pi praised Zhao Zi "for taking on a mission without losing the dignity of his master".

Cao Pi conferred the title of Prince of Wu upon Sun Quan and allowed him to use the "Nine Signs of Honors". An adviser mentioned to Cao Pi that, "If the Shu and Wu fight, heaven will make an end of one of them. If you send an army across the river to attack, and the Shu attack at the same time, the state of Wu will disappear. If Wu is gone, then Shu will be left alone and can be dealt with at your convenience."

Cao Pi's envoy Xing Zhen went to the land of Wu. Gu Yong was opposed to accepting the title offered by Cao Pi and suggested Sun Quan style himself "Supreme Ruler" and "Lord" of the nine territories. However, Sun Quan rejected this suggestion.

Liu Bei launched an attack on Yidu. Zhang Bao stabbed Xie Jing with a spear and took Cui Yu captive. Guan Xing hacked off the head of Li Yi and held Tan Xiong captive.

Guan Xing and Zhang Bao made a sneak attack on the camp of Wu at night. Sun Huan was defeated and escaped to Yiling. Zhu Ran was defeated on the river.

Realising that his army was defeated, Sun Quan ordered Han Dang and some other veteran generals to confront the Shu army with an army of 100,000 soldiers. Liu Bei had arrived in Yiling and had established a line of forty camps, spread out in a two hundred-mile long distance.

Huang Zhong didn't want to admit that he was too old and he was determined to prove this. He marched into battle and won a great victory. When he went to accept the challenge the following day, he fell into the trap set by the Wu army. He was hit by an arrow from Ma Zhong and died after returning to the camp.

When Liu Bei heard of Huang Zhong's death, he led his Imperial Guard in an attack against the enemy. Zhang Bao smote Xia Xun to death and Guan Xing slew Zhou Ping with a mighty slash of his sword. The Wu army was utterly defeated.

Gan Ning was in his ship ill, but he roused himself when he heard that the armies of Shu had come, and mounted himself and prepared to go into battle. King Shamo Ke shot an arrow that pierced the skull of Gan Ning, who died under a tree.

When Guan Xing was in the midst of the army of Wu, he caught sight of Pan Zhang, his great enemy, and he galloped in pursuit. In terror, Pan Zhang took to the hills and disappeared in one of the valleys. Desperately looking for him, Guan Xing lost his way and soon it grew dark and he couldn't find his way out. He found shelter in a small village. During the third watch, Pan Zhang also came to the same village. Guan Xing saw him. Before Pan Zhang could flee, Guan Xing raised his sword; and Pan Zhang lay dead. So, Guan Xing avenged the death of his father.

Fu Shiren and Mi Fang killed Ma Zhong and went to Liu Bei for protection. Liu Bei bade Guan Xing set up an altar to his father in the camp, and thereon the First Ruler offered the head of Ma Zhong in sacrifice before the tablet of Guan Yu. This done, he had Guan Xing strip the two deserters naked and make them kneel before the altar, and with his own hand he hewed them to pieces as a sacrifice.

Fear of the First Ruler was very great among the people of the South Land. Sun Quan ordered that the head of Zhang Fei be enclosed in a sandalwood box; Fan Jiang and Zhang Da were bound and imprisoned in a cage on a cart. All of these were sent to Liu Bei's camp as a peace offering. Liu Bei had Fan Jiang and Zhang Da hewed to pieces and sacrificed upon the altar for Zhang Fei. However, the First Ruler still refused to make peace.

Sun Quan was frightened and bewildered. General Kan Ze recommended Lu Xun to Sun Quan as the man to resist the army of Liu Bei. Zhang Zhao and Gu Yong absolutely opposed this since Lu Xun, who was 39 years old, was only a weakling scholar in their eyes.

Kan Ze grew desperate, and shouted, "It is our only hope. I vouch for him with the lives of all my house!". Sun Quan decided to use Lu Xun. An altar was built. Lu Xun was requested to ascend and make his bow on receiving his appointment as Commander-in-Chief, Senior Leader, General Who Guards the West, and Lord of Fenglou. The sword of authority and the seal of office were presented. Lu Xun was licensed to slay the disobedient and report afterwards.

Lu Xun led the army to the battlefront. Veterans Han Dang and Zhou Tai showed their unhappiness at his appointment by only supporting Lu Xun in a half-hearted manner. They also asked Lu Xun to rescue Sun Huan. Lu Xun said, "There is no need to go to his aid. When the Shu are broken, he can walk free." Next day general orders were issued for the defense and prohibitions were issued against giving battle. The officers preferred to attack instead of defending to the last. Lu Xun, drew his sword and shouted, "I shall put all who disobey to death!"

Hearing that Lu Xun was the author of the villainous and crafty plan to attack Jingzhou, Liu Bei gave orders to advance. But Ma Liang protested and dissuaded him from underestimating the enemy. However, Liu Bei, looking down upon Lu Xun, confirmed the order to move forward, and they attacked the passes and fords and engaged the enemy wherever they were.

The soldiers of the Shu Army shouted all sorts of abuse and sought to humiliate their opponents, but Lu Xun took no notice and bade his troops to hold their ground The weather was scorching. Liu Bei ordered that the camps be moved into the shade of the forest near the streams.

Ma Liang was worried about moving towards the forest, saying "The Prime Minister is on a tour of inspection of the defenses in the eastern portion of Shu, making sure that they are in good order in case of an attack by the Wei. Why not send him a sketch of your present dispositions of troops and ask his opinion?" Liu Bei said, "Well then, you go round to all the camps and make a map and take it to the Prime Minister. If he finds any fault, you may come and tell me." Ma Liang set off.

In accordance with Liu Bei's orders, Wu Ban's soldiers approached and challenged the enemy to battle. They showed their contempt by throwing off their armor and clothing and moving about with a complete lack of caution, naked as the day they were born. The Wu generals Xu Sheng and Ding Feng came to the commander's tent to plead to be allowed to fight. Lu Xun only smiled and said the display was exactly designed to entice us into fight. He urged them to be patient reassuring them that the outcome would be seen in three days.

But on the third day the officers were assembled at a look-out point from where they could see that the Wu army had decamped. When a Shu ambush appeared, the Wu generals were finally convinced.

The First Ruler sent orders for his navy forces to make haste down the river and take up station along the riverbanks deep in Wu territory. Huang Quan spoke against this, but Liu Bei didn't listen.

The Wei spies duly reported these events to the Wei Ruler. Cao Pi laughed aloud when he heard the details of the long line of camps and the encampments among the trees and all the rest of it. "Liu Bei is going to be defeated," he said. He also stated, "If he is successful, Lu Xun will lead all his forces westward into the Western Land of Rivers, and his country will be defenseless. I shall pretend to send an army to help. Instead I shall send them in three divisions, and I shall overcome the Wu easily."

Then orders went out appointing Cao Ren to lead an army via Ruxu. Cao Xiu was appointed to take a second army out by Dongkou, and Cao Zhen was to command a third to go through Nanjun, and the three armies were to converge on a given date to make a sudden attack on Wu.

When he reached Chengdu, Ma Liang lost no time in seeing the Prime Minister and presenting the map of the deployment of Liu Bei's armies as they were set out in the field. "Who advised such an arrangement? He ought to be put to death, whoever it was," said Zhuge Liang in great sorrow. "It is entirely our lord's own work; no other had any hand in it," replied Ma Liang. Zhuge Liang ordered Ma Liang to return as soon as possible and to tell Liu Bei to move the camps immediately. He also told Ma Liang that Liu Bei had to be compelled to shelter in Baidicheng.

Lu Xun perceived that his moment had arrived, and called his generals to his tent to receive their orders. Instead of using veterans such as Han Dang, Zhou Tai and Ling Tong, he called up a junior general, Chunyu Dan, and asked Xu Sheng and Ding Feng to offer support at a point two miles from the camp.

Chunyu Dan went to attack the fourth camp of the Shu army but returned after suffering a bad defeat. Lu Xun didn't blame him; he summoned his generals to receive new orders: "Zhu Ran is to lead our river forces to attack the Shu army. His ships are laden with reeds and straw, which are to be used as I have ordered. Han Dang is to attack the north bank, Zhou Tai the south. Each soldier, in addition to his weapons, is to carry a bundle of straw or reeds. When they reach the Shu camps, they are to start a great blaze. But they are to burn only alternate camps, twenty in all, and leave the others untouched. They are to advance and only stop if they capture Liu Bei."

About the middle of the first watch the wind got up and blew strong from the east. At that time great fires broke out in the camps of Shu. The soldiers trampled on each other in their efforts to escape, and many died.

Behind them came the troops of Wu bent on slaughter. Not knowing the size of the force that was attacking them, the First

Ruler mounted his horse. But Liu Bei was caught between two foes Xu Sheng and Ding Feng. Just at this moment one of his officers broke through and rescued him. The officer was Zhang Bao, and he heroically escorted Liu Bei to Saddle Hill.

Soon Lu Xun arrived with his army and surrounded the hill. In addition, Zhu Ran marched up from the river to try to cut off Liu Bei's escape. The First Ruler thought there was no possibility of escape from this force, and he cried out, "This is the end!" But just at the worst seemed to be upon them, they saw Zhu Ran's soldiers suddenly begin to break up and scatter. This time their saviour was Zhao Yun from Jiangzhou. Zhao Yun happened upon Zhu Ran, and engaged him forthwith and slew him with a spear. The First Ruler escaped safely to the walls of Baidicheng, with only about a hundred men left of his forces.

Lu Xun led his exultant army westward. But as he drew near to the Kui Pass, he suddenly pulled up his horse, suspecting an ambush. They retreated. Lu Xun called in several of the natives and questioned them about the Pass. They said, "This place is called Fishbelly Creek. When Zhuge Liang was going west into the Lands of Rivers, he came along here with a lot of soldiers and heaped up the boulders on the Pass just like those above the Sandy Rapids." The boulders were of such multifarious shapes that he felt they would be equal to a hundred thousand soldiers.

Lu Xun decided to go and look at these boulders himself. So he rode off, with a small escort. They rode down to examine the mysterious arrangement more closely and went in among the stones. A sudden squall came on and the dust whirled up, obscuring both sky and earth. Lu Xun wanted to go back, but he had quite lost his way and could find no way out.

As he stopped to consider what he should do, an old man suddenly appeared, and guided him out. Lu Xun asked his aged guide who he was. "I am Zhuge Liang's father-in-law; my name is

Huang Chenyan. I saw you, General, enter in at the Gate of Death; and as I guessed you were ignorant of the layout of this place, I knew you would get lost. But I am a fair man and I could not bear to see you entrapped without the possibility of escape, so I came to guide you to the Gate of Life."

"This Zhuge Liang is well named as the Sleeping-Dragon. I am not his equal," said Lu Xun. Then, to the amazement of all, he gave orders to retreat. His officers objected, buoyed as they were after their earlier success. Lu Xun said when Cao Pi heard that the Wu army was marching into Shu, he would certainly attack the state of Wu. The homeward march began. On the second day the scouts reported that "Three Wei generals with three armies were converging from three different points and were moving toward the borders of Wu."

Cao Pi went up to the frontline to supervise the battle. However, Cao Ren, Cao Zhen and Cao Xiu were defeated by the Wu generals Zhu Huan, Lu Xun and Lu Fan. The summer of that year was a terrible time, and a great pestilence wiped out half of all the soldiers. So they were marched home to their capital, Luoyang.

Meanwhile the health of the First Ruler was failing. Gradually he became worse and worse. He himself felt the end was near, and he ordered that he be quartered at Baidicheng. Messengers were sent to the capital Chengdu to summon the Prime Minister and the other high-ranking officers of the state to receive the Emperor's last instructions.

The dying Emperor bade Zhuge Liang come and sit beside him. Turning his head, the First Ruler saw Ma Su, Ma Liang's brother, at his bedside. He bade him retire. When Ma Su had left the chamber, the First Ruler said to Zhuge Liang, "I think Ma Su's words exceed his deeds. Do not make much use of him."

Taking paper and pen, the First Ruler wrote down his testament. With one hand the dying man brushed away his tears, while with the other he grasped Zhuge Liang's hand and said, "If my son can be helped, help him. But if he proves a fool, then take the throne yourself and rule." This speech startled Zhuge Liang greatly. His limbs threatened to cease to support him. He fell to his knees, "I will take no other course but to wear myself to the bone in the service of your son, whom I will serve till death." He hit his head upon the ground till blood ran down his face.

The dying man bade his two sons Liu Yong and Liu Li come near, and he said to them, "My sons, remember your father's words. After my death you are to treat the Prime Minister as you would your father and thereby you will fulfill your father's hopes." He made the two Princes pay to Zhuge Liang the obeisance due to a father.

Turning to Zhao Yun, he said, "You and I have marched together through many dangers and difficulties. Now comes the parting of our ways. You must not forget our old friendship, and you must see to it that my sons follow my precepts." "I shall never dare to give other than my best," said Zhao Yun. "The fidelity of the dog and the horse is what I offered you and I shall offer it anew to them."

Liu Bei breathed his last. He was sixty-three, and he died on the twenty-fourth day of the fourth month (222 AD).

The Prime Minister led the procession that escorted the coffin to the capital. His testament was opened and read. Thereupon the ceremonies were performed, and the new Emperor Liu Shan took the throne. The style of the reign was changed to "Beginning of Prosperity".

CHAPTER 27

Calmly Planning the Five Attacks

Hearing of the death of Liu Bei, Cao Pi adopted Sima Yi's plan: to ally with Xianbi State in Liaodong, the Mang Tribes and Sun Quan to form an alliance of five armies. He appointed Cao Zhen as the Commander-in-chief to attack the state of Shu from all sides.

Liu Shan heard the news. He sent one of his personal attendants to summon the Prime Minister to court, but the servants in the Prime Minister's Palace said that Zhuge Liang was ill and could not be seen. He also sent two high ministers Dong Yun and Du Qiong to Zhuge Liang. They went; but they got no farther than the gate.

Zhuge Liang remained at home for several days running and everyone in court was greatly stressed. Du Qiong went again to the Emperor and suggested that he go in person to try to get Zhuge Liang to say what should be done. Liu Shan had to go to meet Zhuge Liang in person.

Zhuge Liang asked Liu Shan not to worry and told him that he was hatching a stratagem to turn back the enemy; but he had only worked out plans to turn back four of the five armies and hadn't yet devised how to circumvent the army from Wu.

Liu Shan was relieved. When Zhuge Liang escorted his master out of the mansion, he saw Deng Zhi, the Minister of Revenue, who was very eloquent and prescient, and he decided to petition Liu Shan to appoint Deng Zhi to take responsibility for dealing with the army from the state of Wu.

After Sun Quan received the letter from Cao Pi in which

Cao asked Sun to dispatch troops, Sun Quan asked Lu Xun for his thoughts. Lu Xun suggested waiting till they saw how the four other armies progressed.

When Sun Quan was about to call in his officers to discuss the attack on the Shu, a Shu envoy was announced. Following Zhang Zhao's advice, a large cauldron was set up, and a quantity of oil was poured in and a fire was lit underneath to frighten Deng Zhi and see what he would say.

Seeing the large cauldron, Deng Zhi laughed aloud at Sun Quan and tried to jump into the cauldron to show his spunk and fearlessness. Sun Quan called Deng Zhi into the hall and treated the envoy as a guest of the highest honor.

Sun Quan was persuaded by Deng Zhi, and sent Zhang Wen, who held the office of Imperial Commander, to Shu to make peace. Following Zhuge Liang's counsel, Liu Shan treated Zhang Wen with great courtesy.

Annoyed at Zhang Wen's arrogance, Qin Mi, one of the nobles of Shu, came in as if he were already drunk, and at once took a seat in the banquet, and began to argue with Zhang Wen. Zhang Wen made no reply to Qin Mi's barbs, fully aware as he was that there was much to fear in the state of Shu. After he returned to Wu, he laid before his lord his proposal for an alliance with Shu against Wei.

Hearing this news, Cao Pi decided to strike first. He led three hundred thousand naval and ground forces against the South Land.

Sun Quan, sent messengers to update Zhuge Liang and to seek the help of the state of Shu, and simultaneously he ordered Xu Sheng to lead an army to confront the enemy.

The Wei army had reached the Yangtze River. Sitting in his dragon boat, Cao Pi looked up and down the south bank, but not one man could be seen. He was wondering why. The next morning, they found that the whole length of the South of the Great River as far as they could see was one long defensive battlement, with towers at regular intervals, with spears and swords glittered in the sun. Unaware that this was all an artifice created by Xu Sheng of the South Lands, Cao Pi was terrified.

Soon a messenger rushed up to give his report, "Zhao Yun is marching through the Yangping Pass and is threatening Chang'an." This frightened Cao Pi so badly that he decided to retreat, and he immediately issued orders to this effect. Xu Sheng asked the soldiers to pour fish oil over the dry reeds and set them afire. The wind spread the flames down river toward the Wei fleets and they were all destroyed.

Cao Pi was taken off his boat to the riverbank. The army of Wei suffered a great defeat, and withdrew to Xudu. Zhang Liao was wounded in the groin by an arrow fired by Ding Feng. He died from the effects of this wound after returning to Xudu.

In the third year of Beginning Prosperity (225 AD), news came to the capital of the state of Shu from Yizhou to the effect that the Mang King, Meng Huo, leading one hundred thousand Mang tribesmen (one of southwest China local ethic groups), had invaded the south and was laying waste to the country; Yong Kai, the Governor of Jianning, had joined Meng Huo in rebellion." When he heard this news, Zhuge Liang went to report to his lord and he decided to lead an expedition to return these rebellious tribespeople to obedience.

CHAPTER 28

Capturing Meng Huo Seven Times

In AD 225, the Shu army launched a southern expedition. Seeking to make mischief, Zhuge Liang made Gao Ding kill Yong Kai and Zhu Bao and then come to surrender with the heads of the two dead men. This solved the problems in Yongchang. Governor Wang Kang of Yongchang then came out of the city and welcomed Zhuge Liang. The defending general Lu Kai presented a map called "The Plan to Subdue the Mangs" to Zhuge Liang. Then Zhuge Liang took Lu Kai into his service as Military Adviser and Guide. With Lu Kai's help, Zhuge Liang advanced and quickly penetrated deep into the country. While the army was advancing, a messenger from the court came to reward the army. When he appeared, Zhuge Liang saw that it was Ma Su.

Zhuge Liang asked Ma Su for his opinion on how to suppress the rebellion of the southern Ma Su said these people were capricious and it was best to focus on their emotions. Zhuge Liang found this idea reasonable.

After Zhuge Liang defeated the chiefs of the "Three Ravines", he set up an ambush and asked Wang Ping and Guan Suo to tempt the enemy in. These two pretended that they had lost the bell in order to lure Meng Huo into the ravine. Zhang Ni and Zhang Yi were pursuing him from two sides and Wang Ping and Guan Suo were ready to launch a pincer movement. Eventually the Mang King was defeated and was captured by Wei Yan.

Meng Huo wasn't convinced and wanted to fight Zhuge Liang again, saying if he was caught once more, he would submit. Zhuge Liang let him go.

Meng Huo camped at the River Lu and asked the chiefs of the two ravines for help. He was afraid of playing into the hands of Zhuge Liang, by only defending instead of doing the unexpected and launching an attack. He wanted to make the Shu army retreat.

Zhuge Liang asked the soldiers to make camp in the forest to prevent sunstroke. He also ordered Ma Dai to cross the river from Shakou with three thousand soldiers to cut off the supply road for the Mangs. He also summoned the chiefs of the two ravines and accepted their surrender and enlisted them as double agents.

Meng Huo, believing that there was no danger during the hot season, was enjoying himself; wine and music were the order of the day. Ma Dai crossed the River Lu at midnight and seized the supplies of Chief Dongtu Na, and also cutting off the supply at the Jiashan Gorge. Meng Huo was angry when he heard the news. He ordered his lictors to give Dongtu Na one hundred strokes with the heavy staff but his death penalty was remitted.

Dongtu Na nursed a grudge against Meng Huo after this. He organised some of his men to tie up Meng Huo and presented him to Zhuge Liang. Meng Huo was still not convinced. After seeing the arrangements and the piles of stores and heaps of weapons, Meng Huo still wouldn't budge. Zhuge Liang let him go again.

Meng Huo said to his brother Meng You that, "I know all the details of the enemy's forces from what I saw in their camp. You must lead a hundred men on the pretext of presenting treasure to Zhuge Liang and seize the opportunity to kill him.

Zhuge Liang asked Ma Su whether he knew of Meng Huo's plot. Ma Su laughed and wrote it down on a piece of paper. Zhuge Liang had no sooner read Ma Su's words than he clapped his hands with joy. Zhuge Liang ordered his attendants to drug the wine and to invite Meng You and the other Mang to have a drink.

During the night, Meng Huo led 30,000 soldiers in a raid to try to capture Zhuge Liang. After they entered the tent, they immediately realised they had been tricked again. Meng You and all his men were dead drunk. Wei Yan, Wang Ping and Zhao Yun led a batallion each to pursue Meng Huo. The Mangs were annihalated. Only Meng Huo escaped to the River Lu.

Meng Huo was captured by the soldiers under the command

of Ma Dai who disguised themselves as Mang soldiers. Ma Dai brought along his prisoner Meng Huo to Zhuge Liang. Meng Huo said he was a prisoner this time only because of the gluttony of his brother and he still wouldn't yield. Hence, Zhuge Liang let him go a third time.

Seeking revenge, Meng Huo amassed one hundred thousand soldiers to fight against the Shu army. Meng Huo was clad in rhinoceros hide mail and wore a bright red helmet The Mang soldiers were naked, their faces painted and their hair all disheveled. They came close up to the Shu camps like barbarians. However, Zhuge Liang ordered the army to retreat within the stockades and to barricade the gates.

When the battle passion of the Mang soldiers gave way to careless idleness, Zhuge Liang launched his attack. Meng Huo was defeated. He escaped and stood under a tree. Seeing Zhuge Liang sitting in a carriage, Meng Huo pushed forward in the hope of capturing Zhuge Liang. Unexpectedly, he stumbled and tumbled into a pit and was captured again. However, he was still not convinced and Zhuge Liang let him go again.

Meng Huo hid in the Bald Dragon Ravine and sought help. Yang Feng, King of twenty-one ravines in the west, who appreciated the fact that Zhuge Liang hadn't killed his clansmen, captured Meng Huo and presented him to Zhuge Liang. Meng

Huo was of course not convinced and determined to fight a decisive battle with the Shu army at the Silver Pit. Zhuge Liang released him again.

Meng Huo gathered over one thousand soldiers at the Silver Pit and asked his wife and younger brother to invite Mu Lu, King of the Bana Ravine. He was a master of witchcraft and rode upon an elephant and was attended by tigers, leopards, wolves, venomous snakes, and scorpions. When Meng Huo was arranging for the decisive battle against the Shu army, the Shu army arrived in front of the ravine. Meng Huo was frightened and his wife Lady Zhurong led an army to go out to face the enemy.

Lady Zhurong wounded Zhang Ni with a flying sword and took him captive. Ma Zhong rushed out to rescue Zhang Ni. The Mangs threw hooks and pulled down his steed, and he was also taken prisoner. The next day, Zhuge Liang captured Lady Zhurong with another cunning trick and then exchanged her for Zhang Ni and Ma Zhong.

Meng Huo asked Mu Lu to go out to fight the enemy. Mu Lu, on his white elephant, was mumbling something that might have been a spell or a curse, and from time to time he rang his bell. He drove a group of serpents and other wild beasts towards the Shu army.

Zhuge Liang took out the constructed huge wooden model creatures, whose mouths vomited flames and whose nostrils breathed out black smoke. The real wild beasts of the Mang turned tail and fled. And thus the Silver Pit Hill was taken.

Next day, as Zhuge Liang was organising parties to search for and capture the King, it was announced that the brother-in-law of Meng Huo, Chief Dai Lai, having vainly tried to persuade the King to yield, had taken him and his wife and all his clan prisoner and was bringing them to Zhuge Liang. Zhuge Liang knew it was a trick and ordered that they all be captured. Then, he called out to his guards to search the prisoners. They did so, and on every man they found a sharp knife. Meng Huo was still not convinced, and he said "If you take me a seventh time, then I will pledge allegiance to you and never rebel again." Hence, Zhuge Liang let him go again.

Meng Huo invited the army from the Wugo Kingdom with their rattan armor to come and fight the decisive battle against Zhuge Liang. Zhuge Liang tried yet another ruse. Oil carts and powder were used to burn numerous Mang soldiers. Meng Huo was captured the seventh time and this time he was convinced sincerely.

After suppressing the Mangs, Zhuge Liang went back to the lands of Shu. Reaching the River Lu, a tremendous storm blew in and hindered them. The locals said it was caused by wild spirits. Zhuge Liang sacrificed the souls of deceased persons and broke into loud lamentations. Then, the River Lu became calm and the Shu army crossed the river.

When the army returned to Chengdu, Liu Shan came out ten miles outside the city to welcome back his victorious minister. The chariots of the Son of God and his minister returned to Chengdu side by side. In the capital there was great rejoicing and banquets for the army. Henceforward over three hundred distant nations sent tribute to the Imperial Court.

CHAPTER 29

Subduing Jiang Wei

Cao Pi fell seriously ill. Some said it was the Empress Zhen who was responsible for exercising a malevolent influence on him. Cao Pi believed this and had the empress killed. However, his illness became even more serious and he died at the age of 40 soon after.

Cao Rui succeeded Cao Pi. He made Sima Yi Imperial Commander of the Flying Cavalry, defending Xizhou and Xiliang. At that time, Zhuge Liang wanted to attack the Central Plains, but he was worried about Sima Yi. He asked messengers to spread the news in Luoyang and other places that Sima Yi was about to rise in rebellion, hoping to fool Cao Rui into taking away the military powers the military powers he had conferred on Sima Yi.

Cao Rui was extremely worried about these rumours. Cao Zhen asked the emperor to go and visit Sima Yi and investigate his intentions. Not knowing the real reason for his visit, Sima Yi went to welcome his ruler with all the pomp of the commander of a great army. The emperor removed Sima Yi from his post and asked Cao Xiu to take over the command.

Hearing that Sima Yi had been removed from the equation, in AD 228, Zhuge Liang presented to the Ruler of Shu a memorial on the expedition to attack the state of Wei. Liu Shan readily agreed. Zhuge Liang appointed the veteran Zhao Yun to lead the vanguard of the army in the march towards the Central Plains.

Hearing this, Cao Rui called in his ministers to discuss possible countermeasures. Xiahou Yuan's son, Xiahou Mao wanted to lead the army against Shu, but he was opposed by Minister Wang Lang. Xiahou Mao blew a fuse, and said "If I cannot capture this Zhuge Liang, I pledge that I will never again look on the Emperor's face."

Xiahou Mao ordered a general from Xiliang, named Han De, and his four sons to lead the vanguard. They confronted Zhao Yun at Phoenix Song Mountain. Zhao Yun killed the three sons of Han

De with his spear and held the other one captive. The Wei army was utterly defeated.

The following day, Xiahou Mao laid an ambush and challenged Zhao Yun to fight. Zhao Yun fell into the Wei ambush but was rescued by Guan Xing and Zhang Bao.

Seeing how Xiahou Mao had defended Nan'an, Zhuge Liang captured Anding with one of his characteristic ruses. The governor of Anding Cui Liang had to surrender. Zhuge Liang knew he was only pretending to surrender, so he asked him to persuade the governor of Nan'an, Yang Ling to also come along to surrender. Cui Liang and Xiahou Mao tried to persuade Zhuge Liang to enter the city.

Cui Liang returned to tell Zhuge Liang that Yang Ling had offered the city to him at midnight. Zhuge Liang asked Cui Liang to take Guan Xing and Zhang Bao along as double agents. He also secretly told Guan Xing and Zhang Bao to kill Cui Liang once they got an opportunity.

Cui Liang opened the gate of Nan'an and Yang Ling came down to the gate to welcome them. As soon as Guan Xing got near, he lifted his sword and smote Yang Ling and cut off his head. Zhang Bao also killed Cui Liang with his spear and took Xiahou Mao captive.

When Ma Zun, Governor of Tianshui led an army to relieve Nan'an, Jiang Wei, who held the military rank of General, tried a ruse, saying he could defend Tianshui and relieve Nan'an.

The following day, Ma Zun led the Tianshui troops out of the city. Zhao Yun attacked the city but was then caught in a pincer attack by Ma Zun and Jiang Wei. Realising he was trapped, Zhao Yun tried to break through the siege. Luckily, Zhang Yi and Gao Xiang came to his rescue and Zhao Yun escaped the danger.

Realising that Jiang Wei was both brave and resourceful, Zhuge Liang led the army personally. In the middle of the night, fires broke out all around and a great shouting was heard. Zhuge Liang mounted his horse and, with Guan Xing and Zhang Bao as escorts, escaped the danger. Looking back, they saw many mounted troops with torches in a winding line like a huge serpent. Zhuge Liang remarked, "An army owes more to its leaders than to its numbers. This Jiang Wei is a true genius."

Zhuge Liang asked the captive Xiahou Mao to persuade Jiang Wei to surrender. On the way back, Xiahou Mao believed a rumour spread by the Shu army and told Ma Zun that Jiang Wei had deserted to Zhuge Liang.

On the night of the same day, Zhuge Liang found among his men one who resembled Jiang Wei and disguised him to meet with Ma Zun under the walls of Tianshui. He ordered his soldiers to attack. The assault continued till dawn, when the besiegers withdrew.

Zhuge Liang then led the army to attack Jicheng. The grain in the city was insufficient to feed the people. Zhuge Liang deliberately asked soldiers to convey wagons of grain and forage to try to lure Jiang Wei out.

Jiang Wei did lead some troops out of the city to attack the train of wagons, but he was immediately attacked from two sides. Jicheng was captured by the Shu army. Jiang Wei escaped to Tianshui and called for the gate to be lowered. But Ma Zun ordered the defenders to shoot at the fugitive.

Jiang Wei was in a terrible situation. He saw Guan Xing leading a company of soldiers coming after him. He was so exhausted that he knew there was no chance of successful resistance, so he turned back. But there soon appeared a small chariot in which sat Zhuge Liang. There was now definitely no way out. So Jiang Wei dismounted and bowed his head in submission. Zhuge Liang at once got out of the chariot and bade him welcome, taking him by the hand and saying, "Ever since I left my humble cottage, I have been seeking some worthy person to whom I might impart the knowledge that my life has been spent in acquiring. I have found no one till this moment, and now my desire is attained. You are the one." Jiang Wei bowed and thanked him.

After losing three cities in succession, Xiahou Mao fled to the Qiangs. Cao Zhen was appointed Commander-in-Chief by Cao Rui, and the ensigns of rank were conferred upon him. Guo Huai was appointed his second-in-command, and Wang Lang was created Instructor of the Army. Cao Zhen camped on the west bank of the River Wei, and confronted the Shu army.

Next day, when the armies were facing each

other, Zhuge Liang sat in a four-wheeled carriage. Wang Lang tried to persuade Zhuge Liang to surrender to the Wei, but Zhuge Liang rejected his offer out of hand and humiliated him. Fierce wrath filled the old man's breast. With one despairing cry Wang Lang fell to the earth dead. He was only 76 years old.

The Wei army came to plunder the camps of Shu but was defeated by Zhuge Liang. Cao Zhen also asked the soldiers of the western Qiang with their iron-clad chariots for help. The Qiang formed long chariot lines one behind the other. The Shu army studied them for a long time quite at a loss as to how to overcome them.

It was now the middle of winter, the twelfth month, and the snows had come. Zhuge Liang asked his soldiers to dig many pits in the snow-covered land. He sat in a small carriage to try to tempt the enemy forward. The iron-clad chariots of the Qiang soldiers tumbled into the pits. The Shu soldiers marched forth and annihalated the Qiang soldiers.

CHAPTER 30

Recall of Sima Yi

The Wei army suffered a number of defeats. Cao Rui was greatly diturbed. The Imperial Guardian Zhong Yao made strenuous efforts to persuade Cao Rui to restore Sima Yi to a position of authority. Cao Rui decided to follow his advice.

Li Feng, the son of Li Yan, came from Baidicheng to tell Zhuge Liang that "Meng Da deserted to the state of Wei, but only because he had no other choice. He proposes to lead an army of three counties —Xincheng, Jincheng, and Shangyong—to attack Luoyang while you are attacking Chang'an."

This was good news. But at that moment there also came the news that Cao Rui was leading an army to Chang'an and had recalled the banished Sima Yi to office. This piece of bad news greatly worried Zhuge Liang. He wrote to Meng Da to ask him to be careful and to take every precaution against Sima Yi.

Meng Da replied immediately: "Should Sima Yi hear of my strategy, it will take a month to contact the capital and get a response. Thus my success is guaranteed." Zhuge Liang sent another message to Meng Da to beware of overconfidence.

Armed with the decree of the emperor, Sima Yi was about to muster his troops when it was reported that Meng Da was about to rise in rebellion. Sima Yi gave ordered to prepare to advance at top speed to Xincheng and he asked Military Adviser Liang Ji to go to Xincheng first to try to control the Meng Da problem.

Still not really taking the threat of Sima Yi seriously, Meng Da had made arrangements

with Governor Shen Yi of Jincheng and Governor Shen Dan of Shangyong and was awaiting the day they had set. But Shen Yi and Shen Dan were only pretending to support him. When Sima Yi's army arrived, Shen Yi and Shen Dan opened the gate and let the army of Sima Yi in. Meng Da was killed by Shen Dan.

Sima Yi reported their success to Cao Rui. The Ruler of Wei conferred upon the successful leader a pair of golden axes and the right to take action in important matters without first obtaining his master's sanction.

Zhuge Liang knew Sima Yi would surely go on the attack and try to capture Jieting, so he ordered some of his generals to guard it. Ma Su came forward to volunteer for the task, offering a written pledge. Zhuge Liang ordered Wang Ping to go along with him and sent Gao Xiang and Wei Yan to lead an army of 10,000 to provide back up support.

In accordance with the instructions of Zhuge Liang, Wang Ping ordered his soldiers to fell trees and build a strong permanent stockade on the road, but Ma Su insisted on camping on a hill. Wang Ping repeatedly tried to persuade him, but Ma Su refused to listen.

Sima Yi ordered his soldiers to surround the hill and Zhang He besieged Wang Ping, cutting off the supplies of water for the people on the hill. The soldiers of Shu were thrown into chaos, and they lost Jieting.

Zhuge Liang was surprised at the loss of Jieting, and he ordered the generals to retreat as soon as possible. He took five thousand troops and set out for Xicheng to gather provisions and then return to Hanzhong.

However a report came that Sima Yi was advancing rapidly on Xicheng with an army of one hundred and fifty thousand troops. Zhuge Liang's officers were all frightened and their faces turned pale. Zhuge Liang smiled and said, "Don't be scared. I have an ambush prepared with a hundred thousand soldiers waiting for Sima Yi."

When Sima Yi got to Xicheng, he saw Zhuge Liang sitting there playing the lute, attended by a couple of boys. His face was all smiles as he played the lute. Sima Yi could hardly believe his eyes and he immediately suspected some subtle ruse. Thus, he retreated with his army. When he learned that Xicheng was in fact deserted, he said with a sigh of resignation, "Zhuge Liang is a cleverer man than I am."

Returning to Hanzhong, Zhuge Liang slew Ma Su. Zhuge Liang lamented bitterly because he remembered the words of Liu Bei who had said, "Ma Su's words exceed the truth, and he is incapable of great deeds."

Next Zhuge Liang petitioned the Throne proposing his own demotion from high office. Thereupon an edict was issued demoting Zhuge Liang to the rank of General of the Right Army, but retaining him in the same position in state affairs and command of the military forces.

Cao Rui wanted to attack the Shu army, but Sima Yi thought it was not advisable to advance their troops for the moment. He recommended the general Hao Zhao to the Wei Ruler to guard Chencang and Cao Rui agreed.

Soon after, a memorial was received from Cao Xiu, Minister of War and Commander of Yangzhou, saying that Zhou Fang, the Wu Governor of Poyang, wished to tender his submission and transfer his allegiance, and had sent a man to present a memorandum with seven headings showing how the power of the South Lands could be broken and to ask that an army be dispatched without delay. Cao Rui asked Sima Yi and Jia Kui to go to help Cao Xiu to take the South Lands.

Cao Xiu suspected that Zhou Fang's surrender was false. Zhou Fang wept in frustration at not being believed. He seized a sword from one of his escort and was about to kill himself when Cao Xiu stopped him. This episode was repeated several times. Finally, Zhou Fang used his sword to cut off his hair and he threw it on the ground to show his sincerity. Then Cao Xiu suspected him no more.

However, Zhou Fang's surrender was in fact false. Sun Quan had ordered Lu Xun with Zhu Huan and Quan Zong to lead a three-pronged army. When the Wei army arrived in Yangzhou, they laid siege to them immediately.

In accordance with the instructions of Zhou Fang, Cao Xiu led his army to Shiting. The Wu General Xu Sheng met with them and Lu Xun, Zhu Huan and Quan Zong made their pincer attack. The Wei army was utterly defeated. When Cao Xiu escaped and went to look for Zhou Fang, Zhou had disappeared.

Lu Xun captured a great number of carts and bullocks, horses and mules and military material and weapons from the Wei army and he led his army home to the Wu lands. Lu Xun suggested Sun Quan send letters to the Shu counseling Zhuge Liang to attack the state of Wei. Sun Quan agreed, and letters were sent.

CHAPTER 31

Jiang Wei Forges a Letter

When Zhuge Liang was about to dispatch troops to attack the Wu, two sons of Zhao Yun, Zhao Tong and Zhao Guang, came to ask for an audience with the Prime Minister. When the two young men came in, they prostrated themselves before him and wept, saying their father had died of illness that night. Zhuge Liang was staggered and burst into great cries of lamentation.

Zhuge Liang once more presented a memorial proposing an expedition against the Wei. The Latter Ruler was convinced, and by edict directed Zhuge Liang to prepare the expedition. In AD 228, Zhuge Liang marched out with three hundred thousand well-trained soldiers, Wei Yan leading the first division, and they marched at top speed towards Chencang.

Cao Zhen recommended Wang Shuang to be leader of the vanguard. Recognising the bravery of Wang Shuang, Cao Rui presented him with a silken robe and a golden breastplate.

The Shu army attacked Chencang for over 20 days but failed to capture it. Wang Shuang stationed his troops outside the city. The two armies clashed. Wang Shuang inflicted damage on several major generals of the Shu army. Jiang Wei advised Zhuge Liang to send a strong force against Qishan. Zhuge Liang agreed and called a halt to the attack on Chencang.

Cao Zhen received a letter from Jiang Wei in which Jiang Wei said he would render service to him and repay his debt to the state of Wei. He added that he would make a great fire as an agreed signal. Cao Zhen asked Fei Yao to take fifty thousand troops by way of the Xie Valley to capture Zhuge Liang.

Fei Yao pursued the Shu army for a day and a night. After such hardship they had to rest, and they were on the point of setting up camp to prepare food when a great hubbub arose all around. They were besieged by the Shu army. Losing all hope, Fei Yao used his sword end his own life.

The Ruler of Wei was in a great panic after getting the news. He called Sima Yi to ask for his counsel. Sima Yi said, "I have a strategy, not only to defeat Zhuge Liang, but to do so without any exertion on our part. They will retreat of their own free will."

Cao Rui accepted the suggestion and asked Cao Zhen to just defend his position and not to attack. Guo Huai also ordered Wang Shuang to make the rounds frequently in order to keep the Shu army from transporting grain. Sun Li suggested a ruse where they would pretend to transport grain with carts which in fact were laden with explosives comprising wood and sulfur; and when the Shu army came to plunder the grain, they would launch a sudden attack and thus would win a great victory. Cao Zhen said, "It seems like an excellent plan."

However Zhuge Liang knew it was all a plot of the Wei army. He met ruse with ruse. He ordered Ma Dai to burn the carts, and directed Ma Zhong and Zhang Ni to deal with the ambush. Wu Ban and Wu Yi were to kill the Wei soldiers and Guan Xing and Zhang Bao were to seize the Wei camp.

At the second watch, Zhuge Liang, on the summit of the Qishan Mountains, saw that the carts were burning and the Shu troops marched to the attack and defeated the Wei army completely.

The Wei troops retreated into Cao Zhen's camp and could attack no more.

Short of food, Zhuge Liang gave orders to break camp and retreat and at the same time he dispatched secret directions to Wei Yan to ask him to kill Wang Shuang when the Shu army retreated. So the retreat began, but to deceive the enemy the watchmen were left in the empty camp to beat the watch drums throughout the night.

Having lost the opportunity for victory, Cao Zhen was greatly saddened. He fell ill and returned to Luoyang.

Following a cunning stratagem, Wei Yan retreated to Hanzhong. Realising the truth of the matter, Wang Shuang led an army in pursuit and when he was just about to catch up with his quarry, a report came that the camp was on fire. When Wang Shuang returned, he confronted by Wei Yan but Wei Yan killed him on the slope. Without their leader, the Wei soldiers fled in all directions.

At that time, Sun Quan wanted to take advantage of the situation to attack the state of Wei. Zhang Zhao suggested Sun Quan proclaim himself emperor first. An altar was prepared on the south of Wuchang, and on that day, Sun Quan ascended to the high altar and assumed the title of "Emperor". "Yellow Dragon" was chosen as the title of the reign. Sun Deng was styled Heir Apparent.

Zhang Zhao sent a memorial to Sun Quan to ask him to make a treaty with the Shu in order to destroy the Wei and share the empire. Sun Quan agreed.

Liu Shan received the Wu envoy and sent emissaries to Hanzhong to ask for Zhuge Liang's counsel. Zhuge Liang said, "Send an envoy with greetings and gifts and ask Sun Quan to send Lu Xun against the Wei. Then Sima Yi will have to focus on the conflict with the Wu, and I may once more march to Qishan and launch an assault on the capital Chang'an." Liu Shan agreed at once.

Lu Xun said, "This is all due to Zhuge Liang's fear of Sima Yi.

However, we must consent since the Shu ask for it. We will make a show of raising an army and we will offer them token support. When Zhuge Liang actually attacks the Wei, we will make for the Middle Lands ourselves." Sun Quan thought it an excellent strategy.

Since Hao Zhao, the defender of Chencang, was ill, Zhuge Liang took Guan Xing and Zhang Bao and they marched day and night and eventually captured Chencang. He also ordered Wei Yan and Jiang Wei to attack Sanguan and Jianwei and then to lead the army out of Qishan.

The Wei Emperor was informed of all the misfortunes in the west and the threats in the east. He called Sima Yi. Sima Yi said they could disregard the menace from the east, and needed only to protect themselves against the Shu. Cao Rui asked him to prepare for a decisive battle with Zhuge Liang.

In AD 229, Zhuge Liang sent Jiang Wei to attack Wudu and Wang Ping to attack Yinping. Sima Yi ordered Guo Huai and Sun Li to launch an attack on the Shu army from the rear. When they were on the march, it was reported that Wudu and Yinping had been captured by the Shu army. They felt like ducks in a thunderstorm.

Sima Yi also ordered Zhang He and Dai Ling to attack the Shu camp, but Zhuge Liang had prepared for this eventuality. As a result, the Wei army was defeated and had to retreat. Liu Shan, buoyed by these victories over the Wei army, issued a decree for Zhuge Liang to resume the post of Prime Minister.

Sima Yi held his ground and didn't attack. Zhuge Liang thought of another ruse. He ordered his soldiers to retreat for half a month. When the Shu army retreated for the third time, Zhang He, afraid of losing the chance of capturing Zhuge Liang, asked that he be allowed to attack. Sima Yi asked Zhang He and Dai Ling to first lead an army in pursuit of the Shu troops.

Guan Xing and others fought with Zhang He and Dai Ling. When the Wei generals were just about to be defeated, Sima Yi came to rescue them. Jiang Wei and Liao Hua took advantage of the chance to attack the Wei camp. The Wei army was defeated.

When Zhuge Liang was about to advance again to fight Sima Yi, a messenger arrived from the capital Chengdu with the sad news that Zhang Bao had fallen from a cliff and died in battle. Zhuge Liang uttered a great cry, blood gushed from his mouth and he fell in a swoon. Afterwards he issued orders to break camp, and the army retreated without delay to Hanzhong. Sima Yi only heard of this five days later.

CHAPTER   32

Eight Arrays

In the autumn of the eighth year of Beginning Prosperity, Cao Zhen sent a memorial to his leader, practically demanding an expedition against the Shu. Cao Zhen was created Commander-in-Chief of the Western Expedition. Sima Yi was Second in command. The army of four hundred thousand troops marched to Chang'an, from where they planned to attack Hanzhong. The army was joined by Guo Huai.

When he heard of the intended attack, in AD 230, Zhuge Liang ordered Zhang Ni and Wang Ping to lead one thousand troops to Chencang and to garrison that road so as to check the march of the Wei army. The two found it difficult—how could a mere thousand troops hope to confront four hundred thousand Wei troops—so they hesitated. Zhuge Liang said that he had observed the stars, and that he saw there would be a tremendous rain this month. The Wei troops would dare not to attack the Shu. This satisfied Wang Ping and Zhang Ni, and they left.

The Wei troops, led by Cao Zhen, were stationed in Chencang. The rain started to fall and it came down in a deluge, continuing for a month so that the surrounding country was soon three feet under water. The soldiers could get no place to sleep and the horses could not be fed. The soldiers were downhearted. The Ruler of Wei issued the command to withdraw troops. Knowing that Sima Yi would not retreat without leaving an ambush to guard against any pursuit, Zhuge Liang ordered that they not be followed.

With no enemy to be seen pursuing them, Cao Zhen ordered the ambushing troops to retreat. Sima Yi said that Zhuge Liang would certainly advance by way of the two valleys and try to occupy Qishan. Cao Zhen was not convinced. The two made a bet. They split their forces, Cao Zhen taking up his station on the west of Qishan in the Xie Valley, and Sima Yi going to the east in the Ji Valley.

Now Wei Yan and Chen Shi, with twenty thousand troops, were sent to enter the Qi Valley. Zhuge Liang ordered them not to advance in a hurry for fear that Wei troops would lay an ambush here. Wei Yan and Chen Shi however, did not listen. Chen Shi took only five thousand troops, and got through the Chi Valley. Chen Shi was ambushed by Sima Yi, and his five thousand troops were reduced to about five hundred. Luckily for him, he was rescued by Wei Yan.

Having seen nothing of the Shu army for over seven days, Cao Zhen grew careless, and he allowed his soldiers to become slack and indisciplined. As a result, Cao Zhen was trapped with his troops and Qin Liang was slain. Sima Yi sent soldiers to rescue Cao Zhen.

After scoring this victory, Zhuge Liang hastened back to Qishan. He sentenced Chen Shi to death according to military rules. Cao Zhen had lost the wager. The fright and excitement made him ill, and he took to his bed. Zhuge Liang wrote a letter to Cao Zhen, saying that his lack of ability and lack of knowledge of astronomy and geography had been the cause of the heavy casualties they suffered in battle. Cao Zhen's wrath rose as he read. In the end it filled his breast and he died that evening.

The Ruler of Wei issued an edict urging Sima Yi to raise a great army and confront Zhuge Liang. Sima Yi wanted a full pitched battle with Zhuge Liang.

Zhuge Liang laid the 'Eight Arrays.' The Wei troops who went to try to break up the formation were each seized and bound. Zhuge Liang set them free to return to their leader, stripped of their arms and armor and with their faces inked. Sima Yi lost his temper at the sight of his people thus humiliated. He gave the signal for the army to charge and attack the enemy. At this time Shu troops under Guan Xing and Jiang Wei rushed up to join the battle. Thus three sides of the Wei army were attacked by three different enemy divisions, At last, with a desperate push, he managed to cut through the enemy toward the south and to free his army. But he had lost six or seven out of every ten of his soldiers.

General Gou An, from Baidicheng with a convoy of grain was a drunkard and he had loitered on the road so that he arrived ten days late. Gou An was sentenced to death by Zhuge Liang according to military rules. But Yang Yi ventured to intervene. Zhuge Liang then bade the executioners give him eighty blows instead. This punishment filled Gou An's heart with bitter resentment so that he went over to the Wei. Sima Yi sent him to go to Chengdu and spread a false report that "Zhuge Liang is angry with the powers there and means to make himself emperor."

Believing the rumors, the Latter Ruler issued an edict recalling the army. Guarding against pursuit by Sima Yi, Zhuge Liang ordered 1,000, 2,000 and 3,000 cooking halls prepared for the next 3 days — just when the various divisions would be retreating. That only the cooking arrangements had been increased, not the soldiers would not be known to the enemy.

Zhuge Liang then went to the capital Chengdu for an audience. He asked what was so important that the emperor had recalled him. For a long time the Latter Ruler made no reply.

Zhuge Liang interrogated the eunuchs and thus found out the base rumors that had been spread abroad by Gou An. He issued a warrant to arrest this man, but Gou An had already fled and gone over to the Wei. The eunuchs who had influenced the Emperor were put to death.

In the spring of AD 231, the Shu army once more took the field against the Wei. Sima Yi ordered Zhang He to guard Qishan against the Shu army, while he himself and Guo Huai would defend Tianshui.

The wheat was ripe. Zhuge Liang sent soldiers to harvest the wheat in Longxi to supplement their grain supplies. Next he bade them bring out three four-wheeled chariots, all exactly alike. Each chariot was driven by a team of twenty-four men, all dressed in black, barefooted and with loosened hair. Each one of the team also had in their hands a sword and a black seven starred flag. He ordered Jiang Wei, Wei Yan and Ma Dai to disguise themselves to frighen the Wei troops.

Next day, it rained. The Wei soldiers saw the cavalcade, and right in the centre Zhuge Liang, and they turned tail. Having thus driven off the Wei soldiers, Zhuge Liang proceeded to reap and harvest the wheat, which was carried into Lucheng and laid out to dry.

The soldiers were still busy with the wheat in Lucheng, Sima Yi led his troops in a surprise raid.

Knowing that the enemy would attack, Zhuge Liang had ordered an ambush laid in the newly reaped fields. Attacked from all sides, the Wei troops suffered heavy casualties.

Just then arrived an urgent letter from Li Yan, then at Baidicheng, who was supplying all things for the army, saying that the Wu had entered into an alliance with the Wei. The plan was for the Wu to attack the Shu. Fearing for the safety of the Eastern lands of the Rivers Zhuge Liang ordered an immediate retreat.

Zhang He wanted to ride in pursuit. Knowing that he was too impulsive, Sima Yi repeatedly cautionded him that Zhuge Liang would leave ambushes at every possible point.

Zhang He quickly set out after the Shu troops and soon he reached the Wooden Path. But suddenly lights appeared, and the sky was all aglow, and at the same time huge boulders and great bulks of timber came rolling down the slopes and blocked his way. Then from the mountains on both two sides flew clouds of arrows and showers of bolts. Zhang He and many of his officers were killed.

Zhuge Liang reached Hanzhong. It then emerged that Li Yan had failed to find sufficient grain to keep the army supplied, and so had lied about the threat of a Wu-Wei alliance so that the army would retreat before the shortage of supplies was revealed. Zhuge Liang sentenced him to death. But Fei Yi interceded for him. Zhuge Liang had to set him free. Li Yan was stripped of all rank and was exiled to Zitong.

CHAPTER 33

Wuzhangyuan

Zhuge Liang had made five expeditions to Qishan without success. Three years later, the troops were strong and supplies ample. The Latter Ruler issued the edict authorising Zhuge Liang to make his sixth expedition to Qishan. Zhuge Liang received the unexpected news of the death of Guan Xing. He was greatly shocked, and fainted away.

The Ruler of Wei named Sima Yi as Commander-in-Chief with the fullest authority to guard against the Shu assault. They were all camped on the southern bank of the River Wei. In addition, fifty thousand troops were stationed farther upstream and they busied themselves preparing nine floating bridges. At the main camp on the east a solid earth rampart was raised to guard against any surprises from the rear.

Zhuge Liang pretended to attack Beiyuan, but really his objective was to set fire to the floating bridges over the River Wei. Unexpectedly, Sima Yi learned of the scheme and the Shu troops were defeated.

When Zhuge Liang met with his army he found, to his sorrow, that he had lost more than ten thousand troops. Just at this time Fei Yi arrived from Chengdu. Zhuge Liang troubled him to carry a letter for him into East Wu, asking Sun Quan to dispatch troops to attack the Wei. Sun Quan had long desired to do so. He raised an army of three hundred thousand troops, who were to attack Wei in three divisions.

Sima Yi sent Zheng Wen to pretend to surrender. Zhuge Liang turned Sima Yi's trick against him. He ordered Zheng Wen to write a letter to Sima Yi telling him to proceed with a raid against the Shu camp. Qin Lang, with ten thousand troops, went on an expedition against the Shu camp, and the leader was killed. The Wei troops were defeated and refused to give battle. Zhuge Liang sent pack teams to transport grain from the Shangfang Valley.

Sima ordered the capture of four or five of the wooden horses and bullocks, some imitated after Zhuge Liang's models, and used them to bring up supplies from Xizhou. Zhuge Liang ordered that five hundred soldiers dress up in the costume of the Deities of the Six Layers to drive off Wei troops and capture a great amount of supplies from the Wei.

Hearing that his Beiyuan troops had been driven off, Sima Yi came to the rescue, but fell into a trap. He was almost killed by Liao Hua. Then the Wei ruler sent a message to inform Sima Yi that the East Wu was to attack the Middle Land in three divisions, and so he ordered Sima Yi to remain on the defensive.

The ruler of Wei, Cao Rui led the main body of troops to confront the army of Wu. At Chaohu, Man Chong raided the Wu camp that night while the Wu troops rested. The Wu were defeated.

Lun Xun proposed moving the troops surrounding Xincheng to cut off the retreat route of the Wei army. Unexpectedly, the letter was intercepted by the Wei. Another plan needed to be considered.

It was hot. Many Wu soldiers fell ill. Sun Quan ordered Lu Xun to retreat. Then Lu Xun withdrew the army to the south lands.

Zhuge Liang ordered Gao Xiang to transport grain from the Shangfang Valley. Sima Yi who had raided the valley was inveigled into the trap by Wei Yan. Zhuge Liang lanuched a fire attack upon them. But suddenly rain poured down in torrents. Sima Yi along with his father and sons, survived.

Zhuge Liang had his army camped on the Wuzhang Hills. He sent women's headgear and funeral clothes to Sima Yi—in effect saying that he was shy like a woman and that he remained strictly on the defensive.

Sima Yi, although inwardly raging, pretended to take it all as a joke and smiled. He accepted the gift and treated the messenger well. Before the messenger left, Sima Yi asked him a few questions about his master's eating and sleeping and hours of labor. The messenger said that Zhuge Liang rose early and retired to bed late. He attended personally to all cases requiring punishment of over twenty strokes. As for food, he did not eat more than a few handfuls of grain every day. Sima Yi thought he surely could not last long living like this.

Just at this time Fei Yi came from Chengdu, to say that the Wu Ruler had marched back to his own country. Zhuge Liang listened to the end; then, without a word, he fell in a swoon. Jiang Wei persuaded him to pray in order to prolong his life. On the floor of the tent he arranged seven lamps, and, outside these, forty nine smaller lamps. In the midst he placed the lamp of his own fate. He said that if the master-lamp remained alight for seven days, then his life would be prolonged for twelve years.

Zhuge Liang invoked the Seven Stars of the North to prolong his life. It was the sixth night of Zhuge Liang's prayers, and the lamp of his fate still burned brightly. He began to feel a secret joy. Xiaohou Ba led a reconnaissance party to the Wuzhang Hills and found out the actual situation of Shu army. Immediately Wei Yan dashed in, to report the news. In his haste Wei Yan knocked over and extinguished the Lamp of Fate. Zhuge Liang threw down his sword and sighed, saying, "Life and death are foreordained."

Zhuge Liang composed a book in twenty four chapters, 104,112 words, treating the Eight Needfuls, the Seven Cautions, the Six Fears, and the Five Dreads of war and left sketches for a multiple crossbow to Jiang Wei, telling him that there was no part of Shu that should cause anxiety, save the Yinping Mountains. That had to be carefully guarded. Next Zhuge Liang sent for Ma Dai, to whom he gave certain whispered instructions. He gave the seal to Yang Yi, saying that after his death, Wei Yan would turn traitor. He gave a silken bag containing certain secret orders to Yang Yi, which would tell him what to do when that happened and his army was in danger.

He rose from his couch, was was helped into a small carriage and he made a round of inspection of all the camps and posts. But the cold autumn wind chilled him to the bone.

Zhuge Liang returned to his tent, and wrote his testament, desiring the emperor to cleanse his heart and limit his desires, to practice self control and to love the people. Li Fu came with the royal command to ask also who should control the destinies of the state for the next century. Zhuge Liang said Jiang Wan. He asked who after Jiang Wan. Zhuge Liang said after him, Fei Yi. When Li Fu asked again, thus died Zhuge Liang at the age of 54 (AD 234).

As the late commander had directed, Jiang Wei and Yang Yi forbade any mourning after his death. Secret orders were given to Wei Yan to command the rearguard to cover the retreat, and then, one by one, the camps were broken up and the army began its homeward march.

Realising that Zhuge Liang was dead, Sima Yi resolved to give chase with a strong force. But just as he passed his camp gates, doubts filled his mind and he gave up the plan. He feared that they might fall victims to one final ambush. Instead he sent Xiahou Ba with a few scouts to reconnoiter the enemy's camps.

The Wei were not going to act as a rearguard for any civil official. He asked Ma Dai to kill Yang Yi. Ma Dai pretended to agree.

By the time Xiahou Ba reached the Shu camps, they were all empty, and he hastened back with this news. Just as he reached the foot of a hill, Sima Yi saw saw a score of generals of rank emerging from the general army, and they were escorting a small carriage, in which sat Zhuge Liang just as he had always appeared, with his feather fan in his hand. Jiang Wei cried out, "You have fallen into one of the Prime Minister's traps! Stay where you are."

The soldiers, seized with panic, fled, throwing off all their arms. They trampled each other in their rush, and many perished. Their leader galloped fifteen miles without pause. In a few days the natives brought news: The figure in the carriage was only a wooden image of the Prime Minister. "While he lived, I could guess what he would do; dead, I am now helpless," reflected Sima Yi.

Yang Yi and Jiang Wei retired slowly and in good order till they neared the Plank Trail, when they donned mourning garb and began to wail for their dead. The soldiers threw themselves on the ground and wailed in sorrow. Some even wailed themselves to death.

Learning that the Prime Minister was dead, the Latter Ruler was overcome with great sorrow, and wept bitter tears. When

Empress Wu, the Empress Dowager, heard the sad tidings, she also grieved. And all the officers were distressed and wept, and the common people showed their grief. Just then Fei Yi arrived. He was summoned into the royal presence and told the story of Wei Yan's revolt. Jiang Wan said that the late Prime Minister would have framed some scheme by which to get rid of Wei Yan.

Wei Yan was sent with troops to take Nanzheng. Yang Yi opened the letter, and the words therein seemed to please him, for he rode forward blithely, saying, " Now if you are able thrice to shout, 'Who dares kill me?', then you will be a real hero, and I will yield to you the whole of Hanzhong." He never finished. Behind him Ma Dai cut him down.

In due course the coffin of the late Prime Minister arrived at Chengdu. The Latter Ruler led out a large cavalcade of officers to meet the body at a point seven miles from the city walls. They chose a propitious day in the tenth month for the interment, and the Latter Ruler followed the funeral procession to the tomb on the Dingjun Mountain.

Hearing that Zhuge Liang was dead, the East Wu increased its garrison at Baqiu by ten thousand troops. Liu Shan contacted Sun Quan, wishing to restore their friendship. Sun Quan took up a gold-tipped arrow and snapped it in two, swearing that he would never attack the Shu.

CHAPTER 34

Sima Yi Usurps the Throne

For the next few years, there was no war between the Wei, Shu and Wu. The world was peaceful. The Wei Ruler, Cai Rui, built himself many magnificent palace complexes at Xuchang. But the strength of the people was used up in this toil, and they cried aloud and complained unceasingly.

It was heard that in the Palace at Chang'an was the Terrace of Cypress Beams, upon which stood the bronze figure of a man holding up a Dew Bowl. Into the bowl was distilled, it was said, the vapor from the great constellation of the north in the third watch of the night. This liquid was called the Celestial Elixir, or Sweet Dew. If mingled with powdered jade and swallowed, it restored youth to the aged. Cao Rui sent workers to Chang'an immediately to bring hither the bronze figure and set it up in the Fragrant Forest Park. Down fell the pedestal, and the platform crumbled, crushing a thousand people to death.

The Wei Ruler and his harem came to the Fragrant Forest Park to enjoy themselves and to feast all day long. Empress Mao complained about that. Then an edict appeared forcing Empress Mao to commit suicide.

Gongsun Yuan, the Governor of Liaodong, rebelled and made himself Prince of Yan. Sima Yi led troops to suppress the rebellion and killed Gongsun Yuan.

Cao Rui fell ill at Xuchang. He entrusted the important affairs of state to

Cao Shuang and Sima Yi and demanded that they support the Heir Apparent, Cao Fang, who was then only eight years old.

No time was lost in enthroning the new Emperor. Following the suggestion of He Yan, Cao Shuang let the whole military authority fall into his own hands. He gathered about him larger and still larger numbers of supporters, till Sima Yi spread rumours that he was ill and remained in seclusion. His two sons also resigned their offices.

Cao Shuang, a son of Cao Zhen, was born of wealth. He now gave himself up to dissipation, spending days and nights in drinking and music. He was devoted to hunting and was often out of the city. He lived an emperor-like life. Cao Xi, a brother of Cao Shuang, remonstrated with him about this and pointed out the dangers of such frequent absences on excursions of pleasure. Cao Shuang would not listen.

When the Ruler of Wei appointed Li Sheng to the governorship of Qingzhou, Cao Shuang bade Li Sheng go to take his leave of Sima Yi, and at the same time to find out the true state of his health. Sima Yi saw through the ruse at once and pretended to be very weak and ill, thus deceiving Cao Shuang.

Sima Yi and his sons Sima Shi and Sima Zhao were secretly plotting and waiting for an opportunity to kill Cao Shuang. One day, Cao Shuang went out of the city to hunt. His departure gladdened the heart of Sima Yi, who at once began quietly to muster his trusted friends and supporters and put the finishing touches to his plot to overthrow his rival. Closing the gates of the city, he told Empress Dowager Guo that Cao had rebelled, and so should be punished. He sent troops to guard the floating bridge, hoping to kill Cao Shuang.

Hearing that Sima Yi rebels in the city, Cao Shuang's generals all advised him to petition the emperor to proceed to Xuchang till regional troops could arrive and deal with Sima Yi. Cao Shuang cried for a whole night and hesitated. The two messengers of Sima Yi said, "The Guardian of the Throne desires only to strip the military power of the Regent Marshal. If the Regent Marshal yields, he may return peacefully to the city." Cao Shuang believed this.

Before long, Sima Yi produced evidence of Cao Shuang's 'revolt' and desire to usurp the throne, so Cao Shuang and his brothers, and all persons connected with them, and their clans, numbering 1,000, were put to death in the market place. After his recovery of power, Sima Yi was made Prime Minister and received the Nine Gifts of Dignities. All state affairs fell under the control of Sima Yi, his father and sons.

Finding that Sima Yi had put to death his kinspeople, Xiahou Ba, a member of Cao Shuang's clan, rose in rebellion, and raised a force of three thousand troops to support him. Defeated by Guo Huai, the Imperial Protector of Yongzhou, Xiahou Ba surrendered to the Ruler of Shu.

Jiang Wei sent an envoy to the Qiang seeking to make an alliance with them. At the same time he ordered the two Shu generals, Li Xin and Ju An, with fifteen thousand troops, to construct two ramparts on the Qushan Mountains, of which Ju An was to hold the eastern and Li Xin the western.

Guo Huai, with his troops, laid siege to the the eastern and western cities. The streams that supplied them with water were cut off. Jiang Wei used Xiaohou Ba's plan to attack Yongzhou, but fell into Guo Huai's ambush and suffered many casualties.

From the walls of Qushan, the Shu general, Ju An, watched anxiously for the help he expected, but ultimately he surrendered. Then Sima Yi died of a serious illness in AD 251.

At this time Lu Xun and Zhuge Jin were both dead, and the power of the government lay in the hands of Zhuge Ke, son of Zhuge Jin. Zhuge Ke immediately placed his late lord's son Sun Liang on the throne,

Because Sun Quan had just died, and the present ruler was a child, the Wei Sima brothers raised an army of three hundred thousand troops and launched an expedition against the Wu. Sima Shi ordered Hu Zun, General Who Conquers the East, to lead one hundred thousand troops in an attack on the county of Dongxing.

Zhuge Ke of East Wu sent reinforcements to Dongxing and ordered Ding Feng to lead three thousand soldiers up the river in thirty ships to confront the Wei army. This expedition however were defeated and fled.

Zhuge Ke took advantage of this to take the Middle Lands. Then Zhang Te, the commander of Xincheng, thought of a cunning plan. He sent a persuasive messenger with all proper documentation to Zhuge Ke.

After careful consideration, Zhuge Ke retreated to his own country.

Mortified by the course of events, Zhuge Ke did not report his return to the Wu Ruler but instead feigned illness. Sun Liang, the Wu Ruler, went to see his general, and his officers too called on him.

In order to silence critical comment, Zhuge Ke assumed an

attitude of extreme severity, investigating every one's conduct very minutely, and punishing rigorously any fault or shortcoming and meting out sentences of banishment, or death, till every one lived in terror of him.

Minister Teng Yin and Sun Jun advised Sun Liang to get rid of Zhuge Ke. Sun Liang gave a banquet and invited him. Sun Jun slew Zhuge Ke at the banquet, and his whole family was also put to death.

Sun Jun was placed in command of all military forces, and became very powerful. The control of all matters was now in his hands.

CHAPTER 35

Iron Cage Mountain

In AD 253, not knowing the army of East Wu had been defeated, Jiang Wei's army of two hundred thousand was ready to march against the north, according to the treaty agreement between the two states. He at once sent Xi Zheng as his envoy to win the help of the King of the Qiang, whose name was Mi Dang.

Xi Zheng as the Shu envoy, carried gifts of gold and pearls and silk, and went to see the King of the Qiang, whose name was Mi Dang. The mission was successful; King Mi Dang accepted the presents and sent fifty thousand troops to Nanan under the Qiang General Ehe Shaoge.

The Shu supplies were coming up along the rear of Iron Cage Mountain, and they were using the wooden oxen and running horses as transport. Sima Zhao ordered Xu Zhi to cut off their supply lines. Xu Zhi fell into a trap and was cut to pieces by the Shu troops.

Xiahou Ba then stripped them of their weapons and clothing and used this raiment to disguise some of his own soldiers. Holding aloft their Wei banners, these disguised soldiers made for the Wei camp. Sima Zhao was deceived. His forces were defeated and fled to the Iron Cage Mountain. Now there was only one road up the hill, which rose steeply on all sides. Jiang Wei had surrounded the hill with his army and he fully thought that Sima Zhao was doomed and would soon fall into their hands.

The hill had but one small spring, enough to supply water for about a hundred people or so, but Sima Zhao's force numbered over six thousand. So the leader went to the summit of the hill and knelt beside the spring and prayed to Heaven for water. Miraculously the waters gushed forth in plenty, so that they all quenched their thirst and lived.

However, news of the dangerous position of Sima Zhao had come to Guo Huai, and he set about organising a rescue. Guo

Huai pretended to surrender to the king of the Qiang. He defeated the Qiang troops by attacking from both inside and outside. He took the king of the Qiangs, Mi Dang and went to Sima Zhao's rescue.

Mi Dang went to the Shu camp to see Jiang Wei. The Wei troops among the Qiang soldiers dashed towards him and looked set to attack him. Jiang Wei was taken aback, leaped on his steed and fled. He had no weapon in his hand— only his bow and quiver hung at his shoulder. Guo Huai knew Jiang Wei had no weapons. He therefore left his spear, took his bow and shot. Jiang Wei caught the arrow as it flew by and fitted it to his own bowstring. He waited till Guo Huai came quite near, and then he pulled the string with all his force and sent the arrow flying straight at Guo Huai's face. Guo Huai fell even as the bowstring sang. The flow of blood could not be stanched, and Guo Huai died.

Jiang Wei was defeated and fled in disorder to Hanzhongwen. Sima Zhao led his army back to Luoyang. Cao Fang bit his finger till the blood flowed, and with his finger-tip traced a command in blood. He gave it to Xiahou Xuan, Li Feng, and Zhang Ji, demanding that they attack the Sima brothers.

Finding that the eyes of the three were red, beside the Donghua Gate of the palace Sima Shi ordered that they be searched. On Zhang Qi was found the blood-stained garment of

the Emperor. Sima Shi was very angry. He ordered his followers to execute the three on the public ground and also to destroy their entire clans.

Sima Shi bade the lictors lead Empress Zhang away, and she was strangled with a white silk cord at the Donghua Gate of the palace.

In AD 254, Sima Shi deposed Cao Fang and raised Cao Mao to the throne. Honors were heaped upon Sima Shi, who also received the right to move freely within the precincts, to address the Throne without using his name, and to wear arms at court.

On hearing the news that Sima Shi had overthrown Cao Fang, Wuanqiu Jian, of the South of River Huai and Wen Qin, Imperial Protector of Yangzhou were very unhappy and mustered their forces South of River Huai and put down this rebellion. Sima Shi, in a padded carriage, resolved to lead an expedition in person to crush these rebels.

The city of Nandun was an excellent camping ground and was occupied by Wei troops. Wuanqiu Jian organised his troops to guard Xiangcheng and defend Lejia, and Shouchun.

Wen Qin and his son Wen Yang were defending Lejia. They attacked the Wei troops before they have had settled into their camp. Wen Yang dashed into the camp, slashing and thrusting right and left, and everyone gave way before him.

Xiangcheng was taken by the Wei army. Wuanqiu Jian led the

way to Shen county. Here Governor Song Bai received him kindly and comforted him with a great feast. At the banquet Guanqiu Jian drowned his sorrows in cups of wine. Soon he was helplessly drunk, and he was slain by his host. His head was sent to the Wei army as proof of his death.

A mole below the left eye of Sima Shi used to pain him at times. Sima Shi grew worse and worse. Seeing that recovery was hopeless, Sima Shi died. Just before he handed the seal of office to Sima Zhao, who was weeping all the while.

Hearing the news that Sima Shi had died, Jiang Wei raised an army for an expedition. His troops were drawn up with the river at his back, so that they had to fight or drown. His generals turned on the enemy and fought with such vigor that the Wei army was defeated. Wang Jing, Imperial Protector of Yongzhou fled to Didao.

The army of Shu marched to Didao and laid siege to the city walls. After many days the city seemed no nearer falling to them. Seeing the army of Deng Ai advancing, Jiang Wei planned to confront this force. However unsure of how many troops Deng Ai had, Jiang Wei had to retreat to Hanzhong.

The Wei army camped outside Didao. Wang Jing welcomed Deng Ai who said that Jiang Wei would return and that he had asked Wang Jing to make camp and guard the important passes.

Jiang Wei himself led the first army; the others followed in due order, and thus the soldiers of Shu marched out of Zhongti towards Qishan. Finding the Wei army had made preparation, Jiang Wei left some forces behind to distract Deng Ai, while he himself led the main army by Dongting to attack Nanan. Deng Ai however saw through Jiang's scheme and laid ambushes at Shanggui and the Block Valley.

When passing Shanggui and Block Valley, Jiang Wei fell

into the Deng Ai's trap. The whole force was in grave danger, but Xiahou Ba came to their rescue, and so Jiang Wei escaped. Soon after Chen Tai came out from the hills, and Jiang Wei was surrounded by a threatening enemy force. He fought in all directions, but could not clear an escape route. However Zhang Ni, who had heard of his critical situation, came to his rescue with a body of cavalry. Zhang Ni cut his way in, and Jiang Wei immediately broke the siege and escaped. Zhang Ni saved his general, but lost his own life in the following struggle.

CHAPTER 36

Crusading against the Simas

Sima Zhao promoted Deng Ai to a higher rank. At that time, Sima Zhao wanted to usurp the throne, but he didn't trust Zhuge Dan who was based to the South of River Huai. Thus, he sent Jia Chong to gauge the attitude of Zhuge Dan. Unexpectedly, Zhuge Dan didn't approve of Jia Chong's proposal. Hence, Sima Zhao privately ordered Yue Chen, Imperial Protector of Yangzhou to kill Zhuge Dan.

Zhuge Dan was fully aware of the plotting of Sima Zhao. He led his army to Yangzhou and killed Yue Chen. Then, he sent to Luoyang a memorial detailing Sima Yi's many faults and he made efforts to unite the South Lands to crusade against Sima Zhao.

At that time, the Prime Minister of Wu, Sun Jun had died of illness and his brother, Sun Chen, had become Prime Minister. Sun Chen sent seventy thousand troops to help Zhuge Dan.

Aware of this, Sima Zhao personally led his army to attack Zhuge Dan. Fearing a popular revolt against him, Sima Zhao took the Empress Dowager and the Son of Heaven with him on the expedition. Wang Ji, General Who Corrects the South, was in command of the vanguard, and Shi Bao, Army Inspector, and Zhou Tai, Imperial Protector of Yangzhou, led the imperial escort. The army moved into the lands south of River Huai like a great flood.

Sima Zhao agreed with the opinion of Zhong Hui and made his plans accordingly, placing herds of oxen, droves of horses, donkeys and mules, and

heaps of military supplies on the battlefield. When the soldiers of Wu saw such huge quantities of booty, theirs seemingly for the taking, they lost all desire to fight and scattered in disorder to try to loot the spoils. Wang Ji led a counterattack and the Wu were annihalated. Zhuge Dan fled to Shouchun.

The Wu general Zhu Yi led an army to offer aid to Shouchun. On the way, his army was defeated and had to return to Anfeng. Sun Chen heard of this fresh defeat. He was very angry and sentenced Zhu Yi to death. He ordered Quan I and his father Quan Duan to fight the Wei army, saying, "If you do not drive off this Wei army, let me never again see your face." With no hope of success, Quan I and his father had no other option but to turn traitor and go over to Sima Zhao.

Zhuge Dan was guarding Shouchun, but they were without reinforcements and were desperately short of food. Wen Qin went to Zhuge Dan with a proposal, "The northern troops should be sent away in order to save food." His suggestion called forth an outburst of fierce wrath from Zhuge Dan. Wen Qin was killed on the spot. His two sons, Wen Yang and Wen Hu, ran amok with rage and they lowered the city walls and deserted to the Wei camp.

The desire to surrender possessed many people in the city of Shouchun. Zhong Hui went in to Sima Zhao to say the moment to attack had come. The commander of the north gate, Zeng Xuan, treacherously opened the gate and let in the Wei soldiers. Zhuge Dan was killed by the Wei soldiers, and soon the country around the River Huai was quiet.

Taking advantage of the opportunity, Jiang Wei asked the Latter Ruler's authority to embark on another expedition against the Wei. He made the young generals Fu Qian and Jiang Shu the leaders of the vanguard, and directed them to attack Changcheng, the great Wei storehouse.

The Commander in Changcheng was Sima Wang, a cousin of Sima Zhao. So when Sima Wang heard of the approach of the Shu army, he and his two leaders, Wang Zhen and Li Peng, made a camp seven miles from the walls to try to repel any attack far from the city walls. Fu Qian was a brave fighter and he killed Wang Zhen and Li Peng. Both generals being dead, Sima Wang fled into the city and barred the gates.

The Shu soldiers shot fire-arrows and firebombs over the ramparts and burned all the buildings on the wall. They next brought up brushwood and piled it against the ramparts and set it alight, so that the flames rose high. When the city seemed just about to fall, Deng Ai and his son Deng Zhong came to rescue Sima Wang. Deng Zhong gave ground in the fight with Jiang Wei but was rescued by Deng Ai.

Deng Ai saw that the army of Shu had the strategic advantage, so he didn't come out to give battle and Sima Wang also stayed in his city. When Jiang Wei was thinking about how he could defeat the enemy, scouts came to give the news of the rout of the army of Zhuge Dan. Jiang Wei led his army in a general retreat.

The Prime Minister of Wu, Sun Chen, was greatly angered by the desertion of so many of his soldiers and officers to the Wei, and revenged himself by putting their families to death. The Ruler of Wu, Sun Liang, disapproved of these acts of cruelty and plotted with Imperial Brother-in-Law Quan Ji to get rid of Sun Chen.

However, Quan Ji let slip word of the plot and Sun Chen immediately acted. He deposed Sun Liang and requested Sun Xiu, Prince of Langye, the sixth son of Sun Quan, to ascend the throne. Sun Chen was confirmed as Prime Minister and made his families all high-ranking officials.

The new Ruler of Wu, Sun Xiu, suspected that Sun Chen had ambitions to be emperor, and so he began to hatch plans to kill him with the old generals Zhang Bu and Ding Feng.

Sun Xiu wrote letters to the Shu saying that beyond doubt Sima Zhao intended to usurp the throne, and when that happened, both Wu and Shu would be invaded. Both should prepare themselves. When he read these letters, Jiang Wei hastened to seek permission to attempt another expedition against the Wei. The Shu troops camped at the entrance to the valley of Qishan, where Deng Ai had tunneled a subterranean road.

At night, Wei army attacked the Shu camp via the subterranean road. Jiang Wei mounted and took his position in front of the center camp. "Let no one move on pain of death!" he shouted. "Stand still, and when the enemy approaches, shoot." A dozen times the Wei troops came forward, only to be driven back before the arrows and bolts of the defenders. Daylight found the Shu camps still standing firm, and the Wei troops withdrew

Next day the two armies were arrayed in front of the Qishan Mountains. Deng Ai was caught in a serpent-shaped manoeuvre but to his great joy Wei soldiers forced their way through and released him. The leader was Sima Wang. Since Deng Ai couldn't defeat Jiang Wei, he sent people to Chengdu to bribe the Eunuch Huang Hao and ask him to sow distrust between the Ruler of Shu and Jiang Wei in order to get Jiang Wei recalled.

On his return to Chengdu, Jiang Wei had an audience with the Latter Ruler, but found there were no major problems at court. He reminded the Latter Ruler not to listen to the babble of mean-spirited persons. The Latter Ruler asked Jiang Wei to return to Hanzhong.

Hearing this, Sima Zhao knew he must act quickly to subdue the Shu. But Jia Chong persuaded him not to leave the capital. Sima Zhao halted the attack on Shu for the moment.

The Wei Ruler Cao Mao wrote a poem titled "Lurking Dragon", indicating that Sima Zhao had the ambition to become an emperor. Sima Zhao had the effrontery to go to court armed to interrogate the emperor. Cao Mao led several hundred old and weak guards and they tried to kill Sima Zhao. Cheng Ji smote Cao Mao to death with his spear at the Dragon Gate.

Sima Zhao assumed an air of not knowing the inside story and beheaded Cheng Ji. Jia Chong and those of his party urged Sima Zhao to assume the Throne but he refused. Sima Zhao supported Cao Huan as the new emperor. Sima Zhao was made Prime Minister and Duke of Jin.

CHAPTER 37

Jiang Wei Takes Refuge

An internal disorder occurred in Wei, so Jiang Wei seized the opportunity to attack it. The Wei general named Wang Guan pretended to surrender to Jiang Wei. Meeting trick with trick, however, Jiang Wei ordered him to transport grain to Qishan and set up an ambush there.

Troops belonging to Shu caught a man carrying a letter from Wang Guan to Deng Ai, telling him that he would divert a convoy of grain to the Wei camps on the twentieth and asked Deng Ai to send troops to Yunshan Valley to help. Jiang Wei beheaded the courier and then sent another letter to Deng Ai carried by someone dressed as a Wei soldier in which the date had been altered from the twentieth to the fifteenth.

Thus, on the fifteenth day, Deng Ai led fifty thousand veteran troops to a site near the Yunshan Valley to give assistance. His force was utterly routed by the troops of Shu. Deng Ai mingled with the footmen in a bid to elude capture. The ruse was discovered. There was no way to escape, so Wang Guan ordered his troops to set fire to the Plank Trail and the pass. Fearing the loss of Hanzhong, Jiang Wei made all haste along by-roads after Wang Guan. Surrounded on all sides, the latter jumped into the Black Dragon River and drowned.

Jiang Wei set about restoring the Plank Trail and gathered provisions and weapons for his troops. He sent a memorial to the Throne for the eighth time seeking permission to resume the attack against Wei and Liu Shan agreed.

The veteran general Liao Hua, however, advised Jiang Wei not to attack Wei. Jiang Wei was annoyed, and, after leaving Liao Hua in charge of the base in Hanzhong, he marched with three hundred thousand troops to Taoyang while Xiahou Ba headed the van of the Shu army.

As he drew near, Xiahou Ba noticed the gates stood wide open. He was wary about going straight in, but his generals were eager to gain merit in battle, so he eventually moved cautiously inside ready to fight. As the itroops neared the curtain wall, the drawbridge rose. As Ba turned to retire, arrows and stones flew down in clouds so that he and many of his soldiers perished.

Jiang Wei detached Zhang Yi to march on Qishan, but Deng Ai had anticipated this and this and repulsed the attack, Zhang Yi being forced to take refuge in the hills. No road was open to him, so Jiang Wei decided to go to his aid. Zhang Yi then took the opportunity to return to the attack and the tables were turned. Defeated, Deng Ai retired to his camp, which Jiang Wei surrounded and attacked vigorously.

Deng Ai remained on defensive for half a month. Unable to raise the siege of the Shu army, he ordered Dang Jun to go to Chengdu to bribe the corrupt Huang Hao, who spread rumors that Jiang Wei would rebel. Hearing this, the astonished ruler ordered Jiang Wei's recall.

Jiang Wei withdrew troops and returned to Chengdu. He

advised Liu Shan to execute the slandering Huang Hao, but this was rejected. Xi Zheng persuaded Jiang Wei to go to Tazhong to take refuge.

In AD 263, hearing that Jiang Wei had gone to Tazhong to save his life and that Liu Shan, the Ruler of Shu, was steeped in dissipation, Sima Zhao ordered Deng Ai and Zhong Hui to march against Shu. Zhong Hui, however, had many large ships built and trained a maritime force. Even his chief, Sima Zhao, was deceived and called him to explain what he was doings. He was told that Zhong was using the strategy of "looking in one direction and rowing in another". Then, he realized how shrewd Zhong Hui was and watched him carefully.

Jiang Wei heard of the intended attack by the Wei army led by Zhong Hui and Deng Ai. He at once sent a memorial to Liu Shan asking that certain defensive arrangements be made and that soldiers in Tazhong be gathered ready for the march.

Liu Shan consulted the eunuch Huang Hao who, in turn, sought the help of a prophetess, who told him that, within a few years, the land of Wei would come under the control of Shu. The pleasure-seeking ruler ignored Jiang Wei's memorial.

Nanzheng Pass was captured by the main army under Zhong Hui after a brief fight. Yangping Pass then became the target for control. The Shu General Fu Qian dared not to go out to fight the enemy and was eventually forced to surrender to the Wei soldiers. Jiang Shu yielded and Fu Qian killed himself.

Jiang Wei at Tazhong heard of the invasion and wrote to his general Liao Hua to give assistance. He himself drove Wang Qi and Qian Hong, but was surrounded by the forces Deng Ai. Presently, he was able to break clear and hastened to the great camp.

Jiang Wei's letters reporting the emergency sent to Chengdu were withheld by the eunuch Huang Hao, so Liu Shan knew nothing of the war situation. Without reinforcements, Jiang Wei led his troops and made a feint as if to take Yongzhou. When Zhuge Xu, who was at the Yinping Bridge, heard this, he feared that the city would be lost, so he sent troops on a rescue mission. Soon after, Jiang Wei crossed the bridge and set out towards the Saber Pass where he planned a last ditch defense.

Soon after this, Zhuge Xu appeared at the pass but was driven off.

Zhong Hui ordered Zhuge Xu to be bound ready for execution. Knowing that Zhuge Xu was really only a subordinate of Deng Ai, those around Zhong Hui urged clemency. Zhong Hui did not put him to death, but sent him as a caged prisoner to the capital to be judged. There was an enmity between Deng Ai and Zhong Hui, it should be noted

In order to make a final reckoning with Zhong Hui, Deng Ai decided to set out upon a long march against Chengdu along mountainous paths. The force was in the most precipitous part of of the Yinping Mountains, which was totally uninhabited. Before them stood a precipice named Heaven Cliffs, which no horse could ascend. First they threw over their weapons; then the leader wrapped himself in blankets and rolled over the edge, followed by the generals and soldiers also wrapped in blankets. Thus, the Heaven Cliffs were passed.

Having crossed this great range of mountains without discovery, Deng Ai marched forward. Presently he came to a large but deserted camp. He was told that while Zhuge Liang lived, a thousand troops had been kept in garrison at this point of danger, but the ruler had withdrawn them. Deng Ai sighed at the thought, "If not for the fatuity of Liu Shan and carelessness of Jiang Wei, we could not arrive here in safety?"

Speed is vital in war. Jiangyou and Fucheng was taken by Deng Ai. His army pressed on toward Mianzhu. Hearing the news that the

Wei army has arrived at Mianzhu, Liu Shan weepingly asked Zhuge Zhan, son of Zhuge Liang, to lead troops to beat off the enemy. With seventy thousand soldiers placed under their command, Zhuge Zhan and his son marched to Mianzhu to find Deng Ai.

Deng Ai laid his plans to surrend Zhuge Zhan. In vain he thrust right and shoved left, killing hundreds of Wei soldiers. The Wei troops, however, unleashed a fusillade of arrows to shatter the enemy ranks. Before long, Zhuge Zhan was wounded and fell. He drew his sword and slew himself. Zhuge Shang whipped his horse and dashed out into the thick of the fight, where he died. Thus, the Wei army was able to break into Mianzhu.

CHAPTER 38

Three Kingdoms Make Way for the Jin Dynasty

As the attacking army led by Deng Ai reached the gates of the city of Chengdu, Liu Shan summoned a council. High Minister Qiao Zhou urged him to surrender to Wei. Liu Shan's fifth son Liu Chen and several key ministers advised the ruler to fight to the last ditch. But he was deaf to the advice and ordered Qiao Zhou to prepare the formal Act of Surrender.

Being told that tomorrow his father and all his ministers were going out of the city to submit formally, Liu Chen slew his wife and three sons and cut off their heads. Bearing the head of the princess in his hand, he went to the Temple of the First Ruler. There he wept until his tears turned to blood, and he then committed suicide.

Nest day, the ruler and all his courtiers, numering sixty, went out three miles from the North Gate to bow their heads in submission. Liu Shan bound himself with cord.

Deng Ai requested him to issue one more proclamation from the Palace to reassure the people. Then, he sent Minister Jiang Xian to order Jiang Wei to surrender. Hearing that theirruler had yielded, Jiang Wei's officers ground their teeth with rage and mortification. They drew their swords and slashed at stones in their wrath. Jiang Wei then revealed his fake surrender scheme to the officers.

The flag of surrender was ordered raised on the ramparts of Saber Pass. Jiang Wei and his general Zhang Yi went to Zhong Hui's camp to

surrender, Jiang telling Zhong Hui he only yielded to him. Had it been Deng Ai, he would have fought to the death. Zhong Hui was so happy that he broke an arrow in two, and they two swore close fealty.

Deng Ai submitted a memorial to Sima Zhao, advising that Liu Shan should be left in Chengdu and made an official, setting an example to the Eastern Wu. Reading this memorial, the thought entered the mind of Sima Zhao that Deng Ai intended to call himself the Prince of Areas of the Western Rivers. He sent Wei Guan to carry a letter to Zhong Hui, ordering him to keep a watch upon Deng Ai and guard against any insubordination.

Zhong Hui told this to Jiang Wei, who made use of this opportunity to lie that Deng Ai had indeed early on intended to call himself the Prince of Areas of the Western Rivers. Zhong Hui envied and hated Deng Ai for he snatched the feat of conquering Shu from him. He submitted a memorial to say that Deng acted wildly against law and public opinion and had won the heart of the Shu people. To support his charges, Zhong Hui's soldiers intercepted Deng Ai's letters and rewrote them in arrogant and rebellious terms.

Sima Zhao ordered Zhong Hui to arrest Deng Ai, and he himself directed a great march under the leadership of the Ruler of Wei, Cao Huang, whom he compelled to go with him, to Chang'an, to watch over Deng Ai and guard against any attempt at insubordination.

Hence Wei Guan was sent by Zhong Hui, with some thirty men, to affect the arrest. Wei Guan first wrote a score or two of letters to various officers who were serving under Deng Ai, to win them over. Deng Ai was kept in the dark about this until Wei Guan forced his way into his bedchamber, seized and bound him and his son. Zhong Hui at once sent the prisoners to Luoyang,

Zhong Hui then entered Chengdu in state. He added all Deng Ai's army to his own forces, so that he became very formidable, planning to call himself the Prince. Using Jiang Wei's plan, Zhong Hui kept all Deng Ai's generals prisoner in the palace under careful guard, planning to kill any who resisted them and bury them in the pit.

Qiu Jian, Zhong Hui's favorite, was unwilling to rebel Wei and let out the secret to Wei Guan, who led troops to capture Zhong Hui. Zhong Hui resisted and managed to slay a lew a few, but he was eventually felled by a volley of arrows and and died. Jiang Wei ran to and fro slaying all he met until seized by a heart spasm that killed him at the age of 59.

Wei Guan was sent to cut down Deng Ai and his son. Liu Shan was created Duke of Anle. Huang Hao, whose evil influence had brought the kingdom to its knees, and who had oppressed the people, was put to death with ignominy in public.

Liu Shan went to the residence of Sima Zhao to thank him for his bounty and a banquet was prepared. There, they performed the music of Wei, with the dances, and the hearts of the officers of Shu were sad; only Liu Shan appeared merry.

Turning to his guest, Sima Zhao said, "Do you never think of Shu?" "With such music as this, I forget Shu," was the reply.

Before long Sima Zhao died of illness, Jia Chong persuaded Siman Yan, his son to become Emperor. Next day he entered the palace armed with a sword. He forced the Ruler of Wei Cao Huan to abdicate. Zhang Jie, one of the ministers, opposed this. Siman Yan bade the lictors take Zhang Jie outside and beat him to death,

In order to save his life, Cao Huan had to resign the throne to the Prince of Jin Sima Yan. Thus Sima Yan reigned in the state called Great Jin. Cao Huan received the the title of Prince of Chenliu. Thus, the Wei

Dynasty ended in AD 265.

When Sun Xiu, the Ruler of Wu, knew that the House of Wei had fallen, he also knew the usurper's next thought would be conquest of his own land. The anxiety made him ill and he died. Finally Sun Hao, a grandson of Sun Quan, was enthroned as Emperor of Wu. Sun Hao ordered Lu Kang, a son of Lu Xun, to base his army at Jiangkou in order to attack Xiangyang.

The Ruler of Jin issued an edict ordering Yang Hu to muster his troops to guard the county. Knowing that Lu Kang was able and crafty, Yang Hu remained on the defensive. Lu Kang also admired Yang Hu. Thus, they carefully kept to their boundaries.

Sun Hao then sent orders for Lu Kang to press forward. The latter was in a quandary. Thereupon Sun Hao deprived Lu Kang of his command and took away his commission. After Yang Hu's death, Du Yu was made Commander-in-Chief by Sima Yan and, with two hundred thousand troops and 10,000 warships, went to attack Wu.

Du Yu was to attack Jiangling, and he sent General Zhou Zhi with eight hundred sailors to sail secretly along the Great River to capture Yuexiang. Three generals of the Wu army were killed, and before long Jiangling was captured.

Sun Hao hastened to summon the chief officers to a council to discuss countermeasures. Zhang Xiang, one of the leaders of Wu, called to the defenders to open the gates of Shitou. In AD 280, the Jin army swarmed into the City. Sun Hao, imitating the conduct of Liu Shan of Shu, went to offer submission to Jin. He was taken to Luoyang to see Sima Yan.

Sun Hao was created Lord of Guining and allowed a seat at court by Sima Yan. Jia Chong asked Sun Hao why he liked to subject people to cruel punishment. "Murders of princes and malicious speech and disloyal conduct were so punished," Sun Hao said sarcastically.

The three states became one empire under the rule of Sima Yan of the Jin Dynasty. The fire of war was quenched for the moment.